Born in India, Chitra Banerjee Divakaruni lives near San Francisco with her husband and two children. She teaches creative writing at a local college, and is the co-ordinator for a helpline for South Asian women. She is the author of several award-winning volumes of poetry, and two novels, *The Mistress of Spices* and *Sister of My Heart*. *Arranged Marriage*, her acclaimed collection of short stories, is already a bestseller in America, and has won the PEN Oakland Josephine Miles Prize for fiction, an American Book Award, and the Bay Area Book Reviewers Award for fiction.

Also by Chitra Banerjee Divakaruni

ARRANGED MARRIAGE
SISTER OF MY HEART

and published by Black Swan

THE MISTRESS
OF SPICES

Chitra Banerjee Divakaruni

BLACK SWAN

THE MISTRESS OF SPICES
A BLACK SWAN BOOK : 0 552 99670 X

Originally published in Great Britain by Doubleday,
a division of Transworld Publishers

PRINTING HISTORY
Doubleday edition published 1997
Black Swan edition published 1997

9 10 8

Set in Sabon.

Black Swan Books are published by Transworld Publishers,
61–63 Uxbridge Road, London W5 5SA,
a division of The Random House Group Ltd,
in Australia by Random House Australia (Pty) Ltd,
20 Alfred Street, Milsons Point, Sydney, NSW 2061, Australia,
in New Zealand by Random House New Zealand Ltd
18 Poland Road, Glenfield, Auckland 10, New Zealand
and in South Africa by Random House (Pty) Ltd,
Endulini, 5a Jubilee Road, Parktown 2193, South Africa.

Printed and bound in Great Britain by
Cox & Wyman Ltd, Reading, Berkshire.

For my three men
Murthy
Anand
Abhay

spicemasters all

My thanks to the following persons and organizations, each of whom helped to make my dream of this book a reality.

To Sandra Dijkstra, my agent, who had faith in me from my first story.

To Martha Levin, my editor, for vision, insight and encouragement.

To Vikram Chandra, Shobha Menon Hiatt, Tom Jenks, Elaine Kim, Morton Marcus, Jim Quinn, Gerald Rosen, Roshni Rustomji-Kerns and C. J. Wallia for their very important comments and suggestions.

To the Arts Council, Santa Clara County, and the C. Y. Lee Creative Writing Contest for financial support.

To Foothill College for giving me, through a sabbatical, the gift of time.

To my family – especially my mother, Tatini Banerjee, and my mother-in-law, Sita Shastri Divakaruni – for their blessings.

And to Gurumayi Chidvilasananda, whose grace illuminates my life, every page and every word.

a warning to readers:
the spices described in this book
should be taken
only
under the supervision
of a qualified
Mistress

The Mistress of Spices

Contents

Tilo

I am a Mistress of Spices.

I can work the others too. Mineral, metal, earth and sand and stone. The gems with their cold clear light. The liquids that burn their hues into your eyes till you see nothing else. I learned them all on the island.

But the spices are my love.

I know their origins, and what their colours signify, and their smells. I can call each by the true-name it was given at the first, when earth split like skin and offered it up to the sky. Their heat runs in my blood. From *amchur* to *zafran*, they bow to my command. At a whisper they yield up to me their hidden properties, their magic powers.

Yes, they all hold magic, even the everyday American spices you toss unthinking into your cooking pot.

You doubt? Ah. You have forgotten the old secrets your mother's mothers knew. Here is one of them again: vanilla beans soaked soft in goat's milk and rubbed on the wrist-bone can guard against the evil eye. And here another: A measure of pepper at the foot of the bed, shaped into a crescent, cures you of nightmare.

But the spices of true power are from my birthland, land of ardent poetry, aquamarine feathers. Sunset skies brilliant as blood.

They are the ones I work with.

If you stand in the centre of this room and turn slowly around, you will be looking at every Indian spice that ever was – even the lost ones – gathered here upon the shelves of my store.

I think I do not exaggerate when I say there is no other place in the world quite like this.

The store has been here only for a year. But already many look at it and think it was always.

I can understand why. Turn the crooked corner of Esperanza where the Oakland buses hiss to a stop and you'll see it. Perfect-fitted between the narrow barred door of Rosa's Weekly Hotel, still blackened from a year-ago fire, and Lee Ying's Sewing Machine and Vacuum Cleaner Repair with the glass cracked between the *R* and the *e*. Grease-smudged window. Looped letters that say SPICE BAZAAR faded into a dried-mud brown. Inside, walls veined with cobwebs where hang discoloured pictures of the gods, their sad shadow eyes. Metal bins with the shine long gone from them, heaped with *atta* and Basmati rice and *masoor dal*. Row upon row of videomovies, all the way back to the time of black-and-white. Bolts of fabric dyed in age-old colours, New Year yellow, harvest green, bride's luck red.

And in the corners accumulated among dustballs, exhaled by those who have entered here, the desires. Of all things in my store, they are the most ancient. For even here in this new land America, this city which prides itself on being no older than a heartbeat, it is the same things we want, again and again.

I too am a reason why. I too look like I have been here forever. This is what the customers see as they enter, ducking under plastic-green mango leaves strung over the door for luck: a bent woman with skin the colour of old sand, behind a glass counter that holds *mithai*, sweets out of their childhoods. Out of their mothers' kitchens. Emerald-green *burfis*, *rasogollahs* white as dawn, and, made from lentil flour, *laddus* like nuggets of gold. It seems right that I should have been here always, that I should understand without words their longing for the ways they chose to leave behind when they chose America. Their shame for that longing, like the bitter-slight aftertaste in the mouth when one has chewed *amlaki* to freshen the breath.

They do not know, of course. That I am not old, that this seeming-body I took on in Shampati's fire when I vowed to become a Mistress is not mine. I claim its creases and gnarls no more than water claims the ripples that wrinkle it. They do not see, under the hooded lids, the eyes which shine for a moment – I need no forbidden mirror (for mirrors are forbidden to Mistresses) to tell me this – like dark fire. The eyes which alone are my own.

No. One more thing is mine. My name which is Tilo, short for Tilottama, for I am named after the sun-burnished sesame seed, spice of nourishment. They do not know this, my customers, nor that earlier I had other names.

Sometimes it fills me with a heaviness, lake of black ice, when I think that across the entire length of this land not one person knows who I am.

Then I tell myself, No matter. It is better this way.

'Remember,' said the Old One, the First Mother, when she trained us on the island. 'You are not important. No Mistress is. What is important is the store. And the spices.'

The store. Even for those who know nothing of the inner room with its sacred, secret shelves, the store is an excursion into the land of might-have-been. A self-indulgence dangerous for a brown people who come from elsewhere, to whom real Americans might say *Why?*

Ah, the pull of that danger.

They love me because they sense I understand this. They hate me a little for it too.

And then, the questions I ask. To the plump woman dressed in polyester pants and a Safeway tunic, her hair coiled in a tight bun as she bends over a small hill of green chillies searching earnestly: 'Has your husband found another job since the layoff.'

To the young woman who hurries in with a baby on her hip to pick up some *dhania jeera* powder: 'The bleeding, is it bad still, do you want something for it.'

I can see the electric jolt of it go through each one's body, the same every time. Almost I would laugh if the pity of it did not tug at me so. Each face startling up as though I had put my hands on the delicate oval of jaw and cheekbone and turned it toward me. Though of course I did not. It is not allowed for Mistresses to touch those who come to us. To upset the delicate axis of giving and receiving on which our lives are held precarious.

For a moment I hold their glance, and the air around us grows still and heavy. A few chillies drop to the floor, scattering like hard green rain. The child twists in her mother's tightened grip, whimpering.

Their glance skittery with fear with wanting.

Witchwoman, say the eyes. Under their lowered lids they remember the stories whispered around night fires in their home villages.

'That's all for today,' one woman tells me, wiping her hands on nubby polyester thighs, sliding a package of chillies at me.

'Shhh baby little *rani*,' croons the other, busies herself with the child's tangled curls until I have rung up her purchases.

They keep their cautious faces turned away as they leave.

But they will come back later. After darkness. They will knock on the shut door of the store that smells of their desires and ask.

I will take them into the inner room, the one with no windows, where I keep the purest spices, the ones I gathered on the island for times of special need. I will light the candle I keep ready and search the soot-streaked dimness for lotus root and powdered *methi,* paste of fennel and sun-roasted asafoetida. I will chant. I will administer. I will pray to remove sadness and suffering as the Old One taught. I will deliver warning.

This is why I left the island where each day still is melted sugar and cinnamon, and birds with diamond throats sing, and silence when it falls is light as mountain mist.

Left it for this store, where I have brought together everything you need in order to be happy.

But before the store was the island, and before the island, the village, when I was born.

How long ago was it, that dry season, that day when heat parched the cracked paddy fields, and my mother thrashed on the birthing mat groaning for water.

Then steel-blue thunder, and jagged lightning that split the old banyan in the village marketplace. The midwife cried out at the veiny purple cowl over my face, and the fortune-teller in the rainfly-filled evening shook his head sorrowfully at my father.

They named me Nayan Tara, Star of the Eye, but my parents' faces were heavy with fallen hope at another girl-child, and this one coloured like mud.

Wrap her in old cloth, lay her face down on the floor. What does she bring to the family except a dowry debt.

Three days it took the villagers to put out the fire in the marketplace. And my mother lying fevered all the while, and the cows run dry, and I screaming until they fed me milk from a white ass.

Perhaps that is why the words came to me so soon.

And the sight.

Or was it the loneliness, the need rising angry in a dark girl left to wander the village unattended, with no one caring enough to tell her Don't.

I knew who stole Banku the water-carrier's buffalo, and which servant girl was sleeping with her master. I sensed where under the earth gold lay buried, and why the weaver's daughter had stopped talking since last full moon. I told the *zamindar* how to find his lost ring. I warned the village headman of the floods before they came.

I, Nayan Tara, the name which also means Star-seer.

My fame spread. From neighbouring towns and beyond, from the cities that lay on the other side of the mountains, people travelled so I could change their luck with a touch of my hand. They brought me gifts never before seen in our village, gifts so lavish that the villagers talked about them for days. I sat on gold-woven cushions and ate from silver plates studded with precious stones, and wondered at how easy it was to learn the habits of affluence, and how right it seemed that I should do so. I cured the daughter of a potentate, foretold the death of a tyrant, drew patterns on the ground to keep the good winds blowing for merchant sailors. When I looked at them, grown men trembled and threw themselves at my feet, and that too seemed easy and right.

And so it was that I grew proud and wilful. I wore muslins so fine they could be drawn through the eye of a needle. I combed my hair with combs carved from the shells of the great tortoises of the Andamans. I gazed long and admiringly in mirrors framed in mother-of-pearl, though I knew well that I was not beautiful. I slapped servant maids if they were slow to my bidding. At mealtimes I ate the best portions and threw the leavings on the floor for my brothers and sisters. My mother and father dared not voice their anger, for they were afraid of my power. But also they loved the luxury-life it brought them.

And when I read this in their eyes I felt disdain, and a bile-black triumph that churned in my belly because I who had been last was now first. There was something else too, a deep wordless sorrow, but I pushed it away and would not look at it.

I Nayan Tara, who had long since forgotten the other meaning of my name: Flower That Grows by the Dust Road. Who did not know then that this would be my name for only a little time more.

Meanwhile the travelling *bauls* sang my praises, gold-smiths impressed my likeness on medallions that were worn by thousands for luck, and merchant sailors carried tales of my powers across the harnessed seas to every land.

That is how the pirates learned of me.

Turmeric

When you open the bin that sits by the entrance to the store you smell it right away, though it will take a little while for your brain to register that subtle scent, faintly bitter like your skin and almost as familiar.

Brush the surface with your hand, and the silky yellow powder will cling to the pads of your palm, to your fingertips. Dust from a butterfly wing.

Bring it to your face. Rub it on cheek, forehead, chin. Don't be hesitant. For a thousand years before history began, brides – and those who long to be brides – have done the same. It will erase blemishes and wrinkles, suck away age and fat. For days afterward, your skin will give off a pale golden glow.

Each spice has a day special to it. For turmeric it is Sunday, when light drips fat and butter-coloured into the bins to be soaked up glowing, when you pray to the nine planets for love and luck.

Turmeric which is also named *halud*, meaning yellow, colour of daybreak and conch-shell sound. Turmeric the preserver, keeping foods safe in a land of heat and hunger. Turmeric the auspicious spice, placed on the heads of newborns for luck, sprinkled over coconuts at *pujas*, rubbed into the borders of wedding saris.

But there is more. That is why I pick them only at the precise moment when night slides into day, those bulbous roots like gnarly brown fingers, why I grind them only when Swati the faith-star shines incandescent in the north.

When I hold it in my hands, the spice speaks to me. Its voice is like evening, like the beginning of the world.

I am turmeric who rose out of the ocean of milk when the devas and asuras churned for the treasures of the universe. I am turmeric who came after the poison and before the nectar and thus lie in between.

Yes, I whisper, swaying to its rhythm. Yes. You are

turmeric, shield for heart's sorrow, anointment for death, hope for rebirth.

Together we sing this song, as we have many times.

And so I think at once of turmeric when Ahuja's wife comes into my store this morning wearing dark glasses.

Ahuja's wife is young and seems even younger. Not a brash, buoyant young but raw and flinching, like someone who's lately been told and told she's not good enough.

She comes every week after payday and buys the barest staples: cheap coarse rice, *dals* on sale, a small bottle of oil, maybe some *atta* to make *chapatis*. Sometimes I see her hold up a jar of mango *achar* or a packet of *papads* with hesitant wanting. But always she puts it back.

I offer her a *gulab-jamun* from the *mithai* case, but she blushes fiercely and painfully and shakes her head.

Ahuja's wife has of course a name. Lalita. *La-li-ta*, three liquid syllables perfect-suited to her soft beauty. I would like to call her by it, but how can I while she thinks of herself only as a wife.

She has not told me this. She has said little to me, in all her times of coming, except 'Namaste' and 'Is this on sale' and 'Where can I find.' But I know it as I know other things.

Such as: Ahuja is a watchman at the docks and likes a drink or two. Or three or four, recently.

Such as: she too has a gift, a power, though she does not think of it so. Every cloth she touches with her needle blooms.

One time I found her leaning over the showcase where

I keep fabrics, looking at the *palloo* of a sari embroidered with *zari* thread.

I took it out. 'Here,' I said, draping it over her shoulder. 'That mango colour looks so nice on you.'

'No, no.' She drew back quick and apologetic. 'I was only seeing the stitching.'

'Ah. You stitch.'

'I used to a lot, once. I loved it. In Kanpur I was going to sewing school, I had my own Singer machine, lot of ladies gave me stitching to do.'

She looked down. In the dejected curve of her neck I saw what she did not say, the dream she had dared to: one day soon, maybe perhaps why not, her own shop, Lalita Tailor Works.

But four years back a well-meaning neighbour came to her mother and said, *Bahenji*, there's a boy, most suitable, living in *phoren*, earning American dollars, and her mother said Yes.

'Why don't you work in this country,' I asked. 'I'm sure many ladies here too need stitching. Wouldn't you like—'

She gave me a longing look. 'O yes.' Then stopped.

Here is what she wants to tell me, only how can she, it is not right that a woman should say such things about her man: all day at home is so lonely, the silence like quicksand sucking at her wrists and ankles. Tears she cannot stop, disobedient tears like spilled pomegranate seeds, and Ahuja shouting when he returns home to her swollen eyes.

He refuses that his woman should work. *Aren't I man enough man enough man enough.* The words shattering like dishes swept from the dinner table.

Today I pack her purchases, meagre as always: *masoor dal*, two pounds of *atta*, a little *jeera*. Then I see her looking in the glass case at a silver baby rattle, her eyes dark as a well to drown in.

For that is what Ahuja's wife wants most of all. A baby. Surely a baby would make everything right, even the heaving, grunting, never-ending nights, the weight pinning her down, the hot sour animal breath panted into her. His voice like the callused flat of a hand arcing out of the dark.

A baby to negate it all, tugging at her with its sweetmilk mouth.

Child-longing, deepest desire, deeper than for wealth or lover or even death. It weighs down the air of the store, purple like before a storm. It gives off the smell of thunder. Scorches.

O Lalita who is not yet Lalita, I have the balm to lay over your burning. But how unless you ready yourself, hold yourself open to the storm? How unless you ask?

Meanwhile I give you turmeric.

A handful of turmeric wrapped in old newspaper with the words of healing whispered into it, slipped into your grocery sack when you are not looking. The string tied into the triple flower knot, and inside, satin-soft turmeric the same colour as the bruise seeping onto your cheek from under the dark edge of your glasses.

Sometimes I wonder if there is such a thing as reality, an objective and untouched nature of being. Or if all that we encounter has already been changed by what we had imagined it to be. If we have dreamed it into being.

I think this most when I remember the pirates.

The pirates had teeth like polished stone and scimitars with handles made from the tusks of boars. Their fingers were laden with rings, amethyst and beryl and carbuncle, and around their necks hung sapphires for luck at sea. Polished with whale oil, their skin gleamed dark as mahogany or pale as birchbark, for pirates come from many races and many lands.

All this I knew from the stories we children were told at bedtime.

They raided and pillaged and burned, and when they left they took the children. Boychildren to make into more pirates, and girlchildren, whispered our old maidservant, shuddering with relish as she blew out our bedside lamps, for their evil pleasures.

She knew no more about the pirates than any of us children. No pirates had been sighted around our little river village for at least a hundred years. I doubt that she even believed in them.

But *I* believed. Long after the stories were done I lay awake and thought of them with yearning. Somewhere out in the great ocean they stood, tall and resolute at the prows of their ships, arms crossed, granite faces turned toward our village, hair whipped free by the salt wind.

That same salt wind would sweep through me. Restlessness. How tiresome my life had become, the endless praise, the songs of adulation, the mountains of gifts, my parents' fearful deference. And these unending nights lying sleepless among a gaggle of girls who groaned out the names of boys in their dreams.

I would turn my face into my pillow to escape the emptiness opening like a black hand inside my chest. I would focus my attention on my discontent until it glittered sharp as a hook, and then I would cast it out over the ocean in search of my pirates.

I was using the calling thought, though only later on the island would I learn its name. The calling thought which, as the Old One told us, can draw to you whoever you desire – a lover to your side, an enemy to your feet. Which can lift a soul out of a human body and place it raw and pulsing in your palm. Which used imperfectly and without control can bring destruction beyond imagining.

And so. Others may blame the merchant sailors who carried tales of me to every land for the coming of the pirates. But I know better.

They arrived at dusk. Later I would think it a fitting time, that moment when day cannot be told apart from night, truth from longing. A black mast cleaving through evening mist, a score of torches flickering their avid red over hut and grainstack and cowbarn, already smelling of charred flesh. And later, the flared eyes of villagers, mouths open to scream and only smoke billowing out.

We had been eating when the pirates splintered the bamboo walls of my father's house and burst upon us. Grease dripped from their blackened faces, and between curled lips, yes, their teeth were polished stone. Their eyes also. Polished and blind as they came toward me, pulled by the force of the calling thought, that gold hook I had sent so heedlessly over the waters. A foot kicked away bowls and pitchers, scattering rice and fish and palm honey, an arm curved casually through the air, driving a sword into my father's chest. Other hands pulled tapestries from walls, dragged women into corners, piled necklaces and earrings and jewelled waistbands onto a green skirt that one of my sisters had been wearing.

Mother, I never thought it would be like this.

I tried to stop them. Cried out all the charms I knew till my throat was raw, made the signs of power with shaking hands. Blew on a pot-shard to turn it into flint and aimed it at the pirate chief's heart. But he flicked it away with a finger and motioned to his men to bind me.

My calling thought had set in motion a juggernaut wheel whose turning even I could not arrest.

They carried me through the burning village, I dazed by shock and shame, by this new helplessness. Smoulder of rubble. Animals bellowing their terror. The pirate chief's voice lifted above dying moans, giving me in awful irony my new name. Bhagyavati, Bringer of Luck, for so I was to be for them.

Father, sisters, forgive me, I who had been Nayan Tara, who had wanted your love but only won your fear. Forgive me, my village, I who in boredom and disappointment did this to you.

Their pain stung like live coals in my chest as the pirates flung me onto the deck of their ship, as we took sail, as the flaming line of my homeland disappeared over the horizon. Long after the calling thought had worked itself out and my powers came to me again, strengthened by hate as power often is, long after I overthrew the chief to become queen of the pirates (for what else I could be I did not know), that pain ate at me. Vengeance did not appease it, as I had thought it would.

This was not the last time I would misguess the workings of my heart.

Ah, I thought I would burn forever, scar and peel and still burn, and I welcomed the punishment.

For a year – or was it two, or three? Time runs into itself at moments in my tale – I lived as queen, leading my pirates to fame and glory, so that bards sang their fearless exploits. I carried this secret pain that branded itself onto each chamber of my heart. This pain, the other face of which was the truth I had learned so hard: the spell is greater than the spellmaker; once unleashed, it cannot be countered.

Nights I walked the decks alone and sleepless, I Bhagyavati, sorceress, pirate queen, bringer of luck and death, my cloak dragging in salt dust like a torn wing.

I would have laughed, except I had no smiles left. Nor tears.

I will never forget them, this pain and this truth, I told myself. Never.

I did not know then that everything is forgotten. Someday.

But now I must tell you about the snakes.

The snakes are everywhere, yes, even in your home, in your favourite room. Under the hearthstone perhaps, or curled in a nest of insulation in the wall, or camouflaged among carpet strands. That flickering at the corner of your eye, gone when you swivel around.

The store? The store is full of them.

You are surprised? You have never noticed any, you say. That is because they have perfected the art of invisibility. If they do not wish, you will never see them.

No, I do not see them either. Not anymore.

But I know they are there. That is why each morning before the customers come I set earthen bowls of milk in the far corners of the store. Behind the extra bags of Basmati, in the thin sliver of space under the shelves of *dals*, near the glass case heaped with gaudy handicrafts that Indians buy only when they need to give gifts to Americans. I must do it just right, feel along the floor for the correct spot, warm as skin and throbbing. I must face the right direction, north-northwest, which is called *ishan* in the old language. I must whisper the words of invitation.

Snakes. Oldest of creatures, closest to the earth mother, all sinew and glide against her breast. Always I have loved them.

Once they loved me too.

In the heat-cracked fields behind my father's house, the land snakes shielded me from the sun when I was tired with playing. Their hoods spread ripple-wide, their smell cool as wet earth at the bottom of banana groves. In the streams that ribboned the village, the river snakes swam with me skin to skin, arrows of gold cutting through sun-flecked water, telling stories. How after a thousand years the bones of drowned men turn to white coral, their eyes to black pearl. How deep in a cavern underwater sits the king snake, Nagraj, guarding mounds of treasure.

And the snakes of the ocean, the sea serpents?

They saved my life.

Listen, I will tell you.

When I had been queen of the pirates for some time, one night I climbed to the prow of the ship. We were in the doldrums. Around me the ocean lay dark and thick, like clotted iron. It pressed in upon me like my life. I thought of the years behind me, all the raids I'd led, all the ships I'd plundered, all the riches I'd amassed meaninglessly and meaninglessly given away. I looked into the years ahead and saw the same, wave upon inky frozen wave.

'I want, I want,' I whispered. But what I longed for I didn't know, except that it wasn't this.

Was it death? It seemed possible.

And so I sent another calling thought over the water.

Sky grew dull like the scales of a *hilsa* fish stranded on sand, air sparked and stung, wind keened in our masts and ripped at our sails. And then it appeared on the horizon, the great typhoon I'd called up from its sleep in the ocean troughs of the east. It came at me, and beneath it the water was boiling.

The pirates screamed their terror in the holds below, but the sound was muffled, like an echo out of my past. When your heart is crusted over with your own pain, it is easy to feel little for others. A question rose in me like the tip of a broken mast in a storm-tossed sea. Had other voices cried to me in these tones once, long ago? But I let it fall back unanswered into the roaring.

O exhilaration, I thought. To be lifted up through the eye of chaos, to balance breath-stopped on the edge of nothing. And the plunge that would follow, the shattering of my matchstick body to smithereens, the bones flying free as foam, the heart finally released.

But when I saw that funnel mouth poised over me, and in it flashes of grey, like whirling knives, a heavy coldness filled my limbs. I knew I was not ready. The world was sweet as never before, suddenly, piercingly, sweet, and I wanted it with all my being.

'Please,' I cried. But to whom I did not know.

Too late Bhagyavati bringer of death.

Then I heard them.

A low sound no more than a hum, no match surely for that shrieking gale. But coming from someplace deep and slow, the centre of the ocean perhaps, the ship vibrating with it and my heart also. And their heads held still above the spinning water, the calm glow from the jewel each wore on its crest. Or was it the glow from their eyes that held me so.

I did not know when the typhoon lifted into the sky, when the waves gentled. My body was filled with their song, and weightless, and shining.

The sea serpents who sleep all day in caves of coral, who ascend to the surface only when Dhruva, star of the north, pours its vial of milk-light over the ocean. Their skin like molten mother-of-pearl, their tongues a ripple of polished silver. Who are seldom seen by the mortal eye.

Later I would ask, 'Why did you save me, why?'

The serpents never answered. What answer is there for love.

It was the sea serpents who told me of the island. And doing so, saved me once again.

Or did they? Some days I am not so sure.

'Tell me more.'

'The island has been there forever,' said the snakes, 'the Old One also. Even we who saw the mountains grow from buds of rock on the ocean bed, who were there when Samudra Puri, the perfect city, sank in the aftermath of the great flood, do not know their beginning.'

'And the spices?'

'Always. Their aroma like the long curling notes of the *shehnai*, like the *madol* that speeds up the blood with its wild beat, even across an entire ocean.'

'The island itself, what does it look like? And she?'

'We have only seen it from far: green slumbering volcano, red sand of beaches, granite outcrops like grey teeth. Nights when the Old One climbs the highest point, she is a pillar of burning. Her hands send the thunder-writing across the sky.'

'Haven't you wanted to go to it?'

'It is dangerous. On the island and also the waters that touch its roots, her power alone prevails. Once we had a brother, Ratna-nag, he with the opal eyes, the curious one. He heard the singing, ventured closer though we warned.'

'And then?'

'His skin floated back to us after many days, his perfect skin still supple as newborn seaweed, smelling of spice. And above it, crying wild, circling till sunset, an opal-eyed bird.'

'The island of spice,' I said, and it seemed that I had finally found a name for my wanting.

'Do not go,' the serpents cried. 'Come with us instead. We will give you a new name, a new being. You will be Sarpa Kanya, snake maiden. We will take you over the seven seas on our backs. We will show you where under the ocean Samudra Puri sleeps, biding its time. Perhaps you will be the one to awaken it.'

If only they had asked before.

The first pale dawnlight gleamed across the water. The serpents' skins grew transparent, took on the colour of the waves. The call of the spices coursed up my veins, un-stoppable. I turned my face from the serpents to where I imagined the island waiting for me.

At once sorrowful and angry, their hissing. Their tails whipping the water white.

'She will lose everything, foolish one. Sight, voice, name. Perhaps even self.'

'We should never have spoken of it to her.'

But the oldest of them said, 'She would have learned some other way. See the spiceglow under her skin, sign of her destiny.'

And before the ocean closed opaque over his head, he told me the way.

I did not see the sea serpents again.

They were the first among all that the spices were to take from me.

*

I have heard that here too in America, in the ocean that lies beyond the red-gold bridge at the end of the bay, there are serpents.

I have not gone to see them. It is forbidden for me to leave the store.

No. I must tell you the real reason.

I am afraid that they will not appear to me. That they have not forgiven me for choosing the spices over them.

I slide the last dish into place under the case of handicrafts, straighten up with a hand pressed to my back. It tires me at moments, this old body which I put on when I came to America, along with an old body's pains. It is as the First Mother had warned.

I think for a moment of her other warnings which too I had not believed.

Tomorrow I will lift out the dish, empty and licked to gleaming, and not even a sloughed-off bit of skin for me to see.

Still, sometimes I think I will try it, stand in evening mist at land's end in a grove of twisted cypress, among foghorns and black seals barking, and sing to them. I will put *shalparni*, herb of memory and persuasion, on my tongue and chant the old words. And even if they do not come, at least I would have tried.

Maybe I will ask Haroun, who drives a Rolls for Mrs Kapadia, Haroun whose footsteps I hear light as laughter outside the door now, to take me there on his day off.

'Lady,' says Haroun rushing in, carrying the scent of pine wind and *akhrot*, the crinkled white walnut from the hills of Kashmir where he was born. 'Oh Lady, Lady, I have news for you.'

His feet fly over the worn linoleum, almost not touching. His mouth is an eager light.

Always he has been like this. From the first time when he came into the shop behind haughty-hipped Mrs K, finding and piling up and carrying and salaaming but always the rueful amusement in his eyes saying, I am playing at this only for a while. And that night he came back alone and said, 'Lady please to kindly read my palm,' and offered me his upturned callused hands.

'I can't read the future,' I told him.

And truly I cannot. The Old One did not teach it to the Mistresses. 'It will keep you from hoping,' she said. 'From trying your best. From trusting the spices fully.'

'O but Ahmad told how you helped him get a green card, no no don't shake your head, and Najib Mokhtar who was about to be fired and on third day after he came to you and you gave him special tea to boil and drink, *subhanallah*, his boss got transfer all the way to Cleveland and Najib was put in his place.'

'Not me. It was the *dashmul*, herb of ten roots.'

But he kept holding his hands in front of me, those hands so hardened and trusting, until finally I had to point to the coarse pads and say 'How did you.'

'O that. Shovelling coals on ship when I came over, and then in car shop. Wrenches and tyre irons and in between road work with jackhammers and pouring pitch.'

'And before that?'

A small trembling in the hands. A pause.

'Yes, before that also. Back home we are boatmen on Dal Lake, grandfather and father and I, we row our *shikara* for tourists from America-Europe. One year money is so good we line the seats with red silk.'

I did not want to hear more. I sensed his past already in
the lines rising ridged and dark as thunder from his palms.

From under the counter I took a box of *chandan*,
powder of the sandalwood tree that relieves the pain of
remembering. I sprinkled its silk fragrance onto Haroun's
hands, careful not to touch. Over the lines of his life.

'Rub it in.'

He obeyed, but absently. And as he rubbed he told me
his story.

'One day the fighting started, and tourists stopped
coming. Rebels rode down from mountain passes with
machine guns and eyes like black holes in their faces, yes,
into the streets of Srinagar, the name which is meaning
auspicious city. I am telling father Abbajan we must leave
now but grandfather said, "*Toba, toba*, where will we go,
this is the land of our ancestors."'

'Hush,' I said, willing away the old lines from his palm,
setting his sorrows free into the dim air of the store. His
sorrows circling and circling above our heads to find a
new home as all released sorrows must.

Still he spoke them, staccato words like chipped stone.

'One night rebels. In our lake village. Came to take the
young men. Abbajan tried to stop them. Shots. Echoing
over water. Blood and blood and blood. Even grandfather
who was sleeping. Red silk of *shikara* turning redder. I
wish I too I too—'

As the last of the *chandan* melted into his palms, he
shuddered to a stop. Blinked dazed as though waking.

'What I was saying?'

'You wanted to know your fortune.'

'O yes.' A smile taking shape so heartbreaking-slow on
his lips as though he were learning it all over again.

'It looks good, very good. Great things will happen to
you in this new land, this America. Riches and happiness

and maybe even love, a beautiful woman with dark lotus-flower eyes.'

'Ah,' he said in a little sigh. And before I could stop him, he bent to kiss my hands. 'Lady I am thanking you.' His curls glinted soft black, a summer sky at night. His mouth was a circle of fire, burning my skin, and his pleasure flaring along my veins, burning them too.

I should have not allowed it. But how could I pull away.

All those things you warned me against, First Mother, I wanted them. His grateful lips innocent and ardent in the centre of my palm, his sorrows shimmering like fireflies alighted in my hair.

At the same time inside me something twisted in fear. A little for me, but for him more. I cannot see the future, true. But that desperate pulsing in his wrists, the blood flowing too fast as if it knew it had only a little time—

He stepped jauntily into the dangerous dark outside the store, Haroun unafraid because hadn't I promised. I who can make it all happen, green cards and promotions and girls with lotus eyes.

I Tilo architect of the immigrant dream.

O Haroun, I sent up a plea for you into the crackling air you left behind. Sandalwood keep safe the brightness in his eye. But there was a sudden explosion outside, a bus backfiring or maybe a gunshot. It drowned out my prayer.

Today I admit gladly that I had been mistaken. For now it is three months and Haroun, smiling with sunshine teeth and new American words, says, 'Lady you not gonna believe this. I quit my job with that Kapadia memsaab.'

I wait for him to explain.

'All these rich people, they think they're still in India. Treat you like *janwaars*, animals. Order this, order that, no end to it, and after you wear out your soles running around for them, not even a nod in thanks.'

'What now, Haroun?'

'Listen, listen. Last night I'm sitting at McDonald's, next to Thrifty Laundromat on Fourth Street, when someone puts his hand on my shoulder. I jump because you remember, how last month there was a shooting, someone asking money and not getting enough. I'm praying to Allah as I turn but it is only being Mujibar from my uncle's village up near Pahalgaon. Mujibar that I didn't even know was in America. He's done good too, owns a couple of taxis already and is looking for driver. Good pay, he is telling me, special for a fellow Kashmiri and maybe even a chance to buy later on. And think, nothing like being your own master. So I say yes and go and tell memsaab I'm leaving. Lady I tell you, her face turned purple like a brinjal. So from tomorrow I am driving a cab black and yellow like sunflowers.'

'A cab,' I repeat foolishly. There is a feeling like clenched ice in my belly, but why.

'Lady I must thank you, it's all your *keramat*, and now come look at my taxi, it's just outside. Come come, the store is being fine without you for a minute.'

O Haroun, in your entreating eyes I see that a joy does not become real until you share it with someone dear, and in this far country who else do you have. So I must step onto the forbidden concrete floor of America, leaving behind the store as I am never supposed to do.

Behind me a hiss like a shocked, indrawn breath, or is it only steam rising from an underground grate.

The taxi is there as Haroun promised in its sculpted butter shell, smooth and sweet but sending a chill into me even before Haroun says, 'Touch' and I put out my hand.

The vision explodes against my eyelids like fireworks

gone wrong. Dark of evening, the car doors swinging crazily open and the glove compartment also, and someone slumped against the steering wheel, is it man or woman? And the curls are they black and sweat-shiny as fear, is it a once-sunshine mouth, and the skin is it broken-bruised, or only a shadow falling?

It passes.

'Lady are you OK, your face is grey like old newspapers, running that big store all by yourself is too much. How many times I said you should put an ad in *India West* for a helper.'

'I'm fine Haroun. It's a beautiful car. But be careful.'

'O Ladyjaan you are worrying too much, just like my old *nani* back home. OK tell you what, you make me a magic packet and next time I come I'll put it in the car for luck. Got to run now. I am promising the boys to meet them at Akbar's and buy them special *khana*.'

He needs he needs—

But before I can think the spicename he's gone. Only the rifle-sharp crack of the car door shutting, the engine's happy hum, the faint smell of gas floating in the air like a promise of adventure.

Tilo don't be fanciful.

In the store the spices' displeasure waits for me. I must beg pardon. But I cannot stop thinking of Haroun yet. In the burnt-brown air my tongue tastes like copper, like a nightmare you escape for a moment, struggling, because if you sleep you will fall into it again, but your eyes are too heavy and force themselves closed.

Maybe I am mistaken this time too.

Why can I not believe it?

Kalo jire, I think, just before the vision comes upon me again, blood and shattered bone and a thin cry like a red thread strangling the night. I must get *kalo jire*, spice of the dark planet Ketu, protector against the evil eye. Spice that is blueblack and glistening like the forest Sundarban where it was first found. *Kalo jire* shaped like a teardrop, smelling raw and wild like tigers, to cover over what fate has written for Haroun.

You may have guessed this already. It is the hands that call power out of the spices. *Hater gun*, they call it.

Therefore the first thing the Old One examines when the girls come to the island are the hands.

This is what she says.

'A good hand is not too light, nor too heavy. Light hands are the wind's creatures, flung this way and that at its whim. Heavy hands, pulled downward by their own weight, have no spirit. They are only slabs of meat for the maggots waiting underground.

'A good hand is not palm-splotched with brown, the mark of a wicked temper. When you cup it tight and hold it up against the sun, between the fingers are no gaps for spells and spices to slip through.

'Not cold and dry as the snake's belly, for a Mistress of Spices must feel the other's pain.

'Not warm and damp as the breath of a waiting lover against the windowpane, for a Mistress must leave her own passions behind.

'In the centre of the good hand is imprinted an invisible lily, flower of cool virtue, glowing pearl at midnight.'

Do your hands fit this litany? Nor did mine.

How then, you ask, did I become a Mistress.

Wait, I will tell you.

*

From the moment the oldest serpent told me the way, I drove my pirates day and night, relentless, till they dropped on the deck exhausted, not daring to ask why or where. Then one evening we saw it on the horizon, a smudge like smoke or seacloud. But I knew what it was. Anchor, I ordered, and would not say more. And while the tired crew slept as though tranced, I dived into the midnight ocean.

The island was far, but I was confident. I sang a chant for weightlessness, and pushed through the waves easy as air. But while the island was still small as a fist pushing up into the sky, the chant died in my throat. My arms and legs grew heavy and would not obey. In these waters charmed by a greater sorceress, my power was nothing. I struggled and thrashed and swallowed brine like any other clumsy mortal until at last I dragged myself onto the sand and collapsed into a dizzy whorl of dreams.

The dreams I do not remember, but the voice that woke me from them I will never forget. Cool and grainy with a hint of a mocking laugh in it, yet deep, deep, a voice to plunge your heart into.

'What has the god of the sea belched up on our shore this morning?'

The Old One, surrounded by her novices, and the sun a halo behind her head and shimmering many-coloured in her lashes. So that I scrambling to my knees felt impelled to lower my own sand-caked ones.

It was then I saw that I was naked. The sea had stripped me of all, clothes and magic and for the moment arrogance even. Had thrown me at her feet bereft of all but my dark, ugly body.

In shame I pulled at my salt-stiff hair to cover me. In

shame I crossed my arms over my chest and bent my head.

But already she was removing her shawl, placing it around my shoulders. Soft and grey as a dove's throat, and the spice-smell rising from it like a mystery I longed to learn. And her hands. Soft, but with the skin burned pink-white and puckered to the elbows as though she had plunged them into a long-ago blaze.

'Who are you, child?'

Who was I? I could not say. Already my name had faded in the rising island sun, like a star from a night that has passed away. Only much later when she would teach us the herbs of memory would I recollect it – and my past life – again.

'What do you want of me?'

Dumbly I stared at her, she who seemed at once oldest and most beautiful of women with her silver wrinkles, though later I would see that she was not beautiful in the way men use the word. Her voice, which I would later learn in all its tones – anger and mockery and sadness – was sweet as the wind in the cinnamon trees behind her. A yearning to belong to her buffeted me like the waves I had fought all night.

I think she read my heart, the Old One. Or perhaps it was merely that all who came to her were drawn by the same desire.

She gave a small sigh. The weight of adoration is hard to bear, I know that now.

'Let me see.' And she took my hands in hers that had passed through fire, who knows where.

Too light, too hot, too damp. My hands freckled as the back of a golden plover. Palms where at midnight thorn-purple bloodwort would burst into bloom.

The Old One had taken a step back, letting go.

'No.'

Each year a thousand girls are sent back from the island because they do not have the right hands. It does not count if they have the second sight, or if they can leave their bodies to travel the sky. The Old One is adamant.

Each year a thousand girls whose hands have failed them throw themselves into the sea as they sail home. Because death is easier to bear than the ordinary life, cooking and washing clothes and bathing in the women's lake and bearing children who will one day leave you, and all the while remembering her, on whom you had set your heart.

They become water wraiths, spirits of mist and salt, crying in the voices of gulls.

I too would have been one of them, but for the bones.

They were why the Old One could not resist taking my hands in hers again. Why she let me stay on the island though all wisdom must have shouted *no*.

Most important in a good hand are the bones. They must be smooth as water-polished stone and pliant to the Old One's touch when she holds your palm between hers, when she places the spices in its centre. They must know to sing to the spices.

'I should have made you go,' the Old One would tell me later, shaking her head ruefully. 'They were volcano hands, simmering with risk, waiting to explode. But I couldn't.'

'Why not, First Mother?'

'You were the only one in whose hands the spices sang back.'

Cinnamon

Let me tell you about chillies.

The dry chilli, *lanka*, is the most potent of spices. In its blister-red skin, the most beautiful. Its other name is danger.

The chilli sings in the voice of a hawk circling sun-bleached hills where nothing grows. *I* lanka *was born of Agni, god of fire. I dripped from his fingertips to bring taste to this bland earth.*

Lanka, I think I am most in love with you.

The chilli grows in the very centre of the island, in the core of a sleeping volcano. Until we reach the third level of apprenticeship, we are not allowed to approach it.

Chilli, spice of red Thursday, which is the day of reckoning. Day which invites us to pick up the sack of our existence and shake it inside out. Day of suicide, day of murder.

Lanka, lanka. Sometimes I roll your name over my tongue. Taste the enticing sting of it.

So many times the Old One has warned us against your powers.

'Daughters, use it only as the last remedy. It is easy to start a flame. But to put it out?'

That is why I hold on, *lanka*, whose name the ten-headed Ravana took for his enchanted kingdom. City of a million jewels turned at the last to ash. Though more than once I have been tempted.

As when Jagjit comes to the store.

In the inner room of the store, on the topmost shelf, sits a sealed jar filled with red fingers of light. One day I will open it and the chillies will flicker to the ground. And blaze.

Lanka, fire-child, cleanser of evil. For when there is no other way.

Jagjit comes to the store with his mother. Stands partly behind her, his fingers touching her *dupatta* although he is ten and a half already and tall as wild bamboo.

'Oi Jaggi don't hang on me like a girl, go get me a packet of *sabu papads*.'

Jagjit with his thin, frightened wrists who has trouble in school because he knows only Punjabi still. Jagjit whom the teacher has put in the last row next to the drooling boy with milk-blue eyes. Jagjit who has learned his first English word. *Idiot. Idiot. Idiot.*

I walk to the back where he stares in confusion at the shelves of *papads*, the packets stamped with hieroglyphs of Hindi and English.

I hand him the *sabu papads*. I tell him, 'They're the bumpy white ones, see. Next time you'll know.'

Shy-eyed Jagjit in your green turban that the kids at school make fun of, do you know your name means world-conqueror?

But already his mother is shouting, 'What's taking you so long Jaggi, can't find the *papads*, are you blind, the hairs on my head will go white waiting waiting by the time you get back.'

In the playground they try to pull it off his head, green turban the colour of a parrot's breast. They dangle the cloth from their fingertips and laugh at his long, uncut hair. And push him down.

Asshole, his second English word. And his knees bleeding from the gravel.

Jagjit who bites down on his lip so the cry will not out.

Who picks up his muddy turban and ties it on slowly and goes inside.

'Jaggi how come you're always dirtying your school clothes, here is a button gone and look at this big tear on your shirt, you *badmash*, you think I'm made of money.'

At night he lies with his eyes open, staring until the stars begin to flicker like fireflies in his grandmother's *kheti* outside Jullunder. She is singing as she gathers for dinner bunches of *saag* green as his turban. Punjabi words that sound like rain.

Jagjit, do they come back when you at last must close your eyes because what else can you do. The jeering voices, the spitting mouths, the hands. The hands that pull your pants down in the playground, and the girls looking.

'*Chhodo mainu.*'

'Talk English sonofabitch. Speak up nigger wetback asshole.'

'Jaggi what you meaning you don't want to go to school, what for your father is killing himself working working at the factory, two slaps will make you go.'

'*Chhodo.*'

At the checkstand I say, 'Here's some *burfi* for you, no no madam, no cost for children.' I see him bite eager into the brown sweet flavoured with clove and cardamom and cinnamon. He smiles a small smile to answer mine.

Crushed clove and cardamom, Jagjit, to make your breath fragrant. Cardamom which I will scatter tonight on the wind for you. North wind carrying them to open your teacher's unseeing. And also sweet pungent clove, *lavang*, spice of compassion. So your mother of a sudden looking up from the washboard, pushing tired hair from her face, 'Jaggi *beta*, tell me what happened,' will hold you in her soapsud arms.

And here is cinnamon, hollow dark bone that I tuck

unseen in your turban just before you go. Cinnamon friend-maker, cinnamon *dalchini* warm-brown as skin, to find you someone who will take you by the hand, who will run with you and laugh with you and say See this is America, it's not so bad.

And for the others with the pebble-hard eyes, cinnamon destroyer of enemies to give you strength, strength which grows in your legs and arms and mostly mouth till one day you shout *no* loud enough to make them, shocked, stop.

When we had passed the ceremony of purification, when we were ready to leave the island and meet our separate destinies, the Old One said, 'Daughters it is time for me to give you your new names. For when you came to this island you left your old names behind, and have remained nameless since.

'But let me ask you one last time. Are you certain you wish to become Mistresses? It is not too late to choose an easier life.

'Are you ready to give up your young bodies, to take on age and ugliness and unending service? Ready never to step out of the places where you are set down, store or school or healing house?

'Are you ready never to love any but the spices again?'

Around me my sister-novices, their garments still wet from the seawater she had poured on them, stood silent, shivering a little. And it seemed to me the prettiest ones kept their eyes lowered longest.

Ah, now I have learned how deep in the human heart

vanity lies, vanity which is the other face of the fear of being unloved.

But on that day I who was the Old One's brightest pupil, quick to master every spell and chant, quick to speak with the spices, even the most dangerous, quick to arrogance and impatience as often I was, had thrown them a glance, half pity and half derision. I had looked the Old One boldly in the eye and said, 'I am.'

I who was not beautiful and thought therefore I had little to lose.

The Old One's stare stung me like the thorn-herb. But she said only, 'Very well.' And called us to approach her, each alone.

Through sea mist the island cast its pearl light around us. In the sky rainbows arced like wings. Each girl knelt, and the Old One bending traced on her forehead her new name. As she spoke it seemed the girls' features shifted like water, and something new came into every face.

'You shall be called Aparajita after the flower whose juice, smeared on eyelids, leads one to victory.'

'You shall be Pia after the *pial* tree whose ashes rubbed on limbs bring vigour.'

'And you—'

But I had chosen already.

'First Mother, my name will be Tilo.'

'Tilo?' Displeasure echoed in her voice, and the other novices looked up fearfully.

'Yes,' I said, and though I too was afraid, I forced my voice not to reveal it. 'Tilo short for Tilottama.'

Ah how naïve I was to think I could keep my heart hidden from the Old One, she who would later teach me to look into the hearts of others.

'You've been nothing but trouble ever since you came,

rulebreaker. I should have thrown you out at our first meeting itself.'

I wonder still that she was not angrier that day, the First Mother. Did she see mirrored, in my headstrong self, her own girlhood?

The roots hanging like dreadlocks from the branches of banyan trees rustled in the breeze. Or was it her, sighing?

'This name, do you know what it means?'

It is a question I expected. I have the answer ready.

'Yes, First Mother. *Til* is the sesame seed, under the sway of planet Venus, gold-brown as though just touched by flame. The flower of which is so small and straight and pointed that mothers pray for their girlchildren to have noses shaped like it. *Til* which ground into paste with sandalwood cures diseases of heart and liver, *til* which fried in its own oil restores lustre when one has lost interest in life. I will be Tilottama, the essence of *til*, life-giver, restorer of health and hope.'

Her laugh is the sound of dry leaves snapping underfoot.

'It is certainly not confidence you lack, girl. To take on the name of the most beautiful *apsara* of Rain-god Indra's court. Tilottama most elegant of dancers, crest-jewel among women. Or had you not known?'

I hang my head. For a moment again I am the ignorant youngster of my first day on the island, sea-wet, naked, stumbling on the sharp slippery stones. Always she can shame me this way. For this I could hate her if I did not love her so, she who was truly first mother to me, who had given up all hope of being mothered.

Her fingertips, light as breath in my hair.

'Ah, child, you've set your heart on it, have you not? But remember: when Brahma made Tilottama to be chief dancer in Indra's court, he warned her never to give her love to man – only to the dance.'

'Yes Mother.' I am laughing with success, with relief, with triumph at this battle fought and won, pressing my lips to the Old One's papery palms. 'Do I not know the rules? Have I not made the vows?'

And now she writes my new name on my forehead. My Mistress name, finally and forever, after so many changes in who I am. My true-name that I am never to tell to any but the sisterhood. Her finger is cool and moves smooth as oil. The air fills with the clean, astringent fragrance of *til* seeds.

'Remember this too: Tilottama, disobedient at the last, fell. And was banished to earth to live as a mortal for seven lives. Seven mortal lives of illness and age, of people turning in disgust from her twisted, leprous limbs.'

'But *I* will not fall, Mother.'

No hint of shaking in my voice. My heart is filled with passion for the spices, my ears with the music of our dance together. My blood with our shared power.

I need no pitiful mortal man to love.

I believe this. Wholly.

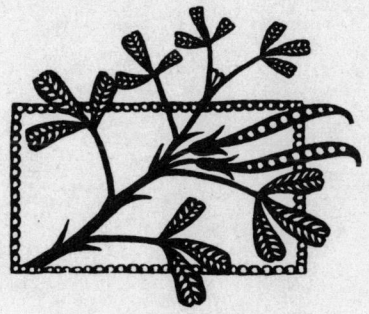

Fenugreek

Give me your hand. Open, then shut. Feel.

Pebble-hard fenugreek lies tight and closed in the centre of your palm, colour of sand at the bottom of an old creek. But put it in water and it will bloom free.

Bite the swollen kernels between your teeth and taste its bitter sweetness. Taste of waterweeds in a wild place, the cry of grey geese. Fenugreek Tuesday's spice, when the air is green like mosses after rain. Spice for days when I want to huddle into a quilt stitched with *peepul* leaves and tell stories like on the island. Except here who would I tell them to.

Fenugreek, I asked your help when Ratna came to me burning from the poison in her womb, legacy of her husband's roving. And when Ramaswamy turned from his wife of twenty years to a newer pleasure.

Listen to fenugreek's song: *I am fresh as river wind to the tongue, planting desire in a plot turned barren.*

Yes I called to you when Alok who loves men showed me the lesions opening avid as mouths on his skin and said, 'I guess this is it.' When Binita raised to me her face like a singed flower. Binita with a lump like a nugget of lead in her breast and the doctors saying cut, and the look in her husband's eyes as he paced and paced the store saying, 'What shall I do, please.'

I fenugreek who renders the body sweet again, ready for loving.

Fenugreek *methi*, speckled seed first sown by Shabari, oldest woman in the world. The young scorn you, thinking they will never need. But one day. Sooner than they think.

All of them, yes. Even the bougainvillaea girls.

The bougainvillaea girls enter in a flock, like dragonflies at noon. Their sudden laughter peals over me. Warm salt waves that take the breath and pull you to drowning. They float through the musty dark of the store, glistery dustmotes on a ray of light. And for the first time I am ashamed and wish everything shiny and new.

The bougainvillaea girls have hair polished as ebony, coiled in agile braids. Or rippling like mountain water around upturned faces so confident you know nothing bad has ever happened to them.

They wear jangly bangles in rainbow colours and earrings that swing against the smooth sides of their necks. Their feet arched high in thin glittery heels, their long swaying legs. Their painted nails like purple bougainvillaea flowers. Their lips also.

Not for them the dullness of rice-flour-beans-cumin-coriander. They want pistachios for *pulao*, and poppy seeds for *rogan josh*, which they will prepare looking at a book.

The bougainvillaea girls don't see me, not even when they raise their voices to ask, 'Where's the *amchur*,' and, 'Is the *rasmalai* fresh, are you sure.' Blackbird voices pitched high as for the deaf, or the feeble-minded.

For a moment I am angry. Fools, I think. Blind fluttering mascara eyes. My hand curls in a fist around the bay leaves they have thrown so carelessly onto the counter.

I could make them empresses. Oceans of oil and honey to bathe in, sparkling palaces of rock-sugar. Leaf of water-hyacinth laid on the palm to turn their touch to gold.

Unguent of lotus root touched to the nipples for men to lie enslaved at their feet. If I wished.

Or I could—

They think themselves so special. Fortune's daughters whom she holds high above harm's touch. But one drop of walnut juice in mandragora, with their names whispered over it. And.

Dust of crushed bay leaf falls from my fist like smoke. A desire leaps clawed like a tiger from its hidden place in me.

I will boil petal of rose with camphor, grind in peacock feathers. Say the words of making and be rid of this disguise I put on when I left the island. This disguise falling like old snakeskin around my feet, and I rising red and new and wet-gleaming. Draped in a veil of diamonds. Tilottama most beautiful, to whom these girls will be like mud scraped from the feet before one crosses the threshold.

My nails cut into my palms. With the blood comes pain. And shame.

'You'll be tempted,' said the Old One before I left. 'You especially with your lava hands that want so much from the world. Your lava heart flying too easily to hate, to envy, to love-passion. Remember why you were given your power.'

Pardon, First Mother.

I wipe contrite hands against my sari. My sari old and patched and stained to guard me against this vanity that presses hot at the walls of my skull, swollen like steam. I breathe it out, red mist. And when I breathe in, I hold on to the smell of the spices. Clean, sharp, sane. Letting me see again.

And so I bless them, my bougainvillaea girls. Bless the round bones of their elbows, the glide of hips beneath their silky *salwaars*, their Calvin Klein jeans. With the fervour of repentance I bless the curve of their moist palms against the bottles of lime pickles they are holding up to the light, the cans of *patra* leaf they will fry tonight for bridegrooms or lovers, for they are always newly wed, the bougainvillaea girls, or not at all.

I crinkle my eyes and see them in evening: the lights turned low, silk cushions the colour of midnight embroidered with tiny mirrors. Perhaps a little music in the distance, sitar or saxophone.

They are serving their men *biriyani* fragrant with ghee, cool bowls of *raita*, *patra* seasoned with fenugreek. And for dessert, dripping with gold honey, *gulab-jamuns* the colour of dark roses.

The men's eyes too darken, like roses under a storm sky.

Later the women's mouths, moist red O's opening as they had for the *jamuns*, the men's breathing hot and uneven, rising and plunging and rising again into a cry.

I see it all. So beautiful, so brief, so therefore sad.

I let the envy drain out. They are only following their natures, the bougainvillaea girls. As I against every advice followed mine.

Envy like green pus, gone now. All of it. Almost.

I breathe a good thought over each purchase as I ring it up. The bay leaves, a new packet, their brown edges crisp and whole, I put in for free.

For my bougainvillaea girls, whose bodies glow saffron in bed, whose mouths smell of my fenugreek, my *elach*, my *paan paraag*. Whom I have made. Musky. Fecund. Irresistible.

I sleep with a knife under my mattress. Have done it for so long that the little bump its hilt makes just below my left shoulder blade feels as familiar as a lover's hand pressing.

Tilo you're a great one to be talking of lovers.

I love the knife (I cannot call it mine) because it was given to me by the Old One.

I remember the day, muted orange of butterfly wings, and a sadness already in the air. She was handing each Mistress a going-away gift. Some received flutes, some incense burners, some looms. A few were given pens.

Only I received a knife.

'To keep you chaste,' she said, speaking for my ears only as she put it in my palm. The knife cold as ocean-water, supple-edged as the yucca leaf that grows high on the sides of the volcano. The knife humming its metal knifesong against my lips when I bent to kiss the blade.

'To keep you from dreaming.'

Knife to cut my moorings from the past, the future. To keep me always rocking at sea.

Each night I slip it under when I unroll my bedding, each morning lift it out and wrap it in its bindings with a thanking thought. Put it in the pouch I wear at my waist, for the knife has other uses also.

All of them dangerous.

You are thinking, what does it look like, such a knife.

Most ordinary, for that is the nature of deepest magic. Deepest magic which lies at the heart of our everyday lives, flickering fire, if only we had eyes to see.

And so. My knife could be a knife bought at any store, Thrifty or Pay Less or Safeway, the wood handle faded smooth with sweat, the flat dark blade with no shine left to it.

But O, how it cuts.

If you ask me how long I lived on the island, I cannot tell you, for time took on a different meaning in that place. We lived our days without hurry, and yet each moment was urgent, a spinning petal borne seaward by a swift river. If we did not grasp it, did not learn its lesson, it would pass beyond our reach for ever.

The lessons we learned on the island might surprise you, you who think our Mistress-lives to be full of the exotic, mystery and drama and danger. Those were there, yes, for the spice-power we were learning to bend to our purposes could have destroyed us in a moment if wrongly invoked. But much of our time was spent in common things, sweeping and stitching and rolling wicks for lamps, gathering wild spinach and roasting *chapatis* and braiding each other's hair. We learned to be neat and industrious and to work together, to protect one another when we could from the Old One's anger, her tongue that could lash like lightning. (But thinking back I grow unsure. Was it real, that anger, or a disguise put on to teach us fellowship?) Most of all we learned to feel without words the sorrows of our sisters, and without words to console them. In this way our lives were not so different from those of the girls we had left behind in our home villages. And though then I chafed and considered such work a waste of my time (I who despised all things ordinary and felt I was born for better), now I sometimes wonder if it might not have been the most worthwhile of the skills I learned on the island.

One day after we had been on the island a long time,

the Old One took us up into the core of the sleeping volcano and said, 'Mistresses, I have taught you all I could. Some of you have learned much, and some little. And some have learned little but think you have learned much.'

Here her eyes rested on me. But I merely smiled, thinking it another of her barbed jokes. For was I not the most skilful among Mistresses.

'There is no more I can do for you,' she said, watching me smile. 'You must now decide where you are to go.'

Night wind wrapped us in its dark secret smells. Black lava dust sifted soft as powder between our toes. The ridges of the volcano rose spiralled around us. We sat in silence wondering what was to come.

The Old One took the branches she had given us earlier to carry and wove them into a lattice fan. What branches they were we did not know. There was still much she chose to keep from us. She waved the fan into the air till its swirling became a fog around us.

'Look,' she said.

Cleaving through the milk-thick fog the images piled one on another, their edges hard and glinting.

Skyscrapers of silver glass by a lake wide as ocean, fur-coated men and women, white like the snow that lines the pavements, crossing the street to avoid dark skin. Brown-sugar girls in flimsy bright dresses, leaning lipsticked on shantytown porches, waiting for customers. Marble mansion walls embedded with glass shards to tear a man's palms to strips. Pothole roads lined with beggars whose skin can't hold in their jagged bones. A woman watching through her barred window a world beyond her reach, while on her forehead the marriage *sindur* presses down like a coin of blood. Narrow cobble streets, shuttered houses, men in fez caps eating *medjool* dates and spitting out *infidel dog* as an Indian passes.

All around us, overpowering like singed flesh, the odour of hate which is also the odour of fear.

'Toronto,' said the Old One. 'Calcutta Rawalpindi Kuala Lumpur Dar es Salaam.'

Burned-out streetlamps, grilled storefronts, brick-lined alleywalls slashed with letters dripping blackness. Wedding canopy, wail of *shehnais*, a girlbride in a *sharara* seeing for the first time the stooped, wrinkled man her father sold her to. Turbaned coolies drinking *daru* and playing cards by open drains. Garment factories smelling of starch and sweat and immigration raids, women hand-cuffed and piled crying into vans. Children coughing and struggling blind out of sleep into lung-burning gas. *Bloody bugger Hindoostani. Fucking Dothead. Paki go home.* Black men in dusty dashikis stalking hot streets, staring through plate-glass windows at air-conditioned Indian shops. Jostling chanting crowd carrying an elephant-headed god down to an ocean made slick with poisons.

'London Dhaka Hasnapur Bhopal Bombay Lagos.'

The lost brown faces looked out at us, unseeing, unknowing, calling. We looked back, silent with shock.

We had known it would be hard to leave this island of women where on our skin the warm rain fell like pomegranate seeds, where we woke to birdcall and slept to the First Mother's singing, where we swam naked without shame in lakes of blue lotus. To exchange it for the human world whose harshness we remembered. But *this*?

'Los Angeles New Jersey Hong Kong.'

'Colombo Singapore Johannesburg.'

The images loomed smoking at their edges, searing themselves into our eyeballs.

Eventually the Mistresses began, their voices low and

filled with misgiving, pointing at pictures that danced on the acrid air. For what else was left for them to do.

'Perhaps I will go here, First Mother.'

'And I here.'

'First Mother, I am too frightened, you choose for me.'

And she inclining her head, assigning to each Mistress what she desired, what she should have desired: the place where she would spend the rest of her life, the place toward which her nature pointed her.

Dubai Asansol Vancouver Islamabad.

Patna Detroit Port of Spain.

Only a few images left now to waver in the night's-end air.

Still I said nothing. I waited, not knowing for what.

Then I saw it. Waves of eucalyptus and ponderosa pine, dry grass the colour of lionskin, gleam of glass and polished redwood, the villas of the California rich poised precariously on restless hills. Even as I watched, the images changed to sooty tenements stacked like crushed cereal boxes, sooty children chasing one another among a crumble of concrete and barbed wire. Now night dropped like a net, and men in torn overcoats huddled around trashcan fires. Beyond, water crested and ebbed dark as mockery, and on the tops of the bridges burned the beautiful, unreachable lights.

And under it all, earth waited with her lead-filled veins, impatient to shrug herself clean.

Even before she spoke I knew its name, Oakland, the other city by the Bay. Mine.

'O Tilo,' she said, 'I must give you what you ask for, but consider, consider. Better you should choose an Indian settlement, an African market town. Any other place in the world, Qatar Paris Sydney Kingston Town Chaguanas.'

'Why, First Mother?'

She sighed and looked away, for the first time not meeting my eyes.

But I waited until she said, 'I have a feeling.'

The Old One seeing more than she told, her spine bent and tired under the weight of it. And I stubborn with youth, with wanting to walk the cliff edge like the lion's tooth. Telling her, 'It is the only place for me, First Mother,' and holding her eye until she said, 'Go then, I cannot stop you.'

I Tilo thinking through a wild wave of joy, I won I won.

In the last hours of the night we piled wood in the centre of the volcano, in readiness. We danced around it singing of Shampati, bird of myth and memory who dived into conflagration and rose new from ash, as we were to do. I was last in line, and as we circled the pyre I watched the faces of my sister-Mistresses. They did not flinch too much when at a word from the Old One the wood burst ablaze.

The fire of Shampati. Ever since we came to the island we had heard the whispers, seen stamped on the lintels and doorposts of the motherhouse the runes of the bird rising, its flame-beak angled toward sky. In one rune only, on the door to the chamber where the Old One slept, forbidden to Mistresses, the rune was reversed, the bird forever plunging into the fierce heart of a blaze. We did not dare ask what it meant.

But she told us, one day.

'Look well Mistresses. Once in a great while a Mistress, grown rebellious and self-indulgent, fails her duty and must be recalled. Warning is sent to her, and she has three days only to settle her affairs. Then Shampati's fire blazes for her once more. But this time entering she feels it fully, scorch and sear, the razors of flame cutting her flesh to strips. Screaming, she smells her bones shatter, skin bubble and burst.'

'And then?'

The Old One had shrugged, spread those palms with the lines melted out of them, and seeing them I had wondered once again, *How?* 'The spices decide. Some Mistresses are allowed to return to the island, learn and labour again. For some it is the end, crumbled charcoal, a last cry dangling in the air like a broken cobweb.'

I remembered all this as I watched my sister-Mistresses. One by one they walked into the fire, and when they reached its centre they disappeared. Watching the empty air flicker where a moment earlier they had been, I was struck by a sorrow deeper than I had thought I could feel. Always I had kept my distance, all these years on the island, knowing this day was to come. And yet when had they slipped into my heart, these girl-women glowing translucent, chaste as alabaster, the last ones in the world to know who I was, and how it felt to be that.

When it was my turn I closed my eyes. Was I afraid? I believed what the Old One had told us: 'You will not burn you will not feel pain. You will wake in your new body as though it has been yours forever.' There had been no agony on the faces of my sisters before they vanished. Still it was a hard thing, to confront for the third time in my brief existence the extinguishing of all I knew life to be.

And so far. So far. I had not thought this before. Between the island and America, a galaxy of nights.

On my elbow, a touch like petals.

'Wait Tilo.'

Behind a veil of smoke, that shimmering in her eyes. Was it tears. And the stinging in my heart, what was that.

Almost I said it. *Mother take back the power. Let me*

stay here with you. What satisfaction can be greater than to serve the one I love.

But the years and days, the moments that had pushed me to this place, inexorable, and made me who I was, would not let me.

'Tilo my daughter,' said the Old One, and by her face I knew she felt my struggle in her own heart, 'most gifted most troublesome most loved, Tilo travelling to America eager as an arrow, I have here something for you.'

And from the folds of her clothing she removed it and placed it on my tongue, a slice of ginger-root, wild island *ada* to give my heart steadfastness, to keep me strong in my vows.

Hot prick of ginger, you were the last taste on my tongue when I stepped into the heart of Shampati's fire. Flametongues licked like a dream at my melting skin, flamefingers pushed down my eyelids.

And when I woke in America on a bed of ash, an age later or was it only a breath, the store already hardening its protective shell around me, the spices on their shelves meticulous and waiting, you were the first taste, ginger, gritty and golden in my throat.

When the sky turns arsenic-red from sunset and smog, and the palm that stands scrawny by the bus stop throws its long ragged shadow in my doorway, I know it is time to close up.

I unpleat the wooden shutters and slide them across the pockmarked curve of a pale moon. In the grey window glass which is the store's only mirror, the shadow of my face wavers for a moment. I shut my eyes, move away. Once a Mistress has taken on her magic Mistress-body, she is never to look on her reflection again. It is a rule that causes me no grief, for I know without looking how old I am, and how far from beautiful. That too I have accepted.

You are wondering if it were always so.

No.

Ah that first waking in the silent store, the smell of damp cement flowing down the walls down my body. How I lifted my arm, so heavy in its loose-lapped skin and felt the scream taking shape like a dark hole in my chest. *Not this not this.* The trembling in my knees as I pushed myself up, the pain that jabbed the twisted bones of my hands.

My beautiful hands.

Anger whose other name is regret surged like wildfire through me. Yet who could I blame. The Old One had warned us a hundred times.

O foolish Tilo always rushing in thinking you know better.

After a while it receded, the anger the pain. Perhaps I grew used to it. Or was it the spicesong? For when I held them in my misshapen hands the spices sang clearer than ever before, their notes true and high like ecstasy, like they knew I was now theirs wholly.

And I was. Am. Happy.

At the store entrance I shut the door. Turn the latch. Hook. Heft the heavy metal bar in place. At each entrance I clap and speak the words to keep out the rats and voles, the goblins that turn the lentils furry-green with mildew and make the chutneys rot inside their sealed jars of glass.

To keep out the boys that prowl the nightstreets. Softchinned apricot-fuzz boys, their bodies hard with the anger of not having. Wanting and not having and shouting inside their heads, *Why. Why when you have.*

The walls of the store grow dim, dimmer, till it is invisible to alien eyes. Even you standing outside will think you see merely shadow-shapes flickering on an empty lot.

Time now to spread my bedding in the centre, where the floor dips just a little. Above, a naked bulb casts great domed shadows, the roof disappears into the colour of smoke. Around me, buckets of *bajra* flour, squat casks of rapeseed oil, reassuring-solid. Sacks of sparkling sea salt to keep me company. The spices whispering their secrets, sighing their pleasure.

I too sigh my pleasure. When I lie down, from every direction the city will pulse its pain and fear and impatient love into me. All night if I wish I can live it, the ordinary life I gave up for the spices, through the thoughts that roll into me.

Tilo whose life is so calm so controlled so always same, is it not fine as wine, this taste of mortal sorrow, and mortal hope.

Each thought is a pattern of heat that will shape itself into words, into a face, and around it a room if I try hard enough.

First come the thoughts of the night boys, a high humming as in electric wires just before storm.

O the power the joy we are high with it when we step along the late street whistling chains swinging, and the people they scuttle into their holes, scuttle and scurry like roaches. We are king. And the orange spurt of flame from the mouths of our lovers our metal lovers our lovers who will give us death, death so much better than love, as many times as we ask.

The night boys with albino eyes colourless as acid.

They curdle my heart. I push back their thoughts into the dark that spawned them, but I know that invisible does not mean gone.

But here is another image. A woman in a kitchen, cooking my rice. She is fragrant as the grains she rolls between her fingers to see if they are done. Rice steam has softened her skin, has loosened hair tied back taut all day. Has gentled the smudges under her eyes. Payday today, so she can begin the frying, mustard seeds sputtering in the pan, brinjal and bitter gourd turning yellow-red. Into a curry of cauliflowers like white fists, she mixes *garam masala* to bring patience and hope. Is she one, is she many, is she not the woman in a hundred Indian homes who is sprinkling, over sweet *kheer* that has simmered all afternoon, cardamom seeds from my shop for the dreams that keep us from going mad?

Inside my head her thoughts knock against one another, falling.

All evening I am running back and forth from kitchen to front window like a wild woman until the children come home. I am this way ever since what happened to the Gupta girl last week and in daylight too, the gods protect us. I am worrying also about their father, layoffs at work, fights with the foreman with the moneylender. Or is he again at Bailey's today with the other men and forgetting the time. When I put the wedding garland around his neck, was I ever knowing that this is what is being a wife and mother, walking the edge of a knife with fear like a wolf waiting on both sides. And worst of all the mouths, the mouths coming to me even after I finally sleep, the mouths crumpled with hunger so many days this month, crying, 'So good Amma give us another half spoon more please Amma please,' and I turning away with eyes like anguished stone.

The men, where are they? Their thoughts give off the smell of parched earth in a year of failed monsoons, lead me into rooms hung with pictures from old calendars. Juhu Beach, the Golden Temple, Zeenat in a spangled sundress. Now I see them, boots kicked off, swollen feet released and lifted heavily to rickety tables. They are breathing in the old comforting smells. Ground coriander, roasted *saunf*, the small tinkling of a woman's bangles. Almost it could be home. They close their hands around sweating brown bottles of Taj Mahal beer they bought at my store, chew the inside of their lips. I feel in my mouth the salt taste of blood as their thoughts come rushing.

Ah, that beer it goes down so foam-sweet and smooth but then in the throat a bitterness, like a long-ago dream unfinished. No one told us it would be so hard here in Amreekah, all day scrubbing greasy floors, lying under engines that drip black oil, driving the belching monster trucks that coat our lungs with tar. Standing behind counters of dim motels where we must smile as we hand keys to whores. Yes, always smile, even when people say 'Bastard foreigner taking over the country stealing our jobs.' Even when cops pull us over because we're in the wrong part the rich part of town. We thought we'd be back home by now, in Trichy, in Kharagpur, in Bareilly. Under the sweet whirr of a ceiling fan in a mosaic room with a seagreen floor, leaning back on satin pillows, and the servant bringing ice-cold lassi *with rose petals floating in it. But the landlord keeps hiking up the rent, last week the car wouldn't start, and the children grow so fast out of their clothes.* Phir bhi, *no matter. This week we'll take the bus up to Tahoe, Dilip bhaiya and I, play a few casinos, maybe get lucky like Arjun Singh, who won the lottery and the next day he went into 7-Eleven and told his boss, 'I spit on you and your job your job your job.'*

But it is dinnertime now. The mothers call out and the children come running from homework, chairs are pulled up, the steaming dishes brought in. Rice. *Rajma. Karela sabji. Kheer.*

A girl. Her hair tied in twin tight braids, oiled and obedient, her legs pressed together the way her mother has told her nice girls sit. She lifts a bowl of *kheer* and her thoughts, flittering like dusty sparrows in a brown back alley, turn a sudden kingfisher blue.

Kheer *today after so long, and there's enough after Father and Elder Brother have been served, enough even for Mother who eats always last of all.* Kheer *with almonds and raisins and crunchy pods of* elaichi *because the old woman at the store said they were on sale when she saw us looking. I dip my mouth into its sweetness, milkwhite lines my lips, and it's like New Year, and like New Year I can wish for anything. So I do, for a house, a big two-storey house with flowers in front and no clothes hanging out of windows, and enough rooms so we don't sleep two to a bed, enough bathrooms for long long baths and hot water also. I am wishing a shiny new car with gold hubcaps and white seats like cat's fur, and maybe a motorcycle as well, a red motorcycle that pulls the breath right out of you when Elder Brother zooms off with you behind. For Mother, a new pair of shoes instead of the one she lines with newspaper, and sparkly earrings like the women on TV. And for me, for me, lots and lots of Barbie dolls, Barbie in a nightgown and Barbie in a prom dress and Barbie in a swimsuit, silver high heels and lipstick, and real breasts. Barbie with a waist so narrow and hair so gold and most of all skin so white, and yes, even though I know I shouldn't, I must be proud like Mother says to be Indian, I wish for that American skin that American hair those blue blue American eyes so that no one will stare at me except to say WOW.*

Asafoetida

At the store each day has a colour, a smell. And if you know to listen, a melody. And Friday, Friday when I am closest to restlessness, hums like a car getting ready. Humming and vibrating, all set to disappear down that neon freeway beyond which surely lie open fields coloured like indigo. You breathe it in all the way because who knows when you will breathe next. And then you find the brake is jammed.

So perhaps it's fitting that the lonely American comes into the store on a Friday evening, the full moon already floating above the shoulder of the woman on the cut-out billboard by the freeway, and she in a black evening gown holding up a glass of Chivas. The headlights of oncoming cars hit the rhinestone straps of her gown so they shine like anticipation. Her eyes are like smoke, her mouth like pomegranates. They hurt me. And when I listen, the speeding cars sound mournful as wind in island bamboo.

I start to say I'm closing, but then I look at him and I can't.

It's not as if I haven't seen Americans. They come in here all the time, the professor types in tweed with patches on jacket elbows or in long skirts in earnest earth colours, Hare Krishnas in wrinkled white kurtas with shaved heads, backpack-toting students in seldom-laundered jeans, leftover hippies lankhaired and beaded. They want fresh coriander seed, organic of course, or pure ghee for a karma-free diet, or yesterday's *burfis* at half price. They lower hoarse voices *Hey lady got any hashish*.

I give them what they want. I forget them.

Sometimes I am tempted. For instance. When Kwesi comes in, with his wine-dark skin, his hair the tight-curled tendrils of night clouds. Kwesi who walks like a warrior, without sound, who holds his body in grace and without fear so I long to ask what he does.

And that scar like lightning on his forehead, that bump of knuckle broken and mended on his left hand.

But I do not. It is not permitted.

'Remember why you are going,' the Old One said. 'To help your own kind, and them only. The others, they must go elsewhere for their need.'

And so I let the clamour of the store drown out Kwesi's heart beating its story. I look away from his desires, which are coloured simple as childhood meadows. I weigh and pack what he has bought, powder of garbanzo, ground cumin, two bunches of cilantro. 'Very nice,' I say when he tells me he's going to make *pakoras* for a special friend, and without more talk wave him good-bye. And all the while I keep the door of my mind firmly shut.

But the lonely American feels different, feels like I might have trouble doing the same with him. It isn't what he's wearing. Black tailored pants, black shoes, a plain black leather jacket – but even I so little experienced in this can tell their expensiveness. Nor how he stands, slim and easy-hipped, a casual hand slipped into a pocket, rocking back a little on his heels. Nor his face, though it is arresting enough with its sharp jawline, its high tilted cheekbones hinting stubbornness, his thick blueblack hair falling onto his forehead in careless elegance. And his eyes, very dark, with little points of light flickering deep within. There's nothing in him to show lonely except a spiderweb thought in the corner of my mind, nothing to account for why I'm drawn so.

Then it comes to me. With the others I have always known what they wanted. At once.

'Oh, just looking,' he says when I ask in my oldwoman voice that I suddenly wish were not so quavery.

Just looking, and gives a surprisingly lopsided smile and gazes at me from under straight brows, as though he's really seeing me, *me* underneath this body, and likes what he sees. Though how can that be.

He keeps on gazing straight into my eyes as no one except the Old One has ever done.

There's a lurching inside me, like something stitched up tearing loose.

O danger.

And now I can't read him at all. I go inside him to search and am wound around in a silk cloud. So all I have for knowledge is the quirk of his eyebrow as though he finds it amusing, all of it, but surely I'm silly to think he knows what I'm doing.

I want it, though. I want him to know. And I want him, knowing, to be amused. How long it has been since someone looked at me except in ignorance. Or awe. As I think this, loneliness fills my chest, a new dull aching weight, like drowning water. It is a surprise. I did not know that Mistresses could feel so lonely.

American I too am looking. I thought all my looking was done when I found the spices but then I saw you and now I no longer know.

I want to tell him this. I want to believe he'll understand.

In my head an echo like a song of stone. *A Mistress must carve her own wanting out of her chest, must fill the hollow left behind with the needs of those she serves.*

It is my own voice, out of a time and place that seems so distant I want to call it not-real. To turn my back on it. But.

'You are welcome to look,' I tell the American, my tone all business. 'I must be getting ready to close the shop.' To give myself something to do I restack packets of *papads*, pour *rawa* into paper sacks and label them carefully, push a bin of *atta* to the other side of the doorway.

'Here, let me help you.'

And before I have stopped thinking that his voice is like gold-roasted *besan* all mixed with sugar, his hand is on the rim of the bin, touching mine.

What words can I choose to describe it, this touch that goes through me like a blade of fire, yet so sweet that I want the hurting to never stop. I snatch my hand away obedient to the Mistress laws, but the sensation stays.

And this thought: no one ever wanted to help me before.

'A great place you have here. I love the feel of it,' says my American.

Yes I know it is a liberty I take, to call him mine. To smile my response when I should be saying *Please go, it is much too late, good-bye good night.*

Instead I pick up a packet. 'This is *dhania*,' I say. 'Coriander seed, sphere-shaped like the earth, for clearing your sight. When you soak it and drink, the water purges you of old guilts.'

Why am I telling him this. Tilo stop.

But that silk cloud pulls my words out of me. And into him.

He nods and touches the tiny globes through the plastic covering, courteous and unsurprised, as though what I am saying is most natural.

'And this' – I open a lid and sift the fine powder through my fingers – 'is *amchur*. Made from black salt and mangoes dried and pounded, to heal the taste buds, to bring back love of life.'

Tilo don't babble like a girl.

'Ah.' He bends his head to sniff, lifts his eyes to smile approval. 'It's like nothing I've ever smelled before – but I like it.'

Then he moves away.

And says in a voice grown formal, 'I've kept you too long already. You should be closing up.'

Tilottama. Fool who should know better. To think he'd be interested.

At the door he raises his hand, in salute or good-bye or maybe just to wave away the hovering moths. I feel a great sorrow because he is leaving empty-handed, because I couldn't find what he was looking for. Because something is twisting inside, telling me I am losing him, the one man whose heart I could not read.

And then.

'I'll be seeing you,' says the lonely American, and smiles a rhinestone smile. As though he really means it. As though he too will be waiting.

After the lonely American leaves, I wander the store, aimless-sad. Dissatisfaction, that old poison I thought I'd been cured of, bubbles up thick and viscous in me. I cannot bear to lock up. Barring the door would be to admit that he is really gone. Outside, streetlights blink on. Men and women turn up the collars of their coats and disappear underground into the dim clank and clatter of the subway. A yellow fog fills the deserted streets, and in the distance sirens begin to wail, reminding us how fugitive happiness is. But of course no one listens.

I am looking for a spice for him.

'Different spices may help us with different troubles,' the Old One told us after she had taught us the common cures. 'But for each person there is one special spice. No, not for you – the Mistresses must never use the spices for their own ends – but for all who come to you it exists. It is called *mahamul*, the root spice, and for each person it is different. *Mahamul* to enhance fortune, to bring success or joy, to avert ill luck. When you do not know how else to help someone, you must go deep into your being and search out the *mahamul*.'

Lonely American, how shall I begin, I who have always prided myself on the quick remedy?

I roam the shelves. *Kalo jire*? *Ajwain*? Powder of mango-gingerroot? *Choon*, the burning white lime that is wrapped in betel leaves? Nothing seems suitable. Nothing feels right. Perhaps the fault is in me, in my distracted soul. I Tilo who cannot stop thinking about those eyes dark as a tropical night, as deep, as filled with peril.

And why do I persist in calling him lonely? Perhaps even now, even as I stalk discontented down the aisle of lentils, as I plunge restive arms elbow-deep in a bin of *rajma* and let the cool red pods roll over my skin, he is turning a key. The door opens, and a woman with hair like gold mist rises from the couch to take him in her—

No. It isn't so. I will not let it be so.

He enters and turns on a light, flips a switch, and the sound of a *sarod* fills the empty room. He leans back against a Jaipuri cushion – for he loves all things Indian – and thinks about what he has seen today, a store smelling of all the world, a woman whose ageless eyes pull at him like—

Idle wishing. Idle, riskful wishing.

'When you begin to weave your own desires into your vision,' the Old One told us, 'the true seeing is taken from you. You grow confused, and the spices no longer obey you.'

Back Tilo, before it's too late.

I force my mind to emptiness. I will trust only my

hands, my hands with their singing bones to know what the lonely American needs.

The store stands unbarred, lucent crystal vial under the poised boot-heel of night. The doorway swarms grey with mothwings. But I cannot tend to it now.

I enter the inner room and close my eyes. In the dark my hands glow like lanterns. I trail my fingers along the dusty shelves.

Phosphorous fingers coral fingers, I wait for you to tell me what I must do.

In his bedroom the lonely American kicks off his shoes, turns down the silk covers of his bed. He shrugs off his shirt and lets it fall to the floor. Candlelight plays liquid on his shoulders, his back, the hard, muscled swell of his buttocks as he lets his pants fall too and stands straight, lithe, made of ivory. In a moment he will turn—

Fluid fills my mouth in a hot sweet rush. In all my lives before, fortune-teller and pirate queen and apprentice of spices, I have never seen a naked man, never desired to see it.

Then my hands shudder to a stop.

Not now, hands, not now. Give me just a moment more.

But they are immovable, adamantine. Mine and not mine. Fisted around something hard and grainy, a pulsing lump whose acrid smell cuts through my vision.

The images crumble, dust or dreaming, and are gone.

Sighing, I open unwilling eyes.

In my hand, a nugget of asafoetida.

A crash in the other room, like something breaking. Or is it the night throwing itself against the store's window-panes?

Spark-hard rock of Mars, urging the receiver to glory and fame, away from Venus's seductions. Baleful yellow asafoetida to leach away softness and leave a man all sinew and bone.

A gust of wind blows in the smell of wet overcoats. The floor is a floe of ice under my stumbling. I force myself to the door. In my hands the bar feels deadly heavy. Almost I cannot lift it. I must use all my strength to push it shaking into place before it is too late.

Asafoetida *hing*, which is the antidote to love.

I lean against the door, spent, knowing what is expected of me, Mistress of Spices, but also their handmaid.

I feel them watching, like a held breath.

Even the air is like iron.

When I can move again, I go to the handicrafts case. I push aside batik scarves and mirrored cushion covers and brass paper knives and terracotta goddesses, let them all tumble to the floor until I find it, a small smooth ebony box lined with velvet like a blackbird's wing. I open it and drop in the asafoetida, and in the precise, angled island script the Old One taught us I write, *For the lonely American.*

Around me arises a soft relieved humming. A breeze caresses my cheek, a gentle exhalation, moist with approval. Or is it tears – I who have never cried before?

I avert my face from the store, from the million spice eyes, tiny, bright, everywhere. Steel points like nails for me to step on. For the first time since I became a Mistress, I pull a covering around my inmost thoughts.

I am not sure it will work, my deception.

But it seems to. Or is it only the spices humouring me?

I slide the box to the back of the shelf under the cash register, to wait in the dust until he comes. I lie down. Around me the spices calm, settle into the rhythms of the night. Their love winds around me heavy as the sevenfold gold Benarasi that women must wear at their wedding.

So much love, how will I breathe?

When the store is lulled into sleep, I uncover the secret chamber of my being and look in. And am not surprised at what I find.

I will not give it to him, heart-hardening asafoetida to my lonely American.

No matter what the spices want.

Not yet, or never?

I do not know the answer to that.

But deep inside I feel the first tremor, warning of earthquakes to come.

The rich Indians descend from hills that twinkle brighter than stars, so bright that it is easy to forget it is only electricity. Their cars gleam like waxed apples, glide like swans over the potholes outside my store.

The car stops, the uniformed chauffeur jumps out to hold open the gold-handled door, and a foot in a gold sandal steps down. Soft and arched and almost white. Rosepetal toes curling in disdain away from what lines the street, wadded paper, rotting peels, dog shit, shucked-off condoms thrown from the back windows of cars.

The rich Indians rarely speak, as if too much money has clogged their throats. Inside the store which they have entered only because friends said, 'O it's so quaint, you *must* go see at least once,' they point. And the chauffeur springs to fetch. Basmati rice, extra-long grain, aged in jute sacking to make it sweet. The finest flour, genuine Elephant brand. Mustard oil in a costly glass bottle, even though sitting right beside are the economy tins. The chauffeur staggers beneath the load. But there's more. Fresh *lauki* flown in from the Philippines, and emerald-leafed *methi saag* that I have grown in a box on the back windowsill. A whole box of saffron like shavings of flame and, by the pound, tiny shelled pistas – the most expensive kind – green as mango buds.

'If you wait one week,' I say, 'they will go on sale.'

The rich Indians look at me with heavy eyes that are almost no colour at all. They nod at the chauffeur and he picks up another two pounds.

I hide my smile.

The rich Indians crane their necks and lift their chins high because they have to be more always than other people, taller, handsomer, better dressed. Or at least richer. They heave their bodies like moneybags out the door and into their satin cars, leaving the crumbly odour of old banknotes behind.

Other rich people send lists instead, because being a rich person is a busy job. Golf cruises charity luncheons in the Cornelian Room shopping for new Lamborghinis and cigar cases inlaid with lapis lazuli.

Still others have forgotten to be Indian and eat caviar only.

For all of them in the evening I burn *tulsi*, basil which is the plant of humility, curber of ego. The sweet smoke of basil whose taste I know on my own tongue, for many times the Old One has burned it for me too. Basil sacred to Sri Ram, which slakes the craving for power, which turns the thoughts inward, away from worldliness.

Because inward even rich people are people only.

I must tell this to myself over and over. And also what the Old One taught us: 'Not for you to pick and choose your compassion. The ones who anger you most, you must bend most to help.'

There is something else that I must tell you.

When I look deep into the lives of rich people, sometimes I am forced to humility, to say Who would have thought. For instance. Anant Soni who at the end of a day of corporate video conferences sits by his mother's bedside to rub her arthritic hands. And Dr Lalchandani's wife who stares unseeing out the bedroom window of her designer home because across town her husband is in bed with another woman. And Prameela Vijh who sells million-dollar houses and sends money to her sister in a battered women's shelter. And Rajesh whose company went public the same day the doctor pushed the biopsy report across the table at him and said *chemo*.

And right now in front of me a woman in oversize Bill Blass jeans and Gucci shoes is buying stacks and stacks of naans for a party tonight, is drumming rubyflash fingers on the counter as I ring up the flat brown bread, is saying shrill as tin 'Come *on* I'm in a hurry.' But inside she is thinking of her teenage son. He's been acting so strange lately, hanging out with boys who frighten her with their razor earrings and biker jackets and heavy boots as though for war, their cold, cold eyes and slits of mouths that are becoming *his* eyes, *his* mouth. Could he be taking— Her mind shudders away from the word she cannot say even inside her clamped lips, and under the layers, foundation and concealer and rouge and thick fuchsia eyeshadow, her face grows bruised with love.

Rich woman I thank you for reminding me. Beneath the shiniest armour, gold-plated or diamond, the beat of the vulnerable flesh.

Into a corner of her matching Gucci purse I place *hartuki*, shrivelled seed in the shape of a womb, which has no American name. *Hartuki* to help mothers bear the pain that starts with the birthing and continues for ever, the pain and joy both, tangled dark and blue as an umbilical cord around an infant's throat.

Saturday comes upon me like the unexpected flash of rainbow under a bird's black wing, like the swirl-spread skirt of a *kathak* dancer, fast and then faster. Saturday is drums bursting from the stereos of the young men who drive by dangerous-slow, and what are they looking for. Saturday takes my breath. For Saturday I put up signs: FRESH-FRESH METHI HOME GROWN; DIWALI SALE LOWEST PRICES; LATEST MOVIES BEST ACTORS, JUHI CHAWLA-AMIR KHAN, RENT 2 DAYS FOR COST OF ONE. And even, daringly, ASK IF YOU CANNOT FIND.

So many people on Saturday, it seems the walls must take a deep breath just to hold them in. All those voices, Hindi Oriya Assamese Urdu Tamil English, layered one on the other like notes from a *tanpura*, all those voices asking for more than their words, asking for happiness except no one seems to know where. And so I must listen to the spaces between, must weigh them in my coral-boned hands. Must whisper chants over packets and sacks even as I weigh and measure and ring up, even as I call out in my pretend-strict voice, 'Please no touching *mithais*' and, 'If bottle breaks you must pay.'

All who come to my store on Saturday, I love them.

You must not think that only the unhappy visit my store. The others come too, and they are many. A father carrying his daughter on his shoulders, picking up *laddus* on the way to the zoo. A retired couple, she holding his elbow as he leans on his cane. Two wives out for an afternoon of shopping and talk. A young computer scientist planning to impress his visiting parents with his new cooking skills. They step through my doors lightly, and as they move from aisle to aisle, choosing, the faintest of radiances flickers around them.

See, bunches of podina *leaves green as the forests of our childhood. Hold them up and smell how fresh and pungent, isn't this cause enough for gladness. Tear open a packet of chilli-cashews and cram a handful into the mouth. Chew. That hot taste, that crumble and crunch against your cheeks, the delicious tears that rise to your eyes. Here's* kumkum *powder red as the heart of a hibiscus flower to put on our foreheads for married luck. And look, look, Mysore sandalwood soap with its calm bright fragrance, the same brand you used to buy me in India so many years ago when we were newlyweds. Ah life, how fine it is.*

I send a blessing behind them as they leave, a whisper of thanks that they have let me share their joy. But already they are fading from my mind, already I am turning from them to the others. The ones whom I need because they need me.

Manu who is seventeen, in a 49ers jacket so shiny red it's like a yell, running in impatient to pick up a sack of *bajra atta* for his mother before he goes to shoot some hoops at school. Angry Manu who is a senior at Ridgefield High, thinking Not fair not fair. Because when he said 'prom' his father shouted, 'All that drinking whisky-beer and dancing pressed up against cheap American girls in miniskirts, what are you thinking of.' Manu poised tip-toe inside furious fluorescent Nike shoes that he bought with money saved up cleaning bathrooms in his uncle's motel, ready to take off if only he knew where he would land.

Manu I give you a slab of sesame candy made with sweet molasses, *gur* to slow you down just enough to hear the frightened love in your father's voice losing you to America.

And Daksha who comes in with her white nurse's uniform starched and shiny, even her shoes even her smile.

'Daksha what do you need today?'

'Aunty today is *ekadasi* you know, eleventh day of the moon, and my mother-in-law being a widow must not eat rice. So I thought maybe some cracked wheat to make a *dalia* pudding for her and as long as I was here, might as well pick up some of your *methi*, my husband is so fond of *methi parathas*.'

As she sifts through the bittergreen leaves I watch her face. Under the edges where the shine has rubbed off, the smile pulls down. Every night coming home from the hospital to cook, rolling out *chapatis* hot hot with ghee because her mother-in-law says old food from the fridge is good only for servants or dogs. Boiling frying seasoning ladling serving wiping up while everyone sits saying, 'Good,' saying, 'Yes, more,' even her husband, because after all isn't the kitchen the woman's place.

In answer to my asking she says, 'Yes Aunty it's hard but what to do. After all we must take care of our old. It makes too much trouble in the house if I say I can't do all this work. But sometimes I wish—'

She stops. Daksha to whom no one listens so she has forgotten how to say. And inside her, pushing up against her palate enormous and silent, the horror of what she sees all day. In the AIDS ward those young, young men grown light as children in their eroding bones. Their fragile bruised skin, their enormous waiting eyes.

Daksha here is seed of black pepper to be boiled whole
and drunk to loosen your throat so you can learn to say
No, that word so hard for Indian women. *No* and *Hear
me now*.

And Daksha before you go, here is *amla* for a different
resistance. *Amla* which I too would like to take some days
to help bear the pain that cannot be changed, pain growing slow and huge like a monsoon cloud which if you let
it will blot out the sun.

Now Vinod sidles in, Vinod who owns India Market on
the other side of the bay and comes sometimes to check
out the competition, who hefts a five-pound packet of *dal*
with practised hands to see if it's just a little less, like in his
store. Who thinks *fool* when it isn't. Vinod who jumps
when I say, 'How's business Vinod-*bhai*' because he has
always thought I don't know who he is. I give him a packet
filled with green-brown-black and say, 'Compliments of
management' and hide my laugh behind my hand while he
sniffs at it suspiciously.

'Ah *kari patti*,' he says finally. Inside he is thinking
Crazy woman, is thinking $2.49 *profit*, as he slips it into
his pocket, astringent leaf dried dark on the stem to
reduce mistrust and avarice.

Saturday when the store is throbbing bloodbeat and
desire, sometimes the future-sight comes to me. I do not
control it. Nor do I trust it fully. It shows me people who
will visit the store, but whether in a day or a year or a lifetime it does not say. The faces are hazy and shapeless, seen
thickly as through Coke-bottle glass. I pay them scant
attention. I am too busy, and happy to let time bring me
what it will.

But today the light is pink-tinted like just-bloomed *karabi* flowers, and the Indian radio channel spills out a song about a slim-waisted girl who wears silver anklets, and I am hungry for the sight. There is a smell like seabirds in the air. It makes me long to open windows. I pace the front aisle looking out, though there is nothing except a bag lady shuffling behind a grocery cart and a group of boys lounging lazy against the graffitied walls of Myisha's Hair Salon Braiding Done. An impatient voice calls me back to the register. A long low aquamarine Cadillac with shark fins cruises by. A customer complains because I have rung up a purchase twice. I apologize. But inside I am trying to remember, did the lonely American come in a car.

Yes I admit it, he's the reason. And yes I want to see him again. And yes I'm disappointed when the sight falls on me like fever, and shuddering I look among the faces to come and do not see his. *He promised*, I tell myself, and am angrier because he didn't really. Suddenly I want to sweep the *mithais* from their case to the floor, *laddus* and *rasogollahs* sent rolling in dust, syrup and splintered glass sticking to shoe soles. And the shock in the eyes of the customers whose desires I'm tired of.

It's *my* desire I want to fulfil, for once.

It would be so easy. A *tola* of lotus root burned in evening with *prishniparni*, a few words spoken, and he would not be able to keep away. Yes it would be *him* standing across from me and not this fat man in round-rimmed glasses who is telling me I'm all out of *chana besan*. If I wanted, he would see not this old body but what I wished, curve of mango breast to cup in one's palm, long lean line of eucalyptus thigh. I would call on the others, *abhrak* and *amlaki* to remove wrinkles and blacken hair and firm the sagging flesh. And king of all, *makaradwaj* rejuvenator whom the Ashwini Kumars, twin physicians of the gods, gave to their disciple

Dhanwantari to make him foremost among healers. *Makaradwaj* which must always be used with greatest care for even one measure too much can bring death, but I am not afraid, I Tilo who was most brilliant of all the Old One's apprentices.

The fat man is saying something, his tongue moving thick and pink in his open mouth. But I do not hear him.

The Old One, the Old One. What would she say to this wanting? I close my eyes in knowing guilt.

'I worry most about you,' she told me the day I left.

We stood on the highest ridge of the volcano, only sky above us. Shampati's fire was not yet lit. Against the dark silhouette of the pyre the evening was violet-grey and soft as moths. Far below us the waves crashed white and silent as in a dream.

Like tendrils of fog, her distress around me.

I wanted to pull her close and place a comfort-kiss on the velvet corrugation of her cheek. As though I were the elder and not she. But I did not dare the intimacy.

So I accused.

'Always you are without faith in me, First Mother.'

'Because I see your nature, Tilo shining but flawed, diamond with a crack running through it, which thrown into the cauldron of America may shatter asunder.'

'What crack?'

'Life-lust, that craving to taste all things, sweet as well as bitter, on your own tongue.'

'Mother you worry needlessly. Before the moon crosses the sky will I not be walking into Shampati's fire that burns up all desire?'

She had sighed. 'I pray it does for you.' And had gestured a blessing sign in the dim air.

'*Chana besan*,' says the fat man now, smelling of garlic pickle and too-large lunches. 'Didn't you hear me say I want some *chana besan*.'

My skull is hot and dry. There is a high buzzing inside, like bees.

Fat man I could take a fistful of mustard seed and say a word, and for a month a fever would burn in your stomach, making you vomit up whatever you ate.

Tilo, is this what you have come to.

Inside my head, a sound like rain. Or is it the tears of the spices.

I bite down on my lip till the blood comes. The pain cleanses me, starts to release the poison from my clenched body.

'So sorry,' I tell the man. 'I have big sack of *besan* inside.'

I measure out a packet and trace on it with my finger a rune for self-control. For him and for me.

O spices I am still yours, Tilottama essence of *til*, giver of life and love and hope. Help me not to fall from myself.

Lonely American, though my body is a sudden soaring whenever I think of you, if you are to come to me, it will have to be by your own desire.

Early morning he steps briskly into the store to do the week's shopping for the family although his son has said many times, '*Baba* why at your age.' Geeta's grandfather still walking like a military major though it has been twenty years. His shirt ironed stiff with pointy collars, his steel-grey pants perfect-creased down the front. And his shoes, his midnight-black Bata shoes spit-polished to match the onyx he wears on his left hand for mental peace.

'But mental peace I am not having, not even one iota, since I crossed the *kalapani* and came to this America,' he tells me once again. 'That Ramu he said Come come *baba* we are all here, what for you want to grow old so far from your own flesh and blood, your granddaughter. But I tell you, better to have no granddaughter than one like this Geeta.'

'I know what you are meaning, *dada*,' I say to placate him. 'But your Geeta, such a nice girl she is, so pretty and sweet-speaking too, surely you are mistaken. She is coming so many times to my store and each time she is specially buying my hot mango pickles and telling me most polite how tasty they are. And so smart, passed out of college with all A marks, is it not, I think her mother is telling me, and now she is doing job in some big engineer company?'

He dismisses my compliments with a wave of his carved mahogany cane.

'May be OK for all these *firingi* women in this country, but you tell me yourself *didi*, if a young girl should work late-late in the office with other men and come home only after dark and sometimes in their car too? *Chee chee*, back in Jamshedpur they would have smeared dung on our faces for that. And who would ever marry her. But when I tell Ramu he says *Baba* don't worry they're only friends. My girl knows better than to get involved with some foreigner.'

'But *dada*, this is America after all, and even in India women are now working, no, even in Jamshedpur.'

'*Hai*, you are talking like Ramu now, and his wife, that Sheela who brought up her girl too lax, never a slap even, and see what has happened. *Arre baap*, so what if this is America, we are still Bengalis, no? And girls and boys are still girls and boys, ghee and a lighted match, put them together and soon or late there's going to be fire.'

I give him a bottle of *brahmi* oil to cool his system. '*Dada*,' I say, 'you and I are old now, time for us to spend our time with our prayer beads and let the young ones run their life as they see best.'

Still each week Geeta's grandfather comes in with newly indignant tales.

'That girl, this Sunday she cut her hair short-short so that even her neck is showing. I am telling her, Geeta what did you do, your hair is the essence of your womanhood. You know what she is replying?'

I can read the answer in his furrowed face. But to soothe him I ask what.

'She is laughing and pushing all those messy ends back from her face, saying, Oh Grandpa I needed a new look.'

Or. 'That Geeta, how much make-up she is using all the time. *Uff*, in my days only the Englishwomen and prostitutes are doing that. Good Indian girls are not ashamed of the face God is giving them. You cannot think what all she is taking with her even to work.'

His tone so full of outrage, I want to smile. But I only say, 'Maybe you are over-imagining. Maybe—'

He stops me, hand held up triumphant. '*Imagining*, you say. Hunh! With my own two eyes I have looked into her purse. Mascara blusher foundation eyeshadow and more whose names I am not remembering, and the lipstick so shameless bright making all the men stare at her mouth.'

Or. '*Didi*, listen to what she is doing this last weekend. Bought a new car for herself, thousands and thousands of dollars it is costing, and such a shiny blue it hurts the eyes. I told Ramu, what nonsense is this, she was using your old car just fine, this money you should save for her dowry.

But that blind fool, he only smiles and says, It's her money from her job and besides, for my Geeta we'll find a nice Indian boy from here who doesn't believe in dowry.'

'Geeta,' I call silently when he is gone, 'Geeta whose name means sweet song, keep your patience your humour your zest for life. I am burning here incense of the *champak* flower for harmony in your home. Geeta who is India and America all mixed together into a new melody, be forgiving of an old man who holds on to his past with all the strength in his failing hands.'

Today Geeta's grandfather comes in, but without his usual striped plastic shopping bag, his hands swinging aimless, his fingers splayed stiff and awkward with nothing to grip. Stands for a while at the counter staring down at the *mithais* but he is not seeing them, and when I ask what he needs today, he bursts out, '*Didi* you will not believe.' His voice is loud with calamity and righteousness, but underneath I hear the raw rasp of fear.

'Hundred times I told Ramu, this is no way to bring up children, girls specially, saying yes-yes every time they want something. Remember in India how all you brothers and sisters got one-two good beatings and after I never had troubles with you. Did I love you less, no, but I knew what was my father-duty. Hundred times I told him, get her married off now she has finished college, why you are waiting for misfortune to knock on your door. And now see what happened.'

'What?' I am impatient, my heart tight with misgiving. I try to look in, but the tunnels of his mind are awhirl with dead leaves and dust.

'Yesterday I am getting a letter from Jadu Bhatchaj, my old army-days friend. They are looking for a match for his grand-nephew, excellent boy, very bright, only twenty-eight and already a district sub-judge. Why not send details of Geeta and a picture also, he has written, maybe the parents will agree. What a fine news I think and offer thanks to Goddess Durga, and immediately as Ramu comes home I tell him. He is not so eager, he says she is brought up here, can she live in a big joint family in India. And Sheela of course is saying O I don't want to send my only daughter so far away. Woman, I tell her, you are simply having no sense. Didn't your own mother have to send you far too? You must do what is best for her. Even from birth a girl's real home is with her future husband's family only. And what better family can we get for our Geeta than Jadubabu's people, such old, respected Brahmins whom everyone is knowing in Calcutta. OK says Ramu at last, we'll ask Geeta.'

He pauses to suck in breath.

I want to shake the slow story out of him, but I press my nails into the counter and wait.

'Well, Madam comes in late as usual, nine p.m., saying I ate already, remember I told you some of the guys were going for pizza. I am wanting to say, Since when are you some of the guys, but I practise self-control. Her father tells her about the letter. Dad, she says, tell me you're joking. She laughs and laughs. Can you see me with a veil over my head sitting in a sweaty kitchen all day, a bunch of house keys tied to the end of my sari. Ramu says Come on Geeta, it's not going to be like that. But I say What's wrong with that, Miss High Nose, your grandmother, God keep her soul at His lotus feet, did that all her life. She says, No disrespect, Gramps, it just isn't for me. And while we're on the subject, arranged marriages aren't for me either. When I marry I'll choose my own husband.

'The look on Ramu's face is not so happy and Sheela's

eyebrows are starting to squeeze together. I begin to tell them, Are you hearing this, for this reason I told you long time back to send her to Ramkrishna Mission boarding school in Chuchura, when she interrupts me and says, the words rushing out all together, I guess this is as good a time as any to let you know that I've already found someone I love.

'*Chee chee*, no shame at all, making talk of love in front of her parents, in front of me, her grandfather.

'After they get over the first shock Ramu asks, What's this now and Sheela asks, Who is it. Then they ask together, What does he do and Do we know him.

'You don't know him, she says. Her face is red and she is holding her breath tight like when underwater and right away I know something even more inauspicious is coming.

'He works at the company, he's a project manager. She is being silent one full minute. Then she says, His name is Juan, Juan Cordero.

'*Hai bhagaban*, I say. She is marrying a white man.

'Dad, Mom, she says, please don't be upset. He's a very nice man, really, you'll see when I bring him home to visit. I'm so glad I finally got it off my chest. I've been wanting to tell you a long time. To me she says, Grandpa, he's not white, he's chicano.

'What is that meaning, I ask. But already I know it is nothing good.

'When she explains I tell to her, You are losing your caste and putting blackest *kali* on our ancestors' faces to marry a man who is not even a sahib, whose people are slum criminals and illegals, don't say *O grandpa you just don't understand*, you think I don't see TV news.

'Sheela is crying and wringing her hands, saying I never thought you'd do this to us, is this how you repay us for giving you so much freedom even though all our relatives warned us not to. But Ramu is sitting total quiet. I want to say to him, Once you let cow out of the barn, you cannot stop it from trampling the paddy field. But when I see his face I don't have the heart. I only say, Ramu you please put me on a plane to India tomorrow.

'Dad, Geeta says, Dad. She shakes his arm. Say something.

'He jerks away like he is getting electric shock. A muscle is jumping small and tight in his cheek. I remember it from when he was a boy, if he got very angry, just before he smashed a pot or beat another boy or similar thing. His hands are fists. I think, he is going to hit her, and everything goes black-black in front of my eyes and then yellow pinpricks like mustard flowers.

'I am too old for this, I am thinking. My head feels so heavy for my neck. I am wishing that misfortunate letter was lost in our Indian post system.

'But then he puts his fists down. I trusted you, he says. His voice, it is worse than hitting.

'After that I must close my eyes. It is like a big wind around me, words flying around in it, mother and daughter.

'Go to your room. I don't want to see your face again.

'You won't have to. I'm leaving. And never coming back.

'Do what you like. Your father and I will think we're childless, and better for it.

'Dad, is that what you want. Dad.

'Silence.

'Very well. I'm going to move in with Juan then. He's been asking me for a long time. I said no, thinking of you guys all this time, but now I will.

'And Sheela shouting through her sobs, Where you go is all the same to us, you shameless bad luck girl.

'Doors slam and crash like breaking. Weeping sounds come and go. Maybe a car engine is roaring, maybe brakes are screeching. When I open my eyes I am all alone in the family room with only the man on TV describing about a big storm out in the ocean soon to be moving in. I go to my room but all night I am not joining my eyelids together in sleep.'

He points in evidence at the veins like brittle red wires in his eyes.

'And this morning,' I ask. 'What happened this morning?'

He lifts his shoulders, helpless.

'I leave the house before anyone wakes. I am walking up and down in front of your shop until you open.'

'But what can *I* do?'

'I know you can help. I am hearing whispered things at Bengali New Year picnic, also when the old people meet together to play bridge. Please.'

Geeta's grandfather holding his proud white head low, the requesting words awkward as strangers in his mouth.

I pound him a powder of almond and *kesar* to boil in milk. 'The whole family must drink it at bedtime,' I say. 'To sweeten your words and thoughts, to remember the love buried under the anger. And you *dada* who made much of this tangle, take special care what you say. No more talk of going back to India. When bitterness boils up in your mouth, wanting out, swallow it down with a spoon of this *draksha* syrup.'

He takes it, thanks me meekly.

'Still, I am not sure it will be enough. For the medicine to work true, Geeta herself must come to me.'

'But she will never.' His words are a dry, hopeless sound. Geeta's grandfather slump-shouldered and shrunken.

Overnight his clothes hang on him like a scarecrow's flapping suit.

Silence pools around us thick as oil. Until finally he coughs it away.

'Perhaps you could go to her?' His voice has learned new tones. Hesitation, apology. 'I can tell you the way.'

'Impossible. It is not allowed.'

He says nothing more. Only looks at me with his hurt-animal eyes.

And suddenly, for no reason at all, I think of my American.

Geeta, like you I too am learning how love like a rope of ground glass can snake around your heart and pull you, bleeding, away from all you should. And so I tell your grandfather, 'O very well, just this once, how much harm can it do.'

That night I dream of the island.

I have dreamed the island often, but this is different.

The sky is black and smoky. There is no sky, and no sea either. The island floats in a dark void, bereft of life.

But I look closer and there we are sitting under a banyan, the Old One questioning us on lessons learned.

'What is a Mistress's foremost duty?'

I raise my hand but she nods at someone else.

'To aid all who come to her in distress or seeking.'

'How must she feel toward those who come to her?'

I raise my hand again, am ignored again.

Another novice gives the answer. 'Equal love to all, particular to none.'

'And what distance must she keep?'

I wave my arm.

Someone else says, 'Not too far nor too near, in calm kindness poised.'

I rise to my knees in anger. Can she not see, or is her ignoring of me a purposed punishment?

'Ah Tilo,' she says, 'Tilo ever too confident, well suited to answer this next question, what happens when a Mistress grows disobedient, when she seeks her own pleasure?'

Shampati's fire, I start to say, but she interrupts.

'Not to her. To the people around.'

First Mother, you never taught us that.

I open my mouth to say this but no sound comes.

'Yes, for I hoped you would not need to know. But you have proved me wrong. Listen well, because now I will teach it.'

As through a telescope her face turns toward me, grows large and looming. Around it all else fades. And then I see.

It is blank. Devoid of nose and eye, lip and cheek. Only a blackness opening where a mouth should be.

'When a Mistress uses her power for herself, when she breaks the age-old rules—'

Her voice grows harsh and hollow, echo of chains clanking on prison stone.

'—she tears through the delicate fabric of the balanced world, and—'

'And what, Mother?'

She does not answer. The black mouth stretches – grimace of sorrow, or a grin? The island begins to rock, the ground grows hot. And then I hear the roaring. It is the volcano, spewing ash and lava.

The Old One is gone now. The other novices also. Only I. Alone on the island that tilts like a plate someone wants to scrape clean. Pellets of scorching rock strike me like shot. I try to hold on, but the ground is smooth as burning glass. I am sliding off its edge into the jaw of nothing.

It is more terrifying than anything I have undergone.

Then I wake up.

And hear myself finishing what the Old One left unsaid.

—and to all whom she has loved as she should not, chaos comes.

Fennel

Ahuja's wife hasn't been to the store for months.

Earlier I would have spared it no more than a shrug. 'What will be, will be,' the Old One told us. 'Your duty is to give the spice only, not to anguish yourself over the consequence.'

But something began to change in me when the American came into the store. The hard husk of a grain removed, a seed moistened, turning soft. The hopes and sorrows of humans slipping under my skin like a razor.

I am not sure it is a good thing.

Now at night I find myself worrying. Has she perhaps not used the turmeric, maybe she has not been cooking Indian food, maybe she is still using a store of old spices bought elsewhere. I imagine the packet slipping from her hand as she goes to pour, the spilled yellow rising in the kitchen air fine as gold dust, lost, lost. The other possibility I push away with all my strength for surely it cannot be, the spice failing which is a failing of my life also.

Instead I remember how at the door when she left, a shaft of sunlight fell on her face, held carefully blank but for that giveaway bruise.

'God be with you,' I had said. And she not answering had inclined her head in thanks, but under the dark glasses was a look that said, After months and months of unanswered prayers, how can I any longer believe.

Recently I catch myself trying to use the sight, to train it like a searchlight on the dark bedroom where she turns her back to the thick sleeping breath of her husband and lets the tears fall cold as pearl onto her pillow. Or are they hot and salt-searing, acid runnels that eat away at her until soon there will be nothing left?

It is forbidden, what I am doing.

'Open yourself to the sight,' the Old One told us, 'and it will show you what you need to know. But never attempt to bend it to your will. Never pry into a particular life that has been brought to your care. That is to break trust.'

Was it me that she looked at as she spoke, her eyes flecked with sad knowing.

'Most important, don't get too close. You'll want to. Even though you've taken the oath to treat all alike, there'll be the special ones whom you'll want to warm at your heart's heat, to whom you'll want to be whatever they lack in life. Mother, friend, lover. But you cannot. When you chose the spices you gave up that right.

'One step too close and the cords of light connecting a Mistress to the one she helps can turn to webs, tar and steel, enmeshing, miring, pulling you both to destruction.'

I believe this. Have I not already approached the edge, felt it begin to crumble underfoot?

And so I repeat to myself the Old One's words at night as I wrench my attention from that apartment across town where a man's voice cracks across a room sudden as a slap, that apartment like a black hole waiting to implode, into which I, raging, could so easily disappear.

Spices I know you will keep her from harm.

Is it doubt I hear beneath my words? The faintest trace, like a whiff of something burning at once whisked away by a stronger wind? Do the spices hear it too?

So when she comes into the store this morning, a little thinner and with deeper circles under her eyes, but well enough, and even a timid, ready-to-take-flight smile quirking up the corner of her mouth as she says '*Namaste*,' relief wells in me. Relief and a slow pleasure like honey, so I must step from behind the counter. Must say, 'How are you, *beti*, I was worried, you didn't come for so long.' Must put my hand – *no, Tilo* – on her arm.

Yes spices I must admit it, this is no accident like the other touchings. I Tilo initiated this joining of skin and blood and bone.

Where my hand meets her, a pulsing. Cold fire, hot ice, all her terrors shooting up my own veins. Light dims as though a giant fist is squeezing the sun. A thick milky grey like cataracts covers my eyes.

This dizzy pain, is this what it is to be mortal human, unpowered by magic?

And Ahuja's wife. What is she feeling?

I hear the spices crying to me, a sound like hot hands pressed over the ears. *Pull away pull away Tilo, before you're welded down.*

I tighten my muscles to snatch me back to safety.

Then she says in a broken voice, 'O *mataji*, I'm so unhappy I don't know what to do.'

Her lips are pale as pressed rose petals, her eyes like broken glass. She sways a little and puts out her other hand. And what can I do except take it in spite of the smell that rises ominous through the floorboards, charred and ashy, take it and hold it tight and say, as mothers have done through time, 'Hush, child, hush. Everything will be all right.'

'*Mataji*, maybe some of it was my fault.'

Sitting in my little kitchen in the back of the store where I should never have brought her, Ahuja's wife tells me this.

My fault my fault. A refrain so many women the world

over have been taught to sing.

'Why do you say that, *beti*?'

'I didn't really want to get married. I had a good life, my sewing, my women friends I would go to the movies with and then to eat *pani-puri*, even my own bank account, enough so I didn't have to ask my father for spending money. Still, when my parents asked, I said, All right, if you want. Because in our community it is a shame if a grown girl sits in the house not married and I did not want to shame them. But till the last moment I was hoping. Maybe something will happen, maybe the marriage plans will break.

'Ah, if only I had been so lucky.'

'But when you met your husband,' I ask as I hand her a stainless-steel glass full of tea, very hot and sweet with a slice of ginger steeped in it for courage, 'what did you think then?'

She takes a sip. 'He arrived from America only three days before the wedding. That was when I met him. I had seen a picture, of course . . .'

She pauses and I wonder if he had sent someone else's photo. I have known it to happen.

'But when I saw him I realized the picture had been taken many years before.' For a moment her voice sparks with an old anger. Then her shoulders slump under their own weight, as they must have at that first encounter. 'It was too late to cancel the wedding. All the invitations sent, already out-of-town relatives arriving, even a news announcement put in the paper. Ah, how much money my poor father had spent because I was his eldest. And if I said no, my sisters would get a bad name too. Everyone would say, O those headstrong Chowdhary girls, better not to arrange a match with that family.

'So I married him. But inside I was furious. Inside I was

calling him all kinds of insults – liar cheater son-of-a-pig. That first night lying in bed I wouldn't talk to him. When he said sweet words, I turned my face. He tried to put his arm around me; I pushed it away.'

She sighs.

I sigh too, feeling for a moment pity for Ahuja, balding and potbellied and knowing it, approaching with guilt this girl tender as green bamboo and yet at her core a hardness. Ahuja wanting so badly (and do we all not want it too) for love to happen.

'One night, two nights,' says Ahuja's wife, 'he is patient. Then he too gets angry.'

I think how it must have been. Maybe his friends were joking and talking, like men do. '*Arre yaar*, tell us, is it sweet as jaggery.' Or, 'Look look, dark circles under Ahuja *bhai*'s eyes, his wife must keep him hard at work all night.'

'And next time I push him away he grabs me and . . .'

She falls silent. Perhaps it is the embarrassment, telling a stranger – for after all I am no more – what good wives should never. Perhaps it is surprise that she has dared so far.

O almost Lalita whose mouth turmeric is beginning to open like a morning flower, how can I tell you there is no shame in speaking out. How can I say I admire.

Inside her head the images, tumbling hot and sere like clothes left too long in a dryer. A hard male elbow holding her down on the mattress, a knee pushing her thighs apart. And when she tries to claw, to bite (soundlessly, for no one outside the bedroom must know this *sharam*), a slap to the head. Not hard, but the shock of it makes her go limp so he can do what he wants. The worst are the kisses after it is over, kisses that leave their wetness on her mouth, and his slaked repentant voice in her ear, lingering.

Pyari, meri jaan, my sweet love queen.

Over and over and over. Every night until he leaves for America.

'I thought of running away, but where could I go? I knew what happened to girls that left home. They ended up on the streets, or as kept women for men far worse than him. At least with him I had honour' – her lips twist a little at the word – 'because I was a wife.'

A question bursts from me, but I know its foolishness even before I have finished forming the words.

'Couldn't you tell someone, your mother maybe. Couldn't you ask them not to send you here to him.'

And now she bows her head, Ahuja's wife who was earlier Chowdhary's daughter, and her tears fall into the glass of tea, turning it salt. Until I must reach across the forbidden distance to wipe them away. Chowdhary's daughter whose parents had brought her up in love and strictness the best they knew, to fit into her destiny, which was marriage. Who sensed her sorrow but were afraid to ask Daughter what is wrong, because what would they do if she answered. And she seeing that fear kept her silence kept her tears, for she loved them too, and hadn't they done the most they could for her already.

Silence and tears, silence and tears, all the way to America. Bloated sack of pain swelling inside her throat until at last today turmeric untied the knot and let it out.

An hour later, and Ahuja's wife is still talking, the words spilling as over the broken lip of a dam.

'I knew better, but still I hoped as women do. For what else is there for us? Here in America maybe we could start again, away from those eyes, those mouths always telling us how a man should act, what is a woman's duty. But ah the voices, we carried them all the way inside our heads.'

I see her in those early days, Ahuja's wife trying to please her husband, sewing new curtains to make the apartment into a home, rolling *parathas* to serve hot when he came home from work. And him too, buying her a new sari, a bottle of perfume, Intimate or Chantilly, a pretty lace nightdress to wear in bed.

'*Hai mataji*, once milk has curdled can all the sugar in the world turn it sweet again?

'In bed especially I could not forget those nights in India. Even when he tried to be gentle I was stiff and not willing. Then he would lose patience and shout the American words he'd learned. *Bitch. Fucking you is like fucking a corpse.*

'And later, *You must be getting it somewhere else.*

'Recently, the rules. No going out. No talking on the phone. Every penny I spend to be accounted for. He should read my letters before he mails them.

'And the calls. All day. Sometimes every twenty minutes. To check on what I'm doing. To make sure I'm there. I pick up the phone and say hello and there is his breathing on the end of the line.'

Now Ahuja's wife tells me in a voice which is frightening-calm, which has run out of tears, '*Mataji*, I used to be afraid of death. I'd hear of women who killed themselves and think how could they. Now I know.'

O almost Lalita, that is not the way out. But what can I say to help you, I who am weeping inside as much as you have done?

'What do I have to live for? Once, more than anything in the world I wanted a baby. But is this any kind of home to bring a new life into?'

Blinded by my tears I cannot see the spice remedy. It is as the Old One warned.

Tilo too close too close.

I breathe deep, holding the air in my lungs like she taught us on the island, until its roaring drives all other sounds from my mind. Until through the red blur a name comes to me.

Fennel, which is the spice for Wednesdays, the day of averages, of middle-aged people. Waists that have given up, mouths drooping with the weight of their average lives they once dreamed would be so different. Fennel, brown as mud and bark and leaf dancing in a fall breeze, smelling of changes to come.

'Fennel,' I tell Ahuja's wife who is plucking at her *dupatta* with restless fingers, 'is a wondrous spice. Take a pinch of it, raw and whole, after every meal to freshen the breath and aid digestion and give you mental strength for what must be done.'

She looks at me despairing. Her crushed velvet eyes say Is this all the help you have to give?

'Give some to your husband as well.'

Ahuja's wife smoothes the sleeve of her *kurta*, which she had pulled up to show me another bruise, and stands. 'I need to get home. He must have called one dozen times. When he comes home tonight—'

Fear rises from her, shimmering, like heat from a cracked summer pavement. Fear and hate and disappointment that I am not doing more.

'Fennel cools the temper as well,' I say. I wish I could tell her more, but that would leach away the spice's power.

She gives a bitter, not-believing laugh. She regrets having confided in me, witless old woman who talks as though a handful of dry seeds can help a breaking life.

'He could certainly do with that,' she says, gathering

her purse. Regrets pound like blood inside her skull.

She will throw the packet I have put between us on the table in the back of a drawer, perhaps even in the trash when she thinks in shame of all she has told me.

Next time she will go to another grocery, even if it means changing buses.

I try to hold her eyes but she will not look. She has turned to leave, she is at the door already. So I must with my oldwoman shuffle catch up and touch her arm once more, though I know I should not.

Pincers of flame pierce my fingertips. She is still now, her eyes changing colour, growing light like mustard oil when heated, intent as though she is seeing something beyond everyday sight.

I reach for the small bag of fennel to press into her palm, but it is not there.

Spices what—

Desperate I look around, feel Ahuja's wife hurrying inside her head. For a moment I am afraid the spice will not give itself to me, I Tilo gone beyond boundaries.

But here is the packet on top of this stack of *India Currents* magazines, where surely I did not place it.

Spices is this a game or is it something you are telling me.

There is no time to ponder. I pick up the packet and a copy of the magazine. Give her both.

'Trust me. Do what I tell you. Every day, after every meal, some for you and some for him, and when you have finished it all come back and tell if it hasn't helped. And here, read this. It'll keep your mind off your troubles.'

She gives a sigh and nods. It is easier than arguing.

'Daughter, remember this, no matter what happens. You did no wrong in telling me. No man, husband or not, has the right to beat you, to force you to a bed that sickens you.'

She does not say yes or no.

'Go now. And don't be afraid. This morning he's been too busy to call home.'

'How do you know?'

'We old women, we sense things.'

From the door she whispers, 'Pray for me. Pray that I die soon.'

'No,' I say. 'You deserve happiness. You deserve dignity. I will pray for that.'

Fennel, I call when she is gone, fennel that is shaped like a half-closed eye accented with *surma*, work for me. I reach into the bin and lift up a fistful. Fennel which the sage Vashistha ate after he swallowed the demon Illwal so he would not come back to life again.

I wait for the tingling, for the song to begin.

Only silence, and the pointed ends of the spice biting my palm like thorns.

Speak to me, fennel, *mouri*, coloured like the freckled house sparrow that brings amity where it nests, spice to digest sorrows and in their digestion make us strong.

When it comes, the voice is no song but a booming, a wave crashing in my skull.

Why should we, when you have done that which you should not? When you have overstepped the lines you willingly drew around yourself?

Fennel equalizer, who can take power from one and give it to the other when two people eat of you at the same time, I entreat you, help Ahuja's wife.

Do you admit your transgression, your greed in grasping for what you promised to give up forever? Do you regret?

I think back to her fingers, light as a bird's hold on my

arm, and as trusting. I think how I wiped away the tears, the feel of her damp eyelashes, her face in my hands. That living, breathing skin. How the band of steel that clenched my chest for so long had given a little.

Ahuja's wife, you who are almost becoming Lalita, I too know what it is to be afraid. I would lie now, if it would do either of us any good. For your life I'd give mine, if they would take it.

Around me the spices, distant and coldly courteous, wait as though they did not know the answer already.

I do not regret, I say finally, and feel the air draining away. My tongue is a slab of wood in my mouth. I have to force the words around it.

I'll pay in whatever way is decided.

It is so silent I could be alone, whirling in a black galaxy. Whirling and burning, and no one to hear when finally I explode to nothing.

Very well, says the voice at last.

What will it be?

You will know. The voice is thin and far now. Appeased. *You will know at the proper time.*

In the half light of evening I am sitting at the counter slicing with the tip of my magic knife *kalo jire* seeds no bigger than a weevil bug's egg.

It requires concentration, this task. Certain words must be said as the knifetip cuts clean into the *kalo jire*'s brittle hardness, the breath must be taken in and held until it is safe to let it go. And so I've had to wait till the store is shut down.

I work without stopping. By the time Haroun comes today, as every Tuesday he does on his way to evening worship at the *masjid*, I must have his packet ready.

Why I can't say, except nowadays whenever I think *Haroun* an ice-hand clutches at my lungs.

The knife rises and descends, rises and descends. The *kalo jire* seeds are humming bright as bees.

I must press just right, split each seed exactly halfway down the middle. I must keep the right rhythm.

Too fast, and the seeds will shatter. Too slow and the invisible chain connecting each split grain will break apart and dissipate their dark energy in the world's air.

Perhaps that is why I do not hear him come in, why I whirl startled when he speaks. And feel on my finger the blade like a thin flame biting.

'You're bleeding,' says the lonely American. 'I'm terribly sorry. I should have knocked or something.'

'It's OK. No, really, it's nothing, just a scratch.'

Inside I'm thinking, I'm sure I locked the door I'm sure I—. And, Who is this man who can enter despite—

Then the words are swept away in a wave of gladness like gold sparks.

Blood drips from my finger onto the pile of *kalo jire*, red-black now and ruined. But filled with gold gladness I cannot find room inside me for regret.

'Here, let me,' he says, and before I can say no he lifts my finger to his lips. And sucks.

Pearl smoothness of teeth, hot moist satin of the inner lip, tongue moving slow over the cut, over my skin. His body my body becoming one.

O Tilo did you ever think—

I want this moment forever but I say, 'Please, I must put something on it.' And pull away though it takes all my will.

In the kitchen I find a bag of dried *neem* leaves. Dipped in honey and pressed against the skin, they are best for healing.

But when I look the finger is not bleeding anymore, and only a faint red crease to show it had happened at all.

Perhaps this body formed of fire and spell-shadow no longer bleeds as humans do.

But inside I am saying, Was it him was it him.

When I return to the front of the store, he is kneeling before the handicrafts case looking through scratched glass at miniature sandalwood elephants.

'You like them?'

'I like everything you've got here.' His smile opening deep petal on petal and at its heart something more than the words.

Tilo you are only imagining he sees through and through this oldwoman body.

I graze my fingers over the elephants until I find one that is perfect-carved – eyes ears line of tail, tiny ivory tusks like toothpick ends. I lift it out.

'I want you to have this.'

Another man would have protested. He does not.

I put the elephant in his palm and see his fingers close over it. His nails flicker translucent in the store's dimness.

'Elephants are for promises remembered and kept,' I say.

'And do you always keep yours?'

Ah. How does he know to ask this.

I tell him, 'Sandalwood is for soothing over hurt, ivory for endurance.'

He smiles, my lonely American, unfooled by my side-stepping. I watch how one corner of his mouth creases, pushing upward, and then a dimple, a taut hollow of sweet flesh that I long to touch.

To stop myself I say, 'Why did you come?'

Tilo what if he says I came for you.

'Is there always a reason?' He is still smiling, silver-edged seductive cloud-smile upon which I could float away so easily and never return.

I make my voice stern. 'Always, but only the wise know it.'

'Perhaps you can tell me, then, what it is.' His face is serious now. 'Perhaps you can read it on my pulses, like I've heard your Indian doctors can do.' And he extends to me a slim arm with skeins of lapis lazuli running under the skin.

'What doctors are these?' I cannot resist saying. 'Our doctors go to medical school, just like yours.'

But forgive me spices, still I take his hand.

I place my fingers on his wrist, light as an unspoken wish. His skin smells of lemon and salt and sun beating down on white sand. Am I only imagining that we are swaying together like the sea.

'Lady! Lady, what the hell is going on?'

Haroun loud as lightning at the door, kicking it shut with his shoe. His forehead is knotted with displeasure with suspicion.

I snatch my hand back, guilty as any village girl. My words stumble over themselves.

'Haroun I didn't realize it is so late already.'

'Please, go ahead and help him, I'm in no hurry,' says my American, his voice cool and unembarrassed. He saunters into the shadows of the far aisle among stacked sacks of mung and *urid* and Texas Long Grain rice.

Haroun turns his head to watch him, lips pressed into a thin line.

'Ladyjaan, you must be more careful who you let in the store after dark. All kinds of bad people roaming around this neighbourhood—'

'Hush Haroun.'

But he goes on, switching to English, his voice raised high so it ricochets off the back walls. His tongue moves thick and awkward through the words he is still not used to. Suddenly I am ashamed of his crude accent, the grammar he hasn't yet mastered. Then a deeper shame, like a slap that leaves my face burning, that I should feel this way.

'How come your door wasn't locked today? Did you read or not in *India Post* just last week how some man broke into one 7-Eleven? Shot the owner – his name was Reddy I think – in the chest three times. Was not so far from here. Better you ask this fellow to leave while I am still being in the store.'

I am mortified because surely my American is hearing.

'Just because he's dressed all fancy-fancy doesn't mean you can trust him. Opposite, in fact. I've heard of men like that, dress up and pretend they're rich, out to cheat you. And if he *is* rich, what does he want with us anyway, a sahib like him? Best to keep away from such. Lady listen, simply you leave it to me, I'll get rid of him.'

I try to remember what the American is wearing and am angry because I cannot, I Tilo who have always prided myself on my deep-seeing. Angry also because there is right in what Haroun advises, which is what the Old One would say also.

A sahib like him. Not one of us. Keep away Tilo.

'Haroun I'm not a child. I can take care of myself. I'd thank you not to insult my customers.'

My voice is sharp and tearing, like rusty nails. Is it the sound of denial.

Haroun flinches from it. Red rises high on his cheeks. His voice is formal with hurt.

'I only spoke my concern. But I see I stepped too far.'

I shake my head exasperated. 'Haroun, I didn't mean it like that.'

'No, no, what right have I, a poor man, a taxi driver, to advise you Lady.'

'Don't go. In a few minutes I'll get your packet done.'

He pushes the door open on a long creak. 'Don't trouble yourself on my account. I'm only a *kala admi* after all, not a white like *him*—'

I know I shouldn't. But.

'Haroun you're acting like a child,' I snap.

He is bowing dignified, silhouetted against a night which opens around him like jaws. '*Khuda hafiz*. I bid you farewell. The mullah will have started the service already and I must not be any more late.'

The door click-closes behind him, such a quiet, final sound, before I can say back to him *Khuda hafiz*, Allah's protection on your head.

When I turn to the counter again I see you, redblack *kalo jire* meant for Haroun, now defiled by my blood, spilled on the counter like a dark stain. A silence that accuses worse than words.

I stare at you a while, then sweep you into the hollow of my *palloo*. Carry you to the trash can.

Waste. Careless, sinful waste. That is what the Old One would say.

Sadness swells inside me with its hot sulphur smell. Sadness and another feeling I dare not look too closely at – guilt, or is it despair.

Later, I tell myself. I'll deal with it later.

But as I walk toward the back of the store where my American is waiting, I know *later* is like a lid clamped over a boiling pot, and inside it the steam building and building.

'Sometimes I have an ache,' says the American. 'Here.' He takes my hand and places it on his chest.

Tilo does he know what he is doing?

In the centre of my palm I feel his heart beating. It is strangely steady, drip of water on old stone. Nothing at all like the wild careening in my chest, horses dashing frantic into cave walls. With effort I direct my seeing to his clothes. Yes, Haroun is right, the silk of his shirt is soft and fine under my fingers, the pants are darkly elegant, the jacket moulds itself around him, perfect-fitted. The muted gleam of leather on his feet and at his waist. And on his ring finger a diamond like white fire. But already I am letting them fall out of my mind because I see his clothes have nothing to do with who he truly is. I keep only the way in which his flesh pulses warm and shining in his throat, the way his eyes soften as I look into them.

We are at the counter, I on the inside, he long-legged and leaning against the glass, and in between us, yes, the spices like a wall, watching.

'Your heart seems fine,' I make myself say. Under the shirt his skin must be golden as lamplight, the little hairs on his chest crisp as grass.

No. A different image comes to me, its edges etched so sharp I know it to be true. His chest innocent of hair, smooth as the sunwarm whitewood we used on the island to carve amulets.

'Yeah, that's what all the doctors say.'

Lonely American, I want to know everything about you. Why you visit doctors, since when this pain. But when I try to look in, there is only my face staring back from a quicksilver lake.

'They probably want to tell me, Maybe the pain's in your head. Except it'd be bad for business to say it out loud.'

His eyes are laughing back at me saying OK I'll give you what you want, just a little. His hair gleams, a bird's black wing with the sun on it.

You are playing with me, my American, and I am charmed. I who have never played. I suddenly light as a girl in these old bones.

'Maybe you need loving to cure your heart,' I say, smiling also. It amazes me how easily I am learning the rules of this flirting game. 'Maybe that's why the ache.'

O shameless Tilo now what.

'You really believe that?' he asks, serious now. 'You believe love can cure the aching heart?'

What should I say, I who have no experience in loving.

But before I can attempt to answer, he laughs away his question. 'Sounds good,' he says. 'You got something for me?'

For a moment I am disappointed. But no, it is better this way. 'Of course,' I tell him, my voice withdrawn already. 'Always, for everyone. Just one moment.'

Behind me I hear him say, 'Wait. I don't just want what you have for everyone. I want—' But I do not stop.

In the inner room I go to the lotus root, weigh its small suppleness in my palm for one breath-catching moment.

Why not Tilo, you who have begun breaking all the rules already.

I set it down with a sigh. Lotus root, *padmamul* aphrodisiac that I plucked from the centre of the island lake, this is not the right moment for you.

When I come back he looks at my empty hands. Raises an eyebrow.

I should give him what's waiting in the ebony box under the counter, hard nugget of *hing*, asafoetida to restore balance to my life and send him forever out of it.

The will of a thousand spices presses on me. I am bending, reaching, already I feel the darkness of the box against my fingers, the grainy asafoetida rock with its bitter smoke-smell.

O spices give me a little time just a little time.

I straighten, pick out a small brown bottle on the shelf behind. Set it on the counter. 'Here is *churan*,' I tell him.

'For loving?' he asks joking, but not-joking too.

'For heartburn,' I say as severe as I can. 'For the too-indulgent life. That's what you really need.' I ring it up and put it in a bag and look pointedly at the door. 'It is very late,' I say.

'I'm terribly sorry for troubling you,' he says, but he isn't. Colour of black water in moonlight, his eyes sparkle amusement. They drag the words I didn't intend out of me.

'Maybe next time I'll have something else for you.'

'Next time,' says my American, his voice like a gift he is offering.

It is morning before I remember the knife.

I throw off the tangled quilt, the spiderweb remnants of a dream I cannot quite remember. Hurry stumbling to the counter where I left it lying, though I fear it is too late already.

'Knife speak to me.'

In my hand the blade is a dull unforgiving grey, colour of a dead thing. The edge rusted with blood. When I rub, metallic flakes of it fall to the floor.

In the cramped alcove of the kitchen, I hold the knife

under running water. Make a paste of lime and tamarind and work it in while I repeat the cleansing mantras.

By the time I give up, my fingers are puckered from the acid.

The stain is clearer now, shape of a pear or maybe a teardrop. Shape of things to come.

I press my forehead into the cold cement wall. The images will not stop pounding their way across my eyelids. Fistful of *kalo jire* flung useless into a garbage can that smells of woman-blood. Haroun's face so young so unprotected, and night spreading behind it like a redblack blotch. The Old One, her sad eyes that see everything.

Forgive me First Mother.

Words only, girl. How can I forgive if you are not ready to give up that which caused you to stumble? And you are not.

This is what she would say, her voice like branches breaking in a storm's hands.

I do not answer her accusation.

Instead I say.

'Knife I will not forget you again. If you want new blood to wash away the old, I am ready.'

I raise the knife and close my eyes, bring it down hard on my fingers, wait for the pain like fireworks in my skull.

Nothing.

When I look again, an inch from my hand the knife quivers embedded in the counter's wood. Deflected. By some hidden desire in me, or its own will?

O foolish Tilo, to think reparation would be so easy.

'I wanted to ask you something,' Kwesi says, coming in with a cardboard tube tucked under his arm. 'Would you mind if I put something up in your store window?'

I am taken aback. Is it allowed? I am not sure.

Indian people do it all the time of course. Just look. All over the window, glossy ads of upcoming cine-star nites, MADHURI DIXIT IN PERSON. Neon-hued flyers inviting you to a DISCO-BHANGRA PARTY, FIVE-DOLLAR-ONLY COVER, MANNY IS YOUR DJ. BHAVNABEN'S FRESH *CHAPATIS* AND *DHOKLA* VERY REASONABLE PRICE. TAJ MAHAL TAILORING, CALL THIS NUMBER FOR BLOUSES STITCHED OVERNIGHT.

But Kwesi, an outsider?

'What is it?' I ask, buying time.

'Here, look.' He pulls it from the tube and lays it carefully on the counter, eye-catching in gold and black, a poster. A man in a belted uniform and bare feet, arms fisted, leg raised to the side in a powerful kick. And under it in simple letters, KWESI'S ONE WORLD DOJO, then the address.

'I knew you were a warrior.' I am smiling.

He smiles too. 'A warrior. I guess you could say that.'

'Have you been doing it long?'

He nods. 'Fifteen years, easy.' He sees my intrigued eyes. 'You want to hear how it started?' And even before I'm done nodding he has begun, settling his elbows comfortably on the counter, Kwesi who loves a good story, who has the telling of them in his bones.

'I was in bad shape back then, heavy into the drug scene, dope, smack, blow, you name it. I lived from high to high, did a lot of crazy things to support the habit. That's how I had a run-in with the man who would become my *sensei*. I challenged him to a fight – I used to think of myself as quite a fighter in those days – but he knocked me out in less than a minute. Next day I made some enquiries, went to his dojo after classes with a gun, planning to make him pay. He opened the door and I jammed the gun up against his head. But he wasn't scared. He said, Why don't you come in, I've just brewed some Japanese tea, you can always shoot me afterward. He wasn't faking, macho stuff like I might've pulled in his place. He really wasn't afraid. I was so amazed I put the gun away and followed him. One thing led to another and I ended up staying six years. Can you believe that?

'I never did develop a taste for that green stuff, though. Give me a strong cup of Darjeeling anytime.'

We are laughing but there's a raw edge to it, a laugh that knows how easily it could have turned to weeping. A laugh like this, when you share it, loosens the knots in the heart. And so I wipe my eyes and tell Kwesi, 'You're welcome to put up your poster here. Though frankly I'm not sure how many people would be interested.'

We look around the store. Two plump middle-aged women in saris argue the respective merits of Patak and Bedekar pickles. An old *sardarji* in a white turban brings a bottle of Original Nilgiris Eucalyptus Oil Excellent for Coughs to the counter for a price check. Someone's children play catch around a bin of *atta*. A long-haired youngish man in Ray Ban glasses and tight Levi's comes in, but he gives Kwesi a suspicious scowl and disappears down the aisle of lentils.

'I see what you mean,' Kwesi says dryly. He starts to roll up his poster. 'I'll find another place for this.'

I am sorry to have disappointed him. I search out a large box of uncut black Darjeeling, the best kind, and pack it for him. 'My compliments,' I say. 'No no, the story was more than worth it.' I walk with him to the door. 'Come again anytime. Good luck with your dojo and your life,' I say, and mean it.

One morning he comes into the store with his mother's list and hair that stands up straight and stiff as brush bristles making him taller, this teenager I almost do not recognize. But then I look some more and it is Jagjit.

'Jagjit how are you?'

He spins around, his hands already fisted. Then sees me and lets them go loose.

'How d'you know my name?'

Jagjit sullen in T-shirt and baggy Girbaud jeans and untied laces, the uniform of young America, speaking its staccato rhythms already.

'You came into my store with your mother three-four times, maybe two and half, three years back.'

He shrugs turning away, not remembering. He has lost interest already.

'Couldn't be that long. I've only been here two years.'

'Only so little?' I make my voice admiring. 'Who would think that, looking at you.'

Jagjit doesn't bother to answer. He knows old women, grandmothers aunts mothers, forever saying Don't don't don't. Don't spend so much time with your friends. Don't miss any more school, they gave us two warnings already. Don't go out so late in the night, it's not safe. *Hai* Jaggi is this why we brought you to Amreekah.

I watch him fill his basket too fast and clatter it down on the counter even though he got only half the list. I watch him tapping his foot because he has places to go.

'Are things better now at school?'

He gives me a hostile stare. 'Who told you?'

I say nothing. Jagjit so busy always fighting always putting on toughness like a second face, look into my eyes. With me you need not struggle so.

A long-ago expression like shyness hovers over his lips, then is gone.

'Yeah, school's cool.'

'You like studying?'

He shrugs. 'I do OK.'

'And the other boys, they don't give you trouble?'

Flash of a smile, showing his teeth sharp as chisels. 'Nobody messes with me no more. I got friends.'

'Friends?'

But even before he nods I see them in his eyes, the boys in their blue satin jackets like midnight embroidered with that special sign, their black berets, their hundred-dollar Karl Kani boots. Thick glittergold chains, bracelets with names engraved, a diamond ring for their little finger.

Yeah, the big boys, Jagjit says inside his head. *Sixteen and already driving a droptop Beamer a seventy-two Cutty a Lotus Turbo. Carrying in their deep pockets sheaves of dead presidents* – what you need, rogue – *peeling off C-notes, even a couple of G's* – no problem, blood, plenty more where that came from. *And hanging on their arms the girls, so many girls, with their wide lacquered eyes.*

Boys rolling and taking a deep drag and passing it on amused to a kid standing nearby. And his mouth opening in wonder.

For me?

My friends.

The big boys who stood at the other end of the school grounds watching and watching, and one day they came over and shoved the others away and said Fuck off. Brushed me clean of dirt and bought me an icecold Coke in that afternoon blazing like brushfire and said We'll take care of you.

And since then I never had no trouble. They're like my brothers, better than my brothers.

I see his eyes glisten gratitude, Jagjit all alone whose parents were too worn with work and worry in a strange land to hear him, Jagjit who went home each day from America to a house so steeped in Punjabi how could they help. Who held his cries in until red swam behind his eyelids like bleeding stars.

Jagjit remembering: *They took me places with them. Bought me stuff, clothes shoes food watches Nintendo games stereos with speakers to make the walls shake, even things I didn't know yet to want. They listened when I talked and didn't laugh.*

They taught me how to fight. Pointed out the soft fleshy parts where it hurts most. Showed me how to use elbow knee fist boot keys and yes, knife.

And in return, so little. Carry this packet here, drop off this box there. Keep this in your locker for a day. Stand on the corner and watch for.

Who needs mother father school? When I'm older, maybe fourteen, I'll be with them all the time. I'll wear the same jacket, carry deep in my pocket the same switchblade with its snake-flick tongue, see the same bright pull of fear in the girls' eyes and the boys running.

Inside me thoughts whirl like dust-devils. I cannot breathe.

O cinnamon strength-giver, cinnamon friend-maker, what have we done.

And one day they'll give it to me, cold and black-shining and heavy with power in my hand, pulsing electric as life, as death, my passport into the real America.

I clasp my fingers to stop the shaking. Clove and cardamom that I scattered on the wind for compassion, how did this happen.

'Jagjit,' I say through cracked lips, a voice with the confidence leached out of it.

His eyes dreaming, not-seeing even when he turns toward me.

'You are such a handsome boy, growing so well, it is a joy for an old woman to see. I have for you a tonic to make you stronger even and more smart, no charge, just wait one small minute while I get it.'

He gives a short scoffing laugh, a sound trying to be so grown-up it twists my heart.

'Shit I don't need no smelly Indian tonic.'

Jagjit slipping away from me, moving toward the door into the maelstrom never to return, so I must go down quick into his past and use whatever I find.

'Jaggi, *mera raja beta.*'

A shudder goes through him at the childhood name, smell of his mother's hair in a simpler time, her hand rubbing his back, smoothing nightmares away into the warm Jullunder night, and for a moment he wishes—

'OK but make it fast. I'm late already.'

In the inner room I fill a bottle with elixir of *manjistha* to cool the blood and make it pure. Rush a prayer over it, missing words because he's at the door already yelling 'Hold on dude' to someone outside. Hand it to him and watch him toss it in the bag and wave a careless Bye now.

A motorcycle roars to life and he's gone.

And I left alone to walk stiffly back to the counter, to lower my aching head into my hands, to wonder in dismay what went wrong. To ask myself over and over, was it him, was it his parents, was it America? Or that other question so devastating I can frame it only phrase by broken phrase.

Spices is this. The way. You have chosen. To. Punish me.

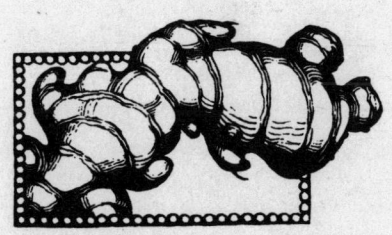

Ginger

This morning when Geeta's grandfather came into the store, the spring gone from his step, he did not speak of Geeta. But his whole face was asking Have you yet and When will you.

Therefore tonight I prepare myself with ginger for my first foray into America.

For as you know, when I woke in this land the store was already around me, its hard, protective shell. The spices too surrounded me, a shell of smells and voices. And that other shell, my aged body pressing its wrinkles into me. Shell within shell within shell, and inmost of all my heart beating like a bird.

Today I plan to stretch my wings, to crack perhaps these shells and emerge into the infinite spaces of the outside world. It frightens me a little. I must admit this.

And so I call on ginger.

Root of gnarled wisdom, *ada* in your hide of banded brown, help me in this my seeking. I weigh your speckled solidness in the hollow of my palm. Wash you three times in lime water. Slice you translucent-thin as the curtain between waking and dream.

Adrak ginger, be with me.

I drop the slices in a pan of boiling water, watch them rise and sink, rise and sink, in a slow whirl. Like lives caught on karma's wheel. Steam fills my kitchen, clings haze-heavy to my lashes so it is hard to see. Steam and that wild smell like bamboo grass torn and chewed that will stay in my sari long after.

Golden ginger used by the healer Charak to relight the fire that simmers in the belly, may your bright burning course up my sluggish veins. Outside, America is flinging itself against the walls of my store, calling in its many-tongued voice. Give me strength to answer.

I wait a long time for the spicesong, but it does not come.

Ah Tilo, bending the rules and sliding through them, what did you expect.

I pour the liquid, colour of palest honey, into a cup. Raise it to my mouth. The pungence is like a blow to the throat. It makes me gasp and cough. When I force myself to swallow, it churns in my bowels, rebelling. Wanting out. But I hold it down with all my will.

Never before have I pitted my strength against a spice's. Never before driven my desire against duty.

Slowly the resistance lessens, is gone.

Tilo now that you have your way, why this sadness, this foolish wish that you had not won?

A prickling starts in my throat, my tongue moving in hot nimbleness, pushing regret aside.

Later Tilo. Later there will be time.

From the pot I lift out the heat-bleached slices. One by one I bite down, feel the fibres catch in my teeth. The top of my skull is lifting off.

When the sting fades, new words begin to come to me, new gestures which will let me move unseen through the streets that coil labyrinthine around the store. Inside my head plans and promises pound.

Geeta wait for me. I am ready I am coming.

But first there is the matter of clothes.

When I came to America I was given no items for outdoor use, just the frayed saris, colour of stained ivory, in which I greet my customers.

I cannot blame the Old One for it. She wanted only to lessen the temptation. To keep me safe.

But now I must attire myself for America.

And so today at the *brahma muhurta*, the holy moment of Brahman when night reveals itself as day, I take poppy seed, *khus khus* that sticks to my fingertips unwilling as wet sand, and crush and roll it with jaggery to form *afim*. Opium, the spice of seeming.

Then I set it on fire.

I can tell the spices are not with me. Three times the *khus khus* ball sputters and goes out, three times I have to chant the flames back into being. And then it burns fit-fully, its odour sour and heavy, reluctant. The rising smoke catches in my throat, making me cough till tears come.

But I am getting better at it, bending the spices' will to mine. This time the heartsickness is less. And the guilt which I will not look in the eye.

Is it always like this when we push into the forbidden, which some call sinning? The first step wrenches, bone and blood, rips out our breath. The second too racks but already it is not so strong. With the third the hurting passes over our bodies like a raincloud. Soon it will not give us pause, or pain.

So you hope, Tilo.

The smoke winds around me, forms itself into a web on my skin. The clothes take shape.

All I know of American clothes is what I have seen customers wear. Glimpses of passers-by. I weave them together into a coat grey as the sky outside. A wisp of a blouse showing the neck. Dark pant legs. And an umbrella, for through the dimness before morning light comes, I can see outside the dull silver strings of falling rain.

But already I know I cannot wear these clothes to Geeta's.

The seeming-spells are hard to work even when all is

well. And today, the spice against me, I feel the power draining away until my brain is dry. And behind it the spice, waiting for my attention to falter. For the spell to break and set it free.

Afim, why do you fight me when it is not for myself I am doing this?

The spice's silence is like a stone in my heart, like ash on my tongue.

Through it I can hear back to long ago, the Old One laughing bitter as bile. I know what she would say were she here.

Hasn't that always been your trouble Tilo, you who think you know best, who choose to forget that the highest motives lead fastest to doom. And are your motives so high, or do you help Geeta because you see in her forbidden love an image of your own.

The clothes thin as fog are tearing already as I lift my hands to my face. I know they will not help me any further, the spices.

And so I am forced to my next plan.

Outside the rain is cold and hard. It stings like needles as I turn to lock the shop door. Under my palm the knob is slick and stubborn. The hinges stick, mutinous. The store's muscles wrestling with mine. I must put down the package, the gift I am carrying to Geeta, to tug and wrench and kick, until at length I can bang the door shut. The sound is sharp as a shot, terminal. I am left shivering on the step. *On the wrong side*, says the voice in my brain. Damp seeps into my bones, settles like silt. I run my hand over the door, which looks so alien in outdoor light, and am struck by the sudden vertigo of homelessness.

I'll be back soon as I can.

The door's nicked green face is mute as a shield and as obdurate. It is not appeased by my promise.

Perhaps it will not let me in when I return?

Stop Tilo, don't create snakes out of ropes. You have enough else to worry about.

The air smells like wet animal pelts. I breathe it in, shrug myself deeper into my coat. I will not be afraid, I tell myself. I open my umbrella, shape of a giant toadstool, over my head.

Resolute, I step down the deserted street, pushing through rain like sheets of frosted glass until I see the sign SEARS, until a door slides open all on its own like the mouth to some magic cave, inviting me in.

You who lounge lazy through Saks and Nordstrom, who pick your ennuied, everyday path through Neiman Marcus, can you understand how I love the anonymity of this my first American store, so different from my spice shop? The blandness of neon lights that fall evenly without shadow on shiny Mop & Glo floors, on shiny carts that roll along pulling dazed shoppers behind. How I love the aisles and aisles of things piled folded hung high, and no one to say, 'Don't touch,' or ask, 'Yes, what do you want.' Aloe vera lotions for youthfulness and false silver platters shinier than real; fishing rods and chiffon nighties transparent as desire; Corning Ware casseroles and video games from Japan; new improved Cuisinarts and tubes of Neet hair remover; a whole wall of TV sets talking at you with different faces. The headiness of knowing you can reach out and take and take, even though you don't need.

I am drunk with it. I who for a moment can become an ordinary old woman feeling through a fabric peering at a label trying a colour against my ridged and freckled skin.

Before I know it my cart is full.

A mirror. A colour TV so I may see into the heart of America, into the heart, I hope, of my lonely American. A make-up kit with everything in it. Perfume of rose and lavender. Shoes, several pairs, in different colours, the last ones red as burnished chillies, high heels like chisels. Clothes and more clothes – dresses pantsuits sweaters, the intricate wispy mysteries of American feminine underwear. And last of all a bed robe of white lace like raindrops caught in a spider's web.

Tilo have you gone crazy is this why you broke the rule of boundary and stepped into America. For this.

That voice, caustic as acid splashing. My face burns with it. First Mother, I think guiltfully, then realize it is my own voice. And am therefore more ashamed of my frivolity.

I abandon the cart in an aisle of hair dyes, taking only what I know I must have. Clothes to wear to Geeta today. And the mirror, though what I will need it for I cannot yet tell.

No Tilo, not that most dangerous of forbidden things.

But this time I do not listen.

I look instead at the cashier women, their sad, sagging underarms, their coloured hair with the roots showing. And wholly innocent of interest, their gaze scanning your face, like the red electric eye of the checkstand is scanning the items they are dragging over.

The cashier women who inside their heads are dreaming of minks bought at Macy's, of high school sweethearts coming back, this time to stay, of cruises to Acapulco on a party boat. Already as their mouths say 'Cash or charge,' say 'You want it delivered, cost you twenty bucks extra,' say 'Have a nice day,' they have forgotten me. Because inside their heads they are spinning it on the

Wheel of Fortune, beautiful as Vanna in her star-spangled mini and even thinner.

O the freedom of it. Almost I envy them.

In a public rest room that smells of ammonia I pull on my no-nonsense pants and polyester top, button my non-descript brown coat all the way to my calves. I lace my sturdy brown shoes, heft my brown umbrella in readiness. This new-clothed self, I and not-I, is woven of strands of brownness with only her young eyes and her bleached-jute hair for surprise. She tries a hesitant smile which resettles her wrinkles. She loosens her muscles, letting go, and the seeming-clothes made of *afim* and mindpower rise off her skin like smoke, stream from her new sleeves to hang in hieroglyphs she cannot read.

For a moment she wonders if they spell a warning.

'Thank you,' says the woman to the spice and is not surprised that there is no answer. She puts the receipt for the mirror, which later someone will bring to the store, into her coat pocket. For a moment a vision hovers at the edge of her eyes: the freeze-cold border of the mirror's mercury against her palm, the blind-silver flash of the moment when she will— But she shakes it away. Geeta is waiting, and her grandfather also. Carefully she picks up the package she has carried all the way from the store. She is thinking so hard about what she must do that she does not even notice when the automatic doors open their glass jaws to let her out.

Outside at a bus stop crowded with other strands of brown and white and black she will get into line, will marvel that no one even raises his eyes, suspicious at her moving through the air of America so awkward-new. She will finger in pleased wonder the collar of her coat, which is better even than a cloak of disappearing. And when the bus comes she will surge at it with the others, her blending so successful that you standing across the street will no longer know who is who.

With a great belch of smoke the bus lets me out in front of Geeta's office and roars away. I stand awhile, craning up in wonder at that glittery tower of black glass. On the lower rectangles I see, shimmering, a face.

Mine?

I move closer to look but it ripples away, this face I have never examined. Have never till now felt the heart-hammering need to. When I retreat it reappears floating, the features remote and unreal, elongated into mystery.

Wisewoman shaman herb-healer, come to make things right.

The receptionist thinks differently.

'Who?' Her magenta lips purse around the pellet of the word. 'Do you have an appointment? No?' In their armour of mascara her eyes rake my cheap coat and boots, the package I have brought all the way from the spice store wrapped in old newspaper. My umbrella pooling dark wetness like pee on her carpet. Her spine is stick-straight with disapproval.

'Then I'm afraid I can't help you.' She smooths her skirt over trim hips with magenta-tipped fingers, turns with finality back to her typing.

But I Tilo did not step over the threshold of prohibited

America, did not risk the spices' retribution to go back so easily empty-handed.

I advance until I stand directly in front of her desk, until her typing stops and she looks up with annoyance and yes, a flicker of fear under the spiked lashes.

'You must tell Geeta I am here. It is important.'

Her eyes say, Crazy bag lady, say, Maybe I should ring for Security, say finally, Heck, why should I get involved. She jabs at buttons on a machine on her desk and speaks in a manicured voice.

'Ms Bannerjee, there's a person to see you. A woman. Yes, I think she's Indian. No, I'm quite sure she isn't representing anyone. She's – uh – different. No, she didn't give a name. OK, if you're sure.' Then she turns to me. 'Fourth floor, ask someone when you get off, elevator's to your left.' Her eyes are saying, Just go.

'You didn't ask,' I say to her gently as I gather my belongings.

'What?' The word startled out of her.

'For my name. And I do represent someone. Why else do you think I'm here.'

Geeta's office is a tiny square and windowless, the kind given to newcomers who should be too busy to look out anyway. A metal table stacked with files and blueprints takes up all the space.

Sitting behind the table she is writing a business report but not really, because the pad is filled with doodles. From where I stand they look like roses with huge thorns. She seems thinner. Or is it just the severity of the dark pantsuit she is wearing today, the lapels slanting hard and angled across her chest, the inkblue cloth pulling the colour out of her face. Its grown-upness only making her look more young.

The last time she came to my store she wore blue jeans. A red T-shirt that said *¡Uxmal!* Her hair in a thick braid down her back, wavy as water as she laughed at something her mother said. Together they were picking out raisins and almonds and sweet white *elachdana* to make desserts for Bengali New Year.

Today her eyes are faintly puzzled as she tries to place me. And dark with disappointment. She was expecting someone else, perhaps her mother come like a miracle to say *I forgive*. She presses her lips together, trying to make them not tremble. There is a small mole on her chin and it too is trembling. I wish I could tell her how beautiful it – she – is.

'Please sit down,' she says finally, straining at politeness. 'This is a surprise. You look different.'

And then because she can't hold it in anymore, 'How did you know where I work? Did someone ask you to come see me?'

I nod.

'My mother.'

When I shake my head no she says, 'Not Dad?' Her voice is high with hoping.

O Geeta my songbird, how I wish I could say yes, wish I could pluck the thorn bleeding in your rose-heart. But I must shake my head again.

Her shoulders crumple. 'I didn't think so.'

'It was your grandfather actually.'

'Oh, *him*.' Her voice is acid now. I can hear the thoughts, gnawing and corrosive in her brain. *He's the one who turned them against me with all that shit about good women and family shame. They never would have behaved so prehistorically otherwise. Dad, especially. If only he'd stayed in India none of this would've—*

'Your grandfather loves you a lot,' I say, to stop the

poison eating at her heart.

'Love, hah.' She spits out the sound like a sickness. 'He doesn't know what the word means. For him it's all control. Control my parents, control me. And whenever he doesn't get his way it's *O Ramu send me back better I die alone in India.*'

Her imitation of the heavy oldman accent is exact, vicious. It shocks me. Still, better hate spoken than hate silent.

'If it weren't for his medieval ideas about arranged marriages I wouldn't have had to tell Mom and Dad about Juan like this. I would've introduced him to them slowly; they would've gotten a chance to see him as a person, not as a—'

Her voice stumbles.

I know what I should say. The Old One taught it to us many times. *Your fate is born with you, stitched into your birth stars. Who can you blame for it?*

But that is not what she needs to hear, Geeta for whom the old words no longer fit her song.

Spices, I know I have no right to ask but spices guide me.

A hot sand wind rubs at my words, eroding them. The minutes fall around us like drops of lead.

What shall I do now.

Then she says, 'What the hell did he think you could do, anyway?' She is staring at me, her brow wrinkled as though trying to recall. But her eyes are no longer crusted over with hate.

'Nothing really,' I say hurriedly. 'Just let you know that angry words like buzzing bees hide the honey underneath. Just see you so I can go back and tell them Don't worry so much she's well.'

'I don't know about that.' Her sigh shakes her whole

body. 'I'm taking pills every night and still I can't sleep. Diana's been getting real concerned. She thinks I should get some help, go see a shrink, maybe.'

'Diana?'

'Oh, I didn't move in with Juan. I couldn't do that to Mom and Dad. Besides, I knew it would be really bad for our relationship, what with me being so stressed and everything. So I called Diana, she's my best friend from college, and she said, Sure, you can stay with me for as long as you need.'

Thankfulness loosens my clenched lungs so I can breathe again. 'Geeta,' I say, 'you are a very intelligent girl.'

She tries to hide her smile but I can tell she is pleased. 'Would you like to see his photo?' she says and wipes the pewter frame sitting on her desk carefully on her blue sleeve. Hands it to me.

Earnest eyes, dark wings of neat-combed hair, a mouth that has learned kindness from growing up with too little. His arm around her a bit awkward as though he isn't yet used to so much luck.

'He looks very intelligent too,' I say.

Now she is openly smiling. 'He's a lot smarter than me. Can you believe, he came out of the *barrio*, went to college on a scholarship, graduated with a 4.0. And so modest you'd never learn any of it from him. I *know* if Dad just talks to him he'll see what a wonderful guy he is.'

'Maybe you will bring him to the store one time so I can meet him?'

'Sure. He'd like that. He's real interested in Indian culture and especially our food. I cook it every once in a while at his apartment. You know Mexicans cook with a lot of the same spices that we—'

Suddenly she stops, Geeta who is nobody's fool. Looks

straight at me, her eyes black as lakes and in them my face floating.

'Now I remember. Grandpa said once that you knew spells.'

'Simply oldman talk,' I say quickly.

'O I don't know,' she says. 'Grandpa can be pretty smart about some things.' She examines me some more. 'It's OK, I don't mind. I have a good feeling about you. I'll bring Juan to you sometime soon, maybe even next week. They have them in his culture too, *curanderas* I believe they're called.'

'Next week then,' I say rising, my work almost done for now, though ahead it will surely be rocks and stumbling. 'Here, I brought you something.'

I take it from its wrappings, bottle of mango pickled in mustard oil into which I've added *methi* for healing breaks and *ada* for the deeper courage which knows when to say no, and also *amchur* for deciding right.

She holds it up to the light, its thick redgold glow. 'Thanks! It's my favourite kind. But of course you know that.' Her eyes glint, mischievous. 'Did you say some magic over it?'

'The magic is in your heart,' I say.

'But seriously, thank you for coming. I feel so much better. Listen, why don't I walk you down.'

In the lobby she gives me a hug, Geeta come down from her glitter-black tower, her arms light as wings around me. Slips something into my hand.

'Maybe you could show them this, you know, if they come to the store or something, and you could maybe tell them also we're not living together?' Her mouth is a hot rose blooming for a moment on my cheek. 'And here's my number, in case – well, just in case.'

A plan stirs inside me, a rustle like wings. I will give

them to her grandfather when next he comes, the phone number and photo both, tell him what to do.

All the way back in the bus my shoulders glow and burn where she touched them. The skin of my face, scorched where she breathed the unsaid words of her wish: *The people I love most, make them love each other.* My eyes too scorching as I stare at the photograph, the two lovers so young, smiling up with wrenching faith as though I could fix it all, I Tilo who is myself in more trouble than ever they could be.

She is sitting by my head when I wake, the store dark except for a radium-green glow coming from I can't tell where, and the smell of the hibiscus oil she would sometimes let us rub into her hair. The Old One sitting crosslegged, her spine curving inward as though something is too heavy for it to hold up, my life or hers, I do not know which. The scars on her hands glow like firelines against that seared-white skin. I start flinching away but then I don't, because on her face is not the anger I imagined but sadness. Such deep sadness it is like a monsoon cloud, like the bottom of the sea. And inside myself someone is twisting and twisting a wet cloth until the last drops are wrung from it.

'First Mother,' I say and put out my hand, but there is nothing to hold. She is spirit-travelling, as I should have known. I am sorry again, for I remember how after such journeys she would lie on a pallet in the healing hut a little longer each time, her breath shallow, the flesh under her eyes loose and purple as with bruising.

'First Mother is it that bad, what I did?'

'Tilo.' Her voice is small and echoing as if caught inside an underwater cave. 'Tilo daughter you should not have.'

'But Mother how else could I have helped Geeta, how else helped her grandfather who came to me asking for the first time in his life.'

'Daughter the help you try to give outside these protected walls turns on itself, don't you know that? Even in here you have seen how all does not work the way you want it to.'

'Jagjit,' I whisper, my voice bowed in failure.

'Yes. And there'll be others. Don't you remember the last lesson?'

I try to think but inside my skull is a jumble of broken parts, thought shards whose ends do not fit each other.

'Ultimately the Mistresses are without power, hollow reeds only for the wind's singing. It is the spice that decides, and the person to whom it is given. You must accept what they together choose and even with failure be at peace.'

'First Mother, I—'

'But when you lean out past what is allowed and touch what is not, when you step beyond the old rules, you increase the chance of failing a hundredfold. The old rules which keep the world in its frail balance, which have been there for ever, before me, before the other Old Ones, before even the Grandmother.'

Her voice fades in and out as though buffeted by a sea storm.

I want to ask so much. I who in my naïveté had thought it had always been her since the beginning. *Who were the other Old Ones who was the Grandmother*. And that question formed of dark curiosity and perhaps a darker desire, which I cannot bring myself to speak.

Who when you are gone.

Then I forget because she is saying, 'Don't let America seduce you into calamities you cannot imagine. Dreaming of love, don't rouse the spices' hate.'

My voice is a stunned whisper. 'You know?'

She doesn't answer. Already her image is growing dim, the phosphorous glow fading from the walls of the store.

'Wait, First Mother—'

'Child I had to fight with all my heart's strength to bring you this warning,' she says faintly through lips blue as air. 'Next time I will not be able.'

'Mother since you know my heart, answer this question before you go. What if a Mistress wants her life back. What will the spices—'

But she is gone. The walls are cold and cobweb-dim again, not even a brief waver of wind to tell she was here. No sigh of sound, no smell of her hibiscus-hair drifting like incense. Only the spices watching, the spices stronger than I ever thought, their dark power clenched in their core. The spices sucking all the store's air into themselves until none is left for me, letting me know this was no dream.

Letting me know they heard it all.

Time passes, time passes. Sun rises, the colour of turmeric, falls in a scatter of *sindur* vermilion. On the naked tree outside, fennel-beaked birds cry their sorrow. Sky presses down so clouds black as *kalo jire* scrape the top of a downtown tower I once travelled to. I think of Haroun I think of Ahuja's wife I think of Geeta and her Juan. I dust the shelves of the store and pile packets up neatly and wonder why they do not come. Cars gun their engines racing by. There are shots there are screams then the keening of the ambulance and lastly the stains hosed off the pavement. *Jagjit Jagjit* I cry inside my heart. But I remember the Old One's face, I remember her warning and do not step even to the window to look.

But maybe I have only dreamed all this, rocking through the night between wishing and not-wishing. Maybe it is only next morning now, for a truck rumbles up to the door and two men in navy overalls with REY and JOSE stitched in red over their pockets are pounding on the door shouting, 'Delivery!' Or is it karma, that great wheel black as death which, once set in motion, cannot be stopped?

The men say, 'Where you want it?' Say, 'Sign here this line, you know English, yes?' Say wiping their brows, 'Hey lady, that was hot work. Got some Coke or better some cold *cerveza*?'

I give them mango juice in ice with mint leaves floating for coolness, for strength that lasts the long day. I chew at my lip waiting for them to wave me *Gracias* and *So long* and take off in their truck which jiggles and stutters over the potholes. Finally the light blinks its green eye at them and I am alone with my carton from Sears.

I try to cut through the tape, a voice inside me calling Hurry hurry, but my knife is unwilling. My knife stained like tears of accusation. It twists in my hand, wanting to leap away. Two, three times I nick myself, almost. Until at last I put it away and rip at the cardboard with fingers. Scrabble through pellets like spongy snow, lift aside Styrofoam sheets brittle as sea salt. How much time it takes, my heart worrying its bars like a caged animal, until at last I catch its slippery hardness in my hands and pull so it rises up gleaming.

My mirror.

All the spices watching me, their eyes one eye their breath one breath united in disapproval, silently asking *Why*.

Ah if only I knew. There is a feeling inside me like someone walking on thinnest ice, knowing at any moment it will crack, but unable to stop.

Here is a question I never thought to ask on the island: First Mother, why is it not allowed, what can be wrong with seeing yourself?

The afternoon sun is a flash on my mirror, making the store so blinding bright even the spices must blink.

Before they can reopen their eyes I have lifted down a picture of Krishna and his *gopis* and hooked it into the waiting nail, with a *dupatta* draped carefully over it.

Mirror, forbidden glass that I hope will tell me the secret of myself.

But not today. It is not time.

Why not Tilo our foolish Mistress for what then did you buy it.

Out of the silence their voice, startling. A question flares like an eye inside me, *Why are they speaking* – then closes in on its dark, suspicious self.

But already I have forgotten it in the joy that floods my whole being. Scoffing yes, annoyed yes, but talking once again to me, my spices.

Ah dear ones, it has been so long.

Who knows when and how a mirror may be needful, I tell them, my voice light as a wind's kiss on a floating thistle.

I feel their attention, curious and grave, like sunlight on my skin. Holding back their power to incinerate. Waiting on judgement.

Perhaps the Old One was mistaken? Perhaps it is not too late for us after all?

Inside my wild caged heart I am saying this over and over: Spices trust me give me a chance. In spite of America, in spite of love, your Tilo will not let you down.

Peppercorn

'This one,' says the American. 'I want this one.'

'Are you sure,' I ask, dubious.

'Absolutely.'

I smile with the irony of it. Tilo he is as certain as you were on the island, and as little-knowing. So now you, like the Old One, must take on the cautioning role.

We are standing in the aisle of snacks. The American holds up a packet of *chanachur* on which is written LIJJAT SNACK MIX VERY HOT!!!

'It really is,' I say. 'Why not try one of the milder brands. What are you trying to prove.'

He laughs. 'My machoness, of course.'

It is Monday. The store is officially closed. For Monday is the day of silence, day of the whole white mung bean which is sacred to the moon. On Mondays I go to the inner room and sit in the lotus asana. When I close my eyes the island comes to me, coconut palms swaying, soft sun floating on the evening sea, smell of wild honeysuckle in the sweet heavy air, so real I could weep. I hear the thin call of ospreys as they dive for salt fish. It is a sound like violins.

The Old One comes to me also, and around her the new girls whom I do not know. But the gleam on their faces is heartbreaking-familiar. The gleam that says *We will change the world*.

On Mondays I talk to the Old One. For Monday is the day for mothers, the day they should know all their daughters' doings. But lately I do not tell everything.

As I will not today.

This is what happened today: The lonely American came to the store. In daylight. For the first time.

Why is this significant, you ask.

Night draped in her glamour-scarf of stars often deceives – especially when we want something just so. It is only in the impartial light of day that we are forced to learn the daytime reality of men.

I sensed his coming long before he stood at the locked door of the shop looking at the dog-eared CLOSED sign. His body had been a column of heat shifting through the busy streets, his gait firm yet gentle as though it were not concrete but the earth's skin he stepped on.

Ah my American, waiting part in dread and part in desire I said to myself, Perhaps now I will see that he is only ordinary after all.

Standing outside in stillness, did he feel me too? Pillar of ice frozen on the other side of the door, and inside me all the old voices clamouring *Don't answer*. Clamouring *Have you forgotten, today is the day consecrated to the First Mother, when you must speak to no one else?*

I think he heard them. For he did not knock. He turned away, my American, giving me a chance. But at the first step he took backward, I opened the door.

Just to look. That is what I told myself.

He didn't speak. Not words. Only the gladness in his eyes telling me he saw something more important than my wrinkles.

What are you really seeing?

American, I am gathering the courage to ask you this. One day soon.

And for the first time inside his mind I caught a swaying, like kelp deep undersea, almost invisible in salt shadows.

A desire. I could not read it yet. I knew only that somehow it included me.

I Tilo who had always been the one who granted wishes, never the one who was wished for.

Gladness tugged at the corners of my mouth also, though we Mistresses are not given much to smiling.

Lonely American you have passed the test of day. You have not dwindled into commonness. But how will I rest until I discover this your desire.

I pushed at the door to open it more, expecting resistance. But it swung easy and wide, like a welcoming arm.

'Come in.' Nor did the words stick raw and jagged in my throat, as I had feared.

'I didn't want to disturb,' he said.

Behind us the door glided shut. In the hushed, listening air of the store my voice floated, a bell of glass.

'How can one be disturbed by those one is happy to see.'

But inside me a question, grating as an eyeful of sand: Spices are you with me truly, or is this a new game you are playing.

'There's something I have to warn you of,' I say as I hand my American the *chanachur*.

Inside my head: No Tilo you don't, why not let it be. After all he chose it himself.

Temptation, soft as a silkbed. It would be so easy to let my body sink into it.

No. Lonely American, later you must never say I used your ignorance.

So I continue. 'The main spice in it is *kalo marich*, peppercorn.'

'Yes?' But his attention is mostly on the packet, which he is smelling. The spices make him sneeze. He laughs, shaking his head, lips pursed in a silent whistle.

'Peppercorn which has the ability to sweat your secrets out of you.'

'So you think I have secrets.' Seeming unconcerned, he

picks up an awkward pinch of the snack, pieces falling from between fingers. Puts it in his mouth.

'I know you do,' I say. 'Because I have them too. Every one of us.'

I watch him, not knowing if the spice will work now that I have told its power. This is a new way I am going, and in front all is bramble bush and dark fog.

'I'm not doing it right, am I,' he says as more *chana* drizzles from his fingers, studding his shirt front yellow and brown.

I have to laugh. 'Here,' I say, 'I'll make you a cone like we use in India.' From under the counter where I keep old Indian newspapers, I shake out a sheet. Roll it up and fill it.

'Pour some onto your palm. When you get really good you can toss it up and catch it in your mouth, but for now lift your hand to your lips.'

'Yes, ma'am,' he says with mock humbleness.

So now my American is sitting on the counter swinging his legs and eating hot snack mix from his paper cone as though he's done it forever. His feet are bare. He took off his shoes at the door. His shoes, handmade of softest leather, whose shine comes not from the surface but somewhere deeper. Shoes Haroun would have loved and hated.

'For respect,' he said. 'Just like Indians do.'

'Not when they are in a store.'

'But you're not wearing any either.'

So many months, so many people coming and going, and only he noticed. Is it foolish to feel pleasure like an electric tingle in my dusty soles?

'I'm different,' I tell him.

'What makes you think I'm not?' He smiles that smile I am learning to watch for.

My American's feet, I decide, are beautiful. (And his

face? Ah, already I have lost the distance needed to discern that.) But his feet, the toes slender and free of hair, the curve arching just enough, the soles pale ivory but not too soft: I can imagine holding them in my hands, rubbing their hollows with the tip of a finger—

Stop Tilo.

He eats with gusto. Strong white teeth crunch unabashed into fried garbanzos, yellow sticks of *sev*, spicy peanuts in their red skin.

'Mmmm, great.' But he is sucking in air, little cool sips of it to lessen the burn on his tongue.

'It's too hot for a white man's mouth. That's why I told you to try something else. Maybe I should get you a cup of water.'

'And kill the taste,' he says. 'Are you kidding.' And sips some more air, but absently. Something distracts him.

After a moment he says, 'So you think I'm white.'

'You look that way to me, no insult intended.'

He half smiles at that but I can see his mind is puzzling something else. I don't try to read his thoughts. Even if I could. I want instead for him to give them to me.

'If you tell me your name maybe,' I say, 'I'd know what you are.'

'Is it so easy, then, to know what one is?'

'I never claimed it was easy.'

He eats in silence until the *chana* is gone, shakes his head when I offer more. He opens up the cone and smooths out the paper on the counter as though he is planning to use it for something important. There is a sharp crease, displeasure or pain, between his brows. His eyes lidded like a hawk's look past me at what only he can see in the air.

Was my question too intimate, asked too soon?

He stands up, dusts off his pants briskly like he's late for somewhere else.

'Thanks a lot for the snack. I'd better get going. How much do I owe you?'

'It was a gift.' I hope my voice does not give away my hurt.

'I can't keep letting you do that,' he says, the words stiff as a wall between us. He puts a twenty-dollar bill on the counter and walks to the door.

Tilo you should have waited. Now you've lost him.

His hand on the doorknob. I feel it as though it were fisted around my heart.

Peppercorn where are you in my time of need.

He twists the knob. The door glides open, treacherous-smooth, not a sound even.

I think, Don't go please. You don't have to say anything you don't want to. Just stay with me awhile.

But I cannot speak them, the asking words that would lay bare my need-full heart. I who have until now been the giver of gifts, the Mistress of desires.

He stands on the threshold for a moment. What he is deciding I do not know. My held breath scrapes my chest, dry like claws.

In one angry motion he pulls the door shut. The thunderclap sound shakes me.

My American, what is it that angers you so.

'What name shall I tell you? I have had so many.'

His voice is harsh and hurting, like rock on rock. He does not look at me.

Still, relief runs through me like a river. When I breathe in, the air is sweet as honey in my throat. *He did not leave he did not leave.*

'I too have had more than one,' I say. 'But only one of them is my true-name.'

'A true-name.' He chews on his lip for a moment. Flicks back a sheet of black satin hair. 'I'm not sure I can tell

which one it is. Perhaps you'll know.'
And that is how he begins.

'I'm not surprised you thought I was white,' says the American. 'For a long time, growing up, I thought so myself. Rather, I didn't think of it at all, like most kids. Just accepted.

'My father was a quiet man, big and slow moving. The kind that when you're with them you feel yourself slowing down too, calmness covering you like a cool blanket, even your heartbeat. Later I would wonder if that was why my mother married him, hoping.

'Of all things about him I remember his hands best. Large and callused from the work he did up at the refinery in Richmond, the knuckles skinned raw. Half-moons of oily dirt under the nails no matter how often he scrubbed them with the brush Mother had bought for him. He was self-conscious about them, I think. How they looked next to my mother's quick, manicured fingers, the nail polish always gleaming perfect no matter what she'd been doing around house or garden. The rare times when company came around, mostly people Mother had met at church, he'd jam his hands in his pockets, where they sat knotted like roots until the visitors left.

'But around me his hands were easy. He'd lay one on my head when I told him about school or a new game I'd made up, and it was the stillest thing I'd ever known. I could feel the listening in it. When I was hurt or upset or sometimes late at night for no reason at all, he would come sit by my bed and rub my back, his callused thumb making little circles over my shoulder blades until I fell asleep. I loved the smell his hands left, on my body, in my hair. An old, wild, patient smell, like a forest swamp.'

My American's voice is glazed and heavy like medicine honey, the words catching in its bitter sweetness, the memory of things lost. They wrench open in me chambers I thought I'd shut for always.

'I guess I idolized him,' he says, 'the way kids do their parents, you know.'

No, American. I do not know. As you speak a memory rises out of my childhood, my parents scolding me – or trying to – for something I'd done. Perhaps a dish I'd thrown to the ground because I did not like its taste, perhaps a fight I'd had with a sister, scratching her face, tearing her hair. I see my father's finger pointed accusing, my mother shaking her head as though I were beyond remedy. And I – how angry I was that they dared criticize *me*, I who was responsible for all their wealth, for how people looked at them with awe in the marketplace. I had fixed my scornful gaze on them until they lowered their eyes and backed away.

But today as I listen to my American's voice I see them newly. I see bafflement and fear in the slumped lines of their shoulders. In their lowered eyes, the desire to be good parents, the desire, even, to love. But not knowing how. I see now that they are the eyes of lost children, and seeing, I want to weep.

Perhaps one day American I will be able to tell you of it. I Tilo who has until now been the patient listener, the solver of everyone else's problems.

But he is speaking, and I must push back my own sorrows to give my attention over to his words which scour the skin of the evening with their sudden harshness. And that is how I know I have come to a hurting place.

'My mother, she was – different.'

I hold my body still as wood earth stone, even my breathing, until he begins again. Now I find his voice has taken on smoothness, his phrases grown full and formal as though this is a long-ago tale of someone else. Perhaps it is the only way he can bring himself to tell it.

'What I remember most about her was how she was always cleaning, with an angry kind of energy. Dirt on anything – Dad or me included – she took as a personal affront. She spent hours at the washboard battling Dad's stained overalls, and every night when he took a bath she scrubbed his back until it was red. We lived in a small house on the edge of a run-down neighbourhood, mostly factory workers and dockhands, men who sat out on the porch in the evenings in undershirts, staring out at the yellowed lawns, nursing bottles of beer. But inside our home you'd never have known this. Everything had a shine to it, the lemon linoleum kitchen floor, the TV in its fake-walnut console, the curtains clean and sweet-smelling from something Mother put in the wash water. Matching silverware on the table, and her watching to make sure I used it right.

'She didn't like the neighbourhood kids, with their loud laughter and curse words and shirts with too-short sleeves on which they wiped their noses. Still, she was a good mother, she knew a boy needed friends. She let me play with them and on occasion bring them into the house. She served them juice and cookies which they ate uneasily, sitting on the edges of chairs that gleamed with furniture polish. But when they left she would make me wash – face, arms, legs, everything – over and over as though to make sure all traces of *them* were removed. She would sit at the dinner table with me as I did my homework, and when I glanced up there would be a look on her face, an intent, pained love I didn't quite know what to make of.

'She had a ritual every night before bed. When I had changed into my pyjamas she would slick my hair down with water and comb it back neatly. So I could go meet my dreams looking good, she said, planting a kiss in the middle of my forehead when she was done. Other boys might have been impatient with such things, but I wasn't. I loved the strong, supple way she moved the comb through my hair, the way she would hum under her breath. Sometimes as she combed she would say she wished my hair was more like Dad's and not so coarse and coalblack, falling over my forehead no matter how much she worked on it. Secretly, though, I was pleased. I loved Dad, but his hair was a thin, brittle red with bald patches already showing through. I was glad my hair took after Mother's, except that where mine was straight as string hers curled around her face in the prettiest way.'

In the opaque evening air of the store, shapes take form. Old desires. A woman, her whole body tensed to lift herself out of her life, a boy looking at his mother with all the world in his eyes.

Is he still speaking, my American, or am I dreaming his dream inside my heart?

Understand this, says the boy-shape. Don't dismiss it as adolescent fancy. I thought my mother the most beautiful woman in creation. Because she was.

I see for a moment the other women that graze the edges of his life, hanging up clothes in the backyards next to his. Mouths full of pins, swollen bellies, the fallen flesh of their arms and throats, their breasts. The sweat that makes their shifts stick to their backs. Or at school, the teachers with their thin mouths, their tired red-rimmed eyes, their fingers curving hard around pointers, chalk, dusters. Dry dead things.

But her. The lacy wrists of her nightdresses, the way she would do sit-ups in the morning, her spine curving cleanly, the smell of the cologne she splashed extravagantly over her throat. Her clothes were few, but always from good stores. Her shoes, high on pointy heels which made her dresses sway around her legs as she moved around the house as if she were in a movie. Even her name, not Sue or Molly or Edith like the neighbour women but Celestina, which she spoke liltingly and never allowed anyone to shorten.

Her hair was always fresh-washed, a halo of wavy black that gave her a radiance which the boy thought was not unlike that of the saints in the holy pictures the nuns handed him in Sunday school. Sometimes she'd pin the curls back with barrettes. Gold, silver, pearl. She kept them in a small carved wooden box and let him play with them and pick out a pair for her to wear.

'She took such good care of them I didn't know until years later that they were fake,' says the American. The word is a hard, hitting sound in his mouth. 'Or that her hair wasn't naturally curly. The day I found the bottle of perming chemicals in the garage behind a stack of old magazines, I was too mad to even speak to her.' His voice shakes again, remembering, then changes to a harsh laugh. 'Except it didn't matter, because by then we weren't talking much anyway.'

'Wait,' I say, puzzled by his vehemence. 'Why did it upset you so much? In America it is common that women curl their hair. Even I know this.'

'Because by then I knew why she'd done it. Why she did everything I'd admired. The lie of it all.'

'Growing up,' says the American, 'I thought of my father

as a rock. And my mother like a river falling onto it from a great height. Or perhaps it was only later I remembered them as such. The silent power of him, her restless beauty. And I – I was the sound of water on stone, which sounds like nothing else, which needs to be related to nothing else. And so I never thought of who my people were, or where I came from.

'My father had been an orphan, brought up in the hard homes of relatives who didn't want him there. Perhaps that was why he so readily believed my mother, a waitress at the roadside diner where he ate his breakfast, when she told him her folks were dead. Kinlessness seemed to him a natural condition, and a terrible one. Perhaps that was what gave him the courage to propose to this startling young woman with hair like wild horses and a look in her eyes like wild horses also. And after a while of being married to him, she began to believe it too.

'But maybe she'd believed it even before. Maybe when she'd left them, run away, not even a note, *Don't look for me*, when she'd cut and styled her hair, when she'd changed the shape of her eyebrows with tweezers and painted on a new mouth, when she'd given herself a name pretty and proper like she'd always wanted to have, it had been the same as dying.'

The store is dark now. A total dark. It is the night of no-moon, and someone has shattered the streetlamp outside, so no dusty lines of light seep through the closed slats. I listen to my American's words and think how darkness changes the timbre of voices, deepens them, cuts them from the body's confines to float free.

American, into what design shall I weave your floating words, with what colour of spice shall I dye them.

'One day when I was about ten, maybe younger,' he says, 'a man came to our house. It was a weekday, Dad was at work. The man wore an old coat torn under one arm and jeans that smelled of animals. His hair, straight and black, fell to his shoulder, and looked vaguely familiar.

'When Mother opened the door and saw him her face turned grey like old rubber. Then a look came over it, hard as the concrete step on which he stood in boots crusted with mud and manure. She started to close the door but he said, Evvie, Evvie, and when I saw her eyes I realized he was calling her by her real name.'

The American's voice takes on the high, wondering tones of someone dreaming again an old childhood dream.

'She sent me in the other room but I could hear her voice, like fork prongs scraping a tin plate: Why you come here to ruin my life? My mother who always spoke perfect grammar, who washed out my mouth with soap if I ever said *ain't*. His voice rumbling louder and louder. You oughta be shamed, Evvie, turning your back on your own people. Look at you, imitating whitefolks, thinking yourself so fine and grand, and your little boy that don't even know who he is. She hissing furious at him to keep it *down*, you no-good bastard.

'After that I heard snatches only. He's dying. So what he's dying, I don't owe him nothing. Words in a language I didn't understand. And finally, Shit Evvie, I promised him I'd find you and tell you. I done my bit. Now you do what you want. The front door slammed and everything went quiet. A long time later I heard her moving slow and shaky, fixing dinner, stumbling like an old woman in her high shoes. I went in the kitchen and she let me peel potatoes. From time to time I shot her a covert glance, trying to read her expression, wishing she would say something about the man who'd come to our door. But she didn't. And before Dad came home she went and washed her face and put on lipstick and a fresh smile.

'That was the first time I realized that there was a place inside of my mother that she kept away from us all, even me, whom she loved more than anyone.

'Early next morning after Dad left she went into the bedroom, and when she came out I saw she was wearing her best dress, navy blue with a matching jacket and little pearl buttons all the way down the front, and her pearl necklace, which she kept in a little velvet case and didn't like me to touch. Come on, she said, we're going somewhere. What about school, I asked, and my mother, who had never let me skip classes before, said, It's OK, let's go. All the way in the car she was silent, not scolding me for fiddling with the radio or having the music on too loud. Once or twice I started to ask her where we were going, but she had on a small, absorbed frown, like she was listening to something inside her head, so I didn't. We drove for a couple of hours this way. And when we turned onto a narrow street with paint-peeled houses and junk cars in the yards and clumps of dandelion grass and garbage spilled from Dumpsters, she made a small sound like something was stuck in her chest, maybe the hook that had pulled her back all the way to that place.

'She jerked the car to a stop and got out very straight and tall, holding my hand so tight it would hurt for days. She walked into a small clapboard house that smelled musty, like wet clothes left too long in a washer, all the way through to the kitchen, like she knew where to go. The kitchen was full of men and women, some of them drinking out of brown bottles, and when I saw their heavy, flat faces, the hair that hung limp and black over their foreheads, it was like looking into a warped mirror. My mother moved past them as though they weren't there. The click of her heels on the scarred linoleum was a precise, confident sound. But her fingers were damp with sweat as they gripped mine, and I knew she felt the eyes on the gleaming pearl buttons of her dress, heard the whisper that went around the room like the frost-wind that kills early fruit.'

The American stops as though he's come up against a wall and doesn't know which way to turn.

I look at him newly, hair and skin colour and shape of bone, trying to see in him the people he is describing. But he is still my American, himself only, not like anyone else.

'At last we were in a narrow room with too many people in it and not enough light. On the bed in the corner was a thin stick-shape covered with a blanket. When my eyes got used to the dimness I saw it was a man. In my eyes he seemed enormously, completely old. Someone was shaking a rattle and singing. I didn't understand the words, but I could feel them weaving thin and snakelike around us, binding us all together.

'When they saw my mother everything stopped. The silence was like a sudden fist slammed against your ear. They propped the old man up in bed, held him so he wouldn't slump over.

'The old man raised his head with such effort that I could feel the slow muscles of his neck creak and pull. He opened his eyes, and in that dark room they glinted like flecks of mica in a cave wall. Evvie, he said. The word came out sharp and clear, like an arrow, not the way I expected an old man to sound. Then he said, Evvie's son. The calling in his voice was like arms around me. Right away I wanted to go to him, though I had always been bashful with strangers. But my mother's hands were on my shoulders, her fingers tight and helpless as the grip of a small, scared bird.'

The American takes a deep, shuddering breath as though he's pushed his way up out of a long, airless tunnel. Then he shakes his head. 'I can't believe I told you all this crap,' he says, shielding himself in the way of men behind that small hard word. 'Whew. This pepper stuff is pretty potent.'

My American, say what you will. It is not the spice only but also you wanting me to hear. This is my belief and my hope.

Aloud I say, 'It isn't – what is that word – *crap*. You know that.'

But I see I will have to wait a long while, perhaps forever, to hear what happened in that dying room.

I am only half sorry that he has stopped. His words have filled the store already, wild water burst from its boundary. It pushes at me with all its opaque weight. It will take me time to swim through, to find out what edges this flooding has erased between us.

Meanwhile I want to tell him, I will carry this moment from your life like a spark in my heart. But I am suddenly shy, I Tilo, once so brash and bold. How the Old One would have laughed at it.

All I can say is, 'Anytime you want to talk, my door is open for you.'

He laughs his old laugh, easy again and mocking. His arm sweeps the shelves. 'All this and free counselling too. What a deal.' But his eyes are holding mine and a deep light in them saying *I'm glad*.

One day you will have to tell me what you see when you look at this shape wrapped in its folds of oldwoman skin. Is it some truth about me that I myself do not know, or merely your own fantasy.

At the door he says, 'You still want to know my name?'

I am almost laughing at his question. Lonely American,

can't you hear my heart singing its red rhythm of *yesyesyes*.

But I make myself say what the Old One told me when I left the island, in warning.

'Only if *you* wish it. Because a true-name has power, and when you tell it you give that power into your listener's hands.'

Why am I telling you this when you will not understand.

'My true-name, that's what you want? Well. Maybe I *can* figure out which one it is.'

'How,' I ask. And inside me: Surely he will not know.

'All the others were given to me, but this one *I* chose.'

American, once again you have amazed me. I who thought that you, being of the West and used always to choosing your own way, would take such a choice for granted.

He hesitates, then says, 'My name is Raven.' And traces a pattern on the floor with his toe. He will not look at me. In tender amusement I see that my American is embarrassed, a little, by his unAmerican name.

'But it is beautiful,' I say, tasting the long wingbeat sound of it in my mouth, smell of hot sky rising and falling, dark wood in evening, bright eye, tailfeather formed of charcoal and smoke. 'And right for you.'

'You think so?' Quick flash of pleasure, as quickly hidden, in his eye, Raven who feels he has made himself vulnerable enough for one day.

'How I got to it,' he says. 'Ah. Another day I'll tell you that story. Maybe.'

I nod assent, I Tilo this once not impatient for knowing. I trust them, the untold stories that stretch between us like filaments of beaten gold. His stories and mine. That will not be lost even if not spoken.

'Raven, now I must tell you my name. Will you believe if I say you are the only man in America, in the entire world, to know it?'

Somewhere ground bucks underfoot, shudders apart. Somewhere a volcano startles awake and coughs fire. Wind turns to ash.

Yes say his eyes, my American letting fall the cloak of his loneliness. He holds out his gleaming goldbrown hand (somewhere a woman is weeping) and into it I place my name.

Kalo Jire

Raven has left, and the store feels too large. Its silence makes a distant ringing in my ears. Like old fluorescent tubes, I think, and am surprised by the thought. For some time now I have been seeing this, my mind invoking impressions of which I have no experience. Are they left behind by those who pass through this space? Are they *his* memories becoming mine?

I wander the aisles, cleaning up though all is tidy already, giving my hands something to do. What I really want is to touch all he has touched. I am hungry for what little I can get. The faint soap-smell of his skin. The last lingering heat from his fingertips.

And thus I come to the newspaper which he left smoothed out on the counter. I lay my hands on it and close my eyes, wait for an image to tell me where he is now, driving down the freeway night perhaps with the windows open, drums on the radio and the sharp clean scent of an unseen ocean, the spices in his hair. What he is thinking. But nothing comes. So after a while what else is there to do but open my eyes and gather up the sheet to store carefully at the bottom of the bin where I keep old papers.

That's when I see the headline. DOTBUSTERS GO FREE. And under it the picture of the two white teenagers, teeth bared in triumphant smiles. Even the blurred photo cannot hide the cocky tilt of their heads.

For a moment I am pulled by an urgent need, an instinct heavy in the pit of myself where the fears lie. *Tilo find out what has pleased them so. Tilo you must.* Instead I fold up the paper with fingers that tremble a little.

I have never read a newspaper, not even the Indian ones that are delivered to the store each week.

Don't you want to, you ask.

Of course I do. I Tilo whose curiosity has pulled me so

often past the limits set by wisdom. Sometimes I put my face to the newsprint. A smell like burning metal rises from the tiny black letters.

Then I move back. Haven't I broken enough rules already.

This is what the Old One told us: 'Events in the outer world are nothing to Mistresses. When you fill your head with inessentials, the true knowledge is lost, like grains of gold in sand. Set your mind only on what is brought to you, search only its remedy.'

'But First Mother, will it not help if I know what is happening elsewhere, to see how this one life given to my care fits the tapestry?'

Her sigh, impatient but not unkind. 'Child, the tapestry is far larger than your seeing, or mine. Turn inward for what you need to know. Listen for the right spice to say its name.'

'Yes, Mother.'

But today I want to ask, Did you First Mother ever feel your thoughts awash around you like the wave-salt ocean, and one voice, *his*, calling like a gull so that all else grows dim and distant, like submarine sounds.

Mother what shall I do. All the certainties of my life are crumbling like cliffs in a sea gale, gritty dust stinging the eye.

My head so heavy I must rest it on the counter where the paper still—

The vision lashes at me, a whip against my eyelids. A young man in a bed with tubes trailing from his nose, from the insides of his elbows. The white of his bandages blends with the white of the hospital pillow. Only his skin stands out in patches, brown like mine. Like mine, Indian skin. Radium blips jerk across a screen. In all the room there is no other movement.

Except inside his head.

Tilo what—

Then I am sucked in. As I go under in a thunderclap of pain I know I am at the start of the story whose end I read in the headlines.

Inside his head evening is falling, the pale sun swallowed up by trees, the downtown park darkened, almost deserted, only a few last office workers clustered tight around the bus stop thinking *home* and *dinner*. He takes down the red awning, the bright yellow letters that say MOHAN INDIAN FOODS crumpling in on themselves. He's a little late but it's been a good day, almost everything Veena cooked got sold, and so many people telling him, 'Tastes good,' bringing back friends. Maybe it's time to hire a helper, put another cart on the other side of town, near the new office complexes. He's sure Veena could find a friend to help her with the cooking . . .

Then he hears the steps, fall leaves breaking under boots, a sound like crushed glass. Why does it seem so loud.

When he turns the two young men are very close. He can smell their unbathed odour like stale garlic. He thinks how Americans always smell different from Indians, even the office *babus* under their cologne and deodorant. And then he realizes it is his own sweat, his sudden prickly fear he is smelling.

The young men's hair is cut severely short. Their bristled scalps gleam white as bone, white as the glitter in their eyes. He guesses them to be in their late teens, not much more than boys. Their tight-fitting camouflage jackets make him uncomfortable.

'Sorry, closed already,' he says, wiping the top of the cart emphatically with a paper towel, kicking out the stones he'd wedged under the wheels. Would it be rude to start walking while they are still standing there? He gives the cart a tentative push.

The young men move deftly, block his way.

'What makes you think we want any of this shitty stuff,' one says. The other leans forward. Casually, elegantly even, he tips over a neat stack of paper plates. The Indian reaches automatically to grab them, and thinks two thoughts at once.

How flat their eyes are, like mud puddles. And *I should have started running already.*

The blunt boot tip catches him in the armpit under his outstretched arm, a hot jolt of pain spurts down his side like molten iron, and through it he hears one of them spit, 'Sonofabitch Indian, shoulda stayed in your own god-damn country.' But the pain's not as bad as he feared, not so bad that he can't pick up the stone and pitch it at the young man who's kicking at the cart until it comes crash-ing down and the kababs and *samosas* that Veena so care-fully rolled and stuffed scatter everywhere in the dirt. He hears the satisfying *thwack* of contact, sees the young man knocked backward with the force of it, his face almost comical in its surprise. The Indian feels good even though it hurts to breathe and a small jagged thought – *ribs?* – spins up for a moment into the lighted part of his mind. (He doesn't know that later a lawyer will show the young man's stone-bruise to the judge and say the Indian had started it all, his clients were only protecting themselves.) He believes for a moment that he can get away, can maybe run to the bus stop, the small safe halo of the streetlight, the handful of commuters (*can't they see what's going on can't they hear?*) waiting. And then the second young man is on him.

Even now that the Indian cannot remember much else

(head yanked up, knuckles cased in metal smashing down), the memory of pain is clear. Pain like a constant throughout whatever happened next. (Kick to the groin, face dragged through gravel.) So many kinds of pain – like fire, like stinging needles, like hammers breaking. But not really. Pain, which is ultimately only like itself. ('Fucking turd, bastard, piece of shit, this'll teach you.') He thinks he shouted for help, only it came out in the old language, *bachao, bachao*. He thinks he saw a red tattoo on a fore-arm, the same *swastic* sign that they used to paint on the walls of village homes for good luck. But surely it couldn't be (a blow to the head so hard that his thoughts splinter into yellow stars), surely it was only the blood in his eyes, the torn nerves playing tricks on him.

In the hospital room it is so peaceful, the pain comes and goes orderly as waves. By now he is almost used to it. Only wish Veena could be here, it would be nice to have someone's hand to hold on to when outside the sky turns inky purple like *that* night, but they took her home to get some rest. 'Don't worry,' they told me. 'Worry will keep you from getting better. We'll take care of things. Try to rest.' But what am I to do with the questions rattling in my skull-box, *will I walk again, how to make a living now, the right eye, is it totally gone, Veena so young and pretty left with a crippled scarred husband.* And over and over, *Those two* haramis, *did the police get them, may they rot in jail.*

Months later in his apartment when he hears of the acquittal he will scream, a high, moaning, on and-on animal sound, will bring down the crutches, hard and shattering, on whatever he can reach. Dishes, furniture, the framed wedding photos on the wall. Down and down and down, not hearing Veena begging him to stop, shak-ing her off. Sweet crash of window glass, the stereo he had saved for so many months to buy caving in easy as a skull under his blows. Until Veena, sobbing, runs to the next apartment to call Ramcharan and his brother. *Calm down bhaiya, calm down.* But he throws himself at the two men, clawing and screaming in that not-human voice that seems to come from a place up behind his eyes, the left one red-veined and bulging, the right one now a dark, shrunken pit. Until finally they grab him from behind and force him onto the bed and tie him down with a couple of Veena's saris. He stops shouting then. Doesn't speak another word. Not then, not in the coming weeks, not in the Air India plane when neighbours finally pool together ticket money to send him and Veena back home, for what else is left for them in this country.

O Mohan broken in body broken in mind by America, I come back from your story in pieces, find myself assembled at last on the chill floor of the shop. My limbs ache as after long illness, my sari is damp with shiver-sweat, and in my heart I cannot tell where your pain ends and mine begins. For your story is the story of all those I have learned to love in this country, and to fear for.

When I can stand again I make my unsteady way to the newspaper bin.

I must know.

Yes, the stories are there. Peeling page off page, going back into the months and years, I discover them slowly. The man who finds his grocery windows smashed by rocks, picks up one to read the hate-note tied around it. Children sobbing outside their safe suburban home over their poisoned dog. Woman with her *dupatta* torn from her shoulders as she walks a city pavement, the teenagers speeding away in their car hooting laughter. The man who watches his charred motel, life's earnings gone, the smoke curling in a hieroglyph that reads *arson*.

I know there are other stories, numerous beyond counting, unreported unwritten, hanging bitter and brown as smog in America's air.

I will split once again tonight *kalo jire* seeds for all who have suffered from America. For all of them and especially Haroun, who is a hurting inside me, whose name each time I say it pulls my chest in two. I will lock the door and stay up all night to do it, through dimness the knife rising and falling steady and silver as holy breath. So that when he comes tomorrow evening (for tomorrow is Tuesday) I can hand him the packet and say, 'Allah ho Akbar, may you be safe, in this life and always.' As penance while I work I will not think once of Raven, I Tilo who have been so self-indulgent already. All night instead I will whisper into air purifying prayers for the maimed, for each lost limb, each crushed tongue. Each silenced heart.

The day passes so slowly it is like being underwater, every movement a huge effort. The light seems dim and green, filtered. Through it the few customers swim lazily to the shelves, then back to lean languid elbows on the counter. Their questions are tiny bubbles breaking against my ears. My limbs too give in, grow seaweed-slippery, swaying to some submarine adagio only they can hear.

Only my mind beats, more furious more helpless than ever.

So much of a Mistress's life is waiting, is inaction. Who would have thought it. Not I, who wanted all the answers at once, who wanted domination immediate as a drug shooting up my veins.

Once upon a time the Old One said, 'Power is weakness. Think on this, Mistresses.'

She said such things often. 'Greatest happiness brings greatest loss.' 'Stare at the sun, bring darkness upon your eyes.' Others which I have forgotten. She would give us the morning to ponder them.

My sister Mistresses would climb the granite cliffs to find a quiet place. Some would sit under the banyans or find a cave mouth. Silent, they would turn their attention inward, try to see.

But I uninterested in riddles spent the time playing in the sea, chasing rainbow fish. If for a moment I grew quiet, if I stopped to stare at the shimmery horizon, it was only to look for my serpents, hoping.

In the afternoon the Old One would ask, 'Mistresses, have you understood?'

I was always the first to shake my head no.

'Tilo, you did not even try.'

'But Mother,' I would say unabashed, 'the others did, and look, they too do not understand.'

'Ah child.'

But too eager to learn the next spice spell, I paid small attention to the disappointment in her voice.

Today, Mother, I am at last beginning to see. Hazily through this air that smells of tar and soot. Power is weakness.

Then Kwesi comes in and I am saved from thought.

It is a pleasure to watch Kwesi shop, I decide.

His movements are precise, not one unneeded gesture. The angle of his arm as it reaches for a packet, a box. The muscles of his back spreading then tightening as he bends to lift a sack. His fingers sifting through lentil grains, knowing what they look for, the bones broken and mended, fused hard and clean.

Not hurrying not wasting time, his body comfortable in its own space.

I can see how he would make a good teacher, having known what it is to be hurt.

Inside me an idea uncurls like a leaf.

Kwesi lays his purchases on the counter. Today he is buying whole mung beans green as moss. A slab of dried tamarind. A coconut which I imagine him breaking in two with the edge of his palm, his hand arcing a brown blur through the air of his kitchen.

'Making coconut-mung *dal*,' I say. 'Getting ambitious, hunh?'

He nods. His smile comes slow, this man who doesn't smile unless he means it, and then he holds nothing back.

It makes me think of Raven, as every beautiful thing does now. Under the happiness that flashes up in me is a fear, when and whether I will see him again. I am never sure. Anchored to this store, I can only wait and hope.

'For my lady,' says Kwesi. 'I like to make something new and uncertain for her once in a while. Do you think it'll be too difficult?'

'No no,' I say. 'Just make sure you soak the mung long enough, and don't add the tamarind paste till the end.' What a fine idea this is, *new and uncertain*. I wish to take it for my own life.

As I ring them up I whisper a success word over the beans, tell him not to forget to sprinkle on a little sugar. 'So it'll be sweet and salt, sour and hot, all the tastes of loving in it, no?' His eyes crinkle in laughing agreement.

If only I could make all who come to me so easily happy.

Tilo be honest. He was happy already when he came.
The ones who are in true need of happiness, you are not
doing too well with them, are you.

I say, 'Remember how you wanted to put a poster
about your karate school in the store? I've been thinking
about it.'

'Yes?'

'It's not a bad idea. You never know who might come
in and see, who might want to learn. Do you have one
maybe in your car?'

I help him tape it up right by the door, that poster spare
and elegant in black and gold so no one coming in can
miss it.

There's a little grey in his hair, like wound-up silver
springs.

'Tell them I'm good but tough. No fooling around in
Kwesi's One World Dojo.'

'Tough is what they need,' I say. And here is what I
don't say: But you're kind also. You've known the hard
streets, their pull. You too have heard death's siren song,
the one she sings especially for the young. Maybe you
will have the power to pull them back from her, to
make them see how beautiful is sunshine, the curve of
a wing in flight, sprinkle of rain on the hair of the one
you love.

As I wave him good-bye I send a calling thought to
search the scarred pitted alleys, the abandoned warehouses, the waterfront disco joints already beginning to
throb in the flame-coloured evening. To search and
bring.

But instead it is Geeta's grandfather who pushes open
the door, who sets down on the counter with defeated
hands the pewter-framed photo I had given him.

'*Didi.*'

'Yes?' Already by his voice I am afraid to ask more.

'I am having no luck with what you said to do. As you said, I am laying the ground carefully, during dinner mentioning how quiet the house is with only us older folks, but Ramu says nothing. Then I tell him maybe we were too hasty, after all she is our only flesh and blood. Still he is silent. Why not you call her just once, I say, or maybe even Sheela can do it. See her number here, I got it from friends. No, he says, his voice like a stone is sitting on his chest. And when I say, Why not, listen, it's the elder people's job to forgive the younger, he just pushes back his plate and gets up from the table.'

'Did you tell him she's staying with her girlfriend and not Juan?'

'I did. Next evening I put the phone number in his hand and said, For my sake Ramu, patch up the fight. The girl has been careful to not do anything immoral, to not hurt you. Why not you tell her to come back home. He gives me a look cold like ice chips. He says, We gave her everything she wanted. This was the one thing we asked her not to do, and still she did it.

'I say, I have been thinking, what if she *does* marry this Mexican boy, it is not so bad, times are changing, other people's children have done similar. Look at Jayanta, married that white nurse, look at Mitra's daughter, what pretty fair-skinned babies she has.

'He says, Baba, what's this new tune you are singing now when all this time it was sighing and slapping your

forehead and *Hai she is putting kali on the ancestors'
faces*. Who has been giving you bad advice? I tell him,
What, you think I cannot reason for myself? The mark of
a wise man is that he changes his mind when he sees mistake. But his face is hard like a brick wall. He says, I
listened to you enough already. When she walked out of
this house slamming the door so proudly behind her, she
slammed herself out of my life.

'All night after this talk I cannot sleep. I am seeing it is
easy to plant a thorn in the heart, not so easy to pluck it
out. I am wishing I never opened my mouth in the business between father and daughter.

'In the midnight I get up and go downstairs. I leave the
photo on the side table where every morning time he sits
to drink his *cha* and read the paper. I think maybe if he
looks at it when he is sitting all by himself he will remember the time when she was small, maybe he will
remember what-all things he did for her. Maybe it will be
a little easier to take off his proud man-face and be a father.

'But when I come in later after he has left for work I see
the photo frame lying facedown on the tiles. And look.'

He points a shaky finger.

Shivering I see a crack, silver-sharp as a launched spear,
cutting the picture in two, separating Geeta from her
Juan.

I pace the inner room, running my hand along the shelves
that hold the spices of power, wanting guidance. But the
spices are silent and I have only the turmoil of my woman
mind to fall back on.

Tilo, what to do?

The moments pool around my feet, spent and chill. No
answers come. Through the walls I can hear Geeta's

grandfather, whom I have left in charge, advising customers. His voice has gathered back a little lost confidence. 'I tell you, *chana dal* will give you gas, better be buying *tur* instead. What you mean your husband refuses to eat it? Boil it soft and mix in lot of fried onion and *dhania* leaf, and he is not knowing any better.'

Disguise, I think. Prevarication. Perhaps he is right. Desperate trickery for a desperate situation.

I search the shelves till I find the package tight-wrapped in tree bark, and next to it the silver-tipped pincers. Gingerly I unroll it, taking care not to touch. And watch it bristling to life, *kantak* the thorn herb with its hair-thin black needles whose sting can be poison.

With the pincers I break off three hairs and drop them on the grinding stone. I measure out ghee and honey to cut the sting, pound them all together, fill a small bottle with it.

Geeta's grandfather is standing military-straight at the counter, drumming his fingers on the glass, when I reenter.

'Ah, *didi*, you are taking a long time. No, no, I am not minding, not impatient slightest even, actually quite the opposite. I am thinking it is a good sign, you are finding something just-right to help us.'

'You said you would do anything for Geeta, to bring her back into the family. Are you sure?'

He nods.

'Here then, mix this into your rice at dinnertime, eat it slowly. It will burn your throat going down, and later it will give you the cramps, maybe for days. But for one hour you will have the golden tongue.'

'What this means?' says Geeta's grandfather, but already in his eyes, hope and fear mixed, I see he has heard the old stories.

'Whatever you say this hour, people must believe.

Whatever you ask, they must obey. Listen now.'

And I tell him what he is to do.

At the door I say, 'Use the gift with care. It is yours once only. And remember, the cramps will be bad.'

He squares his shoulders, lifts his head, Geeta's grandfather, and I see that he is a small man, has always been so behind his bluster-words. But today there is a bigness in his eye.

'The worst cramp I am happy to suffer,' he says very simply and closes the door behind him with gentleness.

I wait until all the customers have left, until moths float around the doorlight and I hear the soft thump of their bodies against the hot domed glass. Until the puppet moon dangles in the centre of my window from its invisible string, and rush-hour sounds are swallowed by a terrible night stillness, and it is long past closing time. And then I can no longer hide from it, the fear that has been lying cold and coiled all this time in the centre of my chest: Haroun will not come. Not now. Not perhaps ever.

How then to make amends. How help him past the dark which is reaching for him with its hungry hand.

The answer comes so quickly and with such sureness it surprises me, shows me I am no longer the Tilo who left the island.

You must go to him. Yes, out one more time into America.

But the Old One?

The voice knows my weak places. *Will you sit here, your hands folded in your lap, and let him be destroyed,* it says. *Is that what the Old One in your place would have done, would have wanted.*

I see her face, deep lines creasing the forehead, corner of the mouth, laughter and frowning both. The eyes sometimes dark and still, sometimes sparking irony. At once kind and stern. 'Eyes that could in anger scald your skin,' said the older Mistresses when they were story-talking to us.

I cannot tell what she would have wanted, but I know what she would have done. What I too should.

I think for a long moment before I choose the other path, which hurts through my whole body like bones wrenched from sockets.

If you were to ask me why I am doing so, I couldn't answer. Only this: I who have held Haroun's hands in mine and felt the hope pulsing wild through them, cannot let night cast her ink-net over him without a fight. Is it rebellion, is it compassion? Perhaps you know better than me, for to me they sit side by side, their edges bleeding into each other till all becomes one colour.

But now I am faced with a more immediate problem: I must find Haroun. I have no address, and when I send out a calling thought, it is slammed back into my skull as though I were ringed with a well of impassable stone. My head throbs with the impact of it, with the question that I cannot push away.

Tilo are your powers leaving you.

But slowly out of the throbbing comes a word: *telephone.* An image forms behind my eyelids, and though I have never seen one in real life, I know what it is: a pay phone enclosed in its tiny crystal cubicle, the rectangular box glowing faintly in the fitful streetlight, the steel cord looped and glinting like the thin ridged body of some pre-historic reptile, the hard black bulbous head. Whose memory is this? I have no idea. But I know to pick the correct coins to feed the machine's slit mouth.

I search out my Sears plastic bag and lift from it a sheet with a number (for I must call Geeta also). I steel myself for the spices' stare and lock the door behind me. (But why are there no reproving glances, why does the door not hold itself back stubbornly from my hands?) I am not surprised to find my feet following without falter all the twists and turns of alleyways that will lead me to the phone call.

I make the easy call first. To Geeta, the number she had given me that day hoping, high in her glitter-black tower. And when I get the replica of her voice spooling thin and metallic from the machine, I know what it is. I know to wait for the beep and then to tell her clearly, slowly, to come to the store, alone, day after tomorrow at seven, evening hour when the light of sun and moon fall mixed upon our longings, and all is perhaps possible.

Now it is Haroun's turn. But I have no number for him, no inkling of where he lives. Once I could have divined it with ease. But today when I start to chant the song of find-ing I stutter, come to a halt. I Tilo of whom the Old One once said that the parrot, bird of memory, must live in my throat. Too late I begin to see the price I have unknow-ingly paid for each step I took into America. Inside me a voice cries *What else is lost.*

No time now to worry this thought, no time now to mourn. I must grope for the fat metal-bound book that hangs from the booth wall and sift its pages, praying.

He is not there.

The booth is full of crumbling desires, the countless desperations of all those who lifted this receiver trying to connect across miles of humming wires. I lean my head into its wall. I would weep if I believed weeping could help.

Tilo weakened in magic through your wilfulness, who can you blame but yourself.

No time for blame either. Inside me the minutes are swooping wild, colliding against the walls of my chest, falling back stunned.

You must use what you have, your own frail mortal wits, your imperfect remembering. Your heart's pain.

I focus back to that first night at the store, Haroun reciting the tales of friends I had helped. I squeeze shut my eyes till I smell it plain, the sandalwood dust in his palm. Feel the press of his just-ripe lips in my hand's hollow. Ah it hurts to look in his face, to see it blazing with trust, Haroun who stands on a stage built of dreams, under a spotlight about to be extinguished.

Out of the pain a name comes finally: *Najib Mokhtar.* I hold on to it as though it is a raft in drowning water, or perhaps it is a blade of grass only. I hope I have not conjured it out of my desperate wanting.

But see, here it is in the phone book, the letters small and black as the skeletons of ants pressed into the page, but plain enough. I swallow down the questions crowding my mouth, What if it's the wrong Najib what if he doesn't know where Haroun lives what if he won't tell, what if what if what if, and punch in the numbers.

Ringing, ringing, ripples of rings echoing out with me at the centre, and when I've almost given up hope, a woman's voice.

'Hello.' Pronounced the Indian way, the word hangs in the air, hesitant, questioning.

'I'm looking for Haroun. Do you know where I can find him.'

As soon as I say the sentences I know their wrongness. I feel her suspicion course like electricity through the wires. Her fear. *Immigration? Creditors? Old-country enemies following his ocean trail?* Her fingers tighten around the receiver, ready to slam it down.

'I'm a friend,' I say quickly.

She is unconvinced, I hear it in her cut-short sentences. 'I am not knowing any Haroun-maroun. No one of that name living here.'

'Wait, don't hang up. I'm from the Indian grocery, you know, the Spice Bazaar, next to the burned-down hotel on Esperanza Street. I helped your husband one time long ago.'

Only the sound of her listening, her held-in, half-believing breath.

'Now you must help me. I have something I must give Haroun, something to protect him from—' I search for a phrase out of her understanding, a story she would have been told as a girl '— the jinn's breath.'

'The jinn's breath,' she whispers. She knows it, black ice which can suck away your name your life.

'Yes. That's why you must tell me where he is.'

She considers. In her head I hear her husband warn, 'Woman, open your mouth and let out one word of this even, and I'll make you sorry you were born.'

'Please. No harm will ever come to him from me.'

We both wait. Between us the moment stretches taut as steel.

Then she says, 'I will tell you. He has no phone, but I will tell you how to get to his house and when to find him there.'

She gives me names of streets and parks which I jot

down on the back of the small square sheet stamped with Geeta's employer's name. Neighbourhood schools, gas stations, Quik-Stops, police headquarters. Take this bus and then this one, turn right here, then left twice, pass the massage parlour and the lot full of junk cars, climb up the rickety steps to the topmost apartment. Go early, eight a.m. latest. He leaves home right after morning *namaaz* and comes home only ten minutes at sundown for it again. Then back to his taxi, sometimes all night because that's when the best tips are.

'*Shukriyah*,' I say, 'heartfelt gratitude. I will go tomorrow morning itself early-early before the store opens.'

Walking home through the smoky air I dodge shadows and worse than shadows and keep my eyes on the moon, white as a polished jawbone. I rehearse all I will say to Haroun, apology and affection and warning of the nightmare which is the back-side of his immigrant dream. Ah, we will argue, I know it. He will stomp up and down and wave his hands in angry spirals, but at the end he will say, 'OK Ladyjaan, just to make you happy I am doing as you say.'

I am smiling with the thought of it already as I lean to unlock the shop door.

Then I see it, a small rectangle white as the sari of a widow or an ascetic, caught in the crack as though someone closed the door too quickly.

My throat so tight I cannot breathe. *First Mother?* I start to cry out.

Then I see it is a note only.

I open it and when my hands have stopped shaking I read the large, looping letters.

I came hoping to see you, but you were gone. I

didn't know you ever left the store, but knowing it I feel better asking this. Will you come with me tomorrow to the City, to share with me the places I love? I'll come by early to take you, and bring you back by night.

Please say yes.

My Raven, I think, and like any woman in love I lay my cheek where his hand rested on the paper. 'Yes,' I whisper, 'yes. Tomorrow will be our pleasure day.' Already I can smell the bracing salt air of the City, long-imagined, feel under my feet the roll of its hills.

But then the thoughts come. What of the censuring curious eyes, when they see my handsome American with this sag-skinned brown woman?

And (O foolish woman-thought) I have nothing to wear.

What of Haroun says the thorn-voice.

I put the directions for safekeeping into a small leather bag which I borrow from the gift cabinet. 'I will not neglect him,' I reply. If doubts lurk somewhere within, I choose not to pamper them with attention. 'Do I not know my duty as well as I do my pleasure? First thing tomorrow I will ask Raven to take me to him.'

Neem

All evening I cannot sit still. I must pace the shop, front and back, front and back, thinking What can make me look better. Not beautiful, I do not expect that, but perhaps younger just a little, so the stares will not be so bad.

Tilo since when do you care what people whisper.

Not for me. But him I would protect from the world's ridicule.

In a bowl I mix boiled milk and powder made of the neem leaf which kills disease. Smooth the paste over neck and cheekbone, the hollow under the eye. Into my hair I rub soaked *ritha* pulp, pile the grey into a mass on my head. I scrub my one American outfit in the sink with a bar of chemical-smelling Sunlight soap. Night passes, each minute dripping like washwater from the hung-up clothes. Neem dust dries and pulls at my skin. My scalp itches. Spikes of *ritha* hair poke at my face.

Yet when I have bathed and dried myself, I feel on my face the same crumpled skin, around my shoulders the same locks, coarse and grey as the *shon* jute women weave into sacking.

O Mistress what did you think. The voice of the spices is like skipping water, cool laughter that dances over my chagrin. *If you want true change you must use us differently, must call on our powers. You know the words.*

Spices, what are you saying. My spells were not given for myself to use.

For you, for him, where do you separate the desires. Their voice is a shrug as though this were a little thing.

I who know it is not, think in startlement, Why do they say this, they who know right and wrong better far than I.

The singing rises now from the inner room. *Come Tilo use us, we give ourselves gladly to you who have tended us so faithfully. Lotus root and* abhrak, amlaki *and most of all* makaradwaj *kingspice, we are yours to command. Use us for love for beauty for your joy, because that is why we were made.*

The song is like little hooks in my flesh, pulling. *Come Tilo come.* My head fills with pictures, the Tilo I could be, Raven's face when he sees. Our bodies together, supple and twined in ecstasy.

I begin the walk to the inner room. The song is husky, syllables that enter my body itching.

My hand on the door now, throb of my palm on wood that feels soft as water. All the molecules of the universe dissolving and gathering into new shapes.

Then sudden as lightning I see it, how they are luring me. To break the most sacred promise, to doom myself beyond recall.

O spices who have these many years been my one reason to live, do not punish me with temptation. I Tilo who still hold you high in my heart. Do not battle me, push me down where later I will hate us both.

Silence.

Then: *So be it for now. We are patient. We know you will come to us soon. Once you have heard our song, have paced the rhythms of desire whose seat is deep in the body's core, you cannot resist.*

O spices, I say as I lower my stiff body onto the hard floor where I will toss unsleeping all this night. My voice is tired with persuading, tinged with doubt. Can I not love you and him both. Why must I choose.

The spices do not answer.

At the window the morning is like an orange split open, soft and juice-sweet. But on my skin it etches the lines deeper, highlights the cording veins. I stand in my brown outfit, sad as old leaves, and almost wish for Raven not to come.

But then he is here, and again that pleased glance in his eyes as if he has lifted off the coat of my skin and is seeing beneath. He takes my hand in his, and against my surprised cheek his lips are at once hard and soft.

'You'll come? I wasn't sure. I stayed awake most of the night wondering.'

'I too,' I smile. My heart has taken over my body till it is one beat of joy. Raven who does not know, who I want never to know, how much I will have to pay for this excursion, how gladly I will count the cost.

Is this what love is.

'Look.' He is opening a package. 'I brought you something.'

It spills across the counter, gossamer and spiderweb, spangled like dew. When I lift it up it is long and loose to my feet and white as the first dawn. The loveliest dress I have seen.

I lay it down.

First Mother who warned us, who watched sorrow-eyed as our bodies twisted into age in Shampati's flames, did you foresee this moment. This regret raking me inside and out.

'I can't wear it,' I say.

'Why not?'

'It's too fancy. A young-woman dress.'

'No,' he says. 'A beautiful-woman dress. And you are that woman.' He runs a wingtip finger over my cheekbone.

The spices are watching intently, their thoughts veiled.

Tuned to my every trembling breath.

'How can you say that, Raven.' My voice comes out tears. I brush the anger from my eyes, pull him to the window to the cruel light.

Inside me a voice implores *Let it be*.

No. If I am to lose him, make it now. Before the insidious splinter of love has worked a deeper way into my heart.

'Can't you see,' I cry. 'I'm ugly. Ugly and old. That dress on me would be mockery. And you and I together, that too is mockery.'

'Hush,' he says. 'Hush.' Then his arms are around me, his lips like reassurance in my hair. My face presses into his chest, into the softness of a white shirt that smells clean as wind. Through it his skin is warm like polished silkwood.

How can I tell you how it feels, you around whom so many men have set their casual arms that you cannot even remember where it began.

But I who have never been held. Not by father or mother. Not by my sister Mistresses. Not even by the Old One, not like this, heart to thudding heart. I Tilo, the child who could never cry, the woman who never would. I smile through wet lashes as the smell of his skin fills me, the warm riffle of his breath on my lashes. My bones are melting in this desire to be always so held, I who never thought I would want a man's arms to protect me.

His thumbs rub gently at the ridges of my shoulderbones. 'Tilo. Dear Tilo.'

Even my name takes on new texture in his mouth, the vowels shorter and sharper, the consonants more defined. My American, in all ways you are reshaping me.

'Put on the dress,' he says. Puts a gentle hand over my mouth to stop my protesting. 'This body, I know it's not the real you.'

My lips want to rest quiet against the firm curves of his fingers, the cool platinum band of a ring, the palm lines which tell his future and mine, if only I could read them.

But I pull back. I must ask.

'How do you know? You, the one who earlier said it's not easy to know the real self one is.'

He smiles. 'Perhaps we can see each other better than we can ourselves.' He lays the dress in my arms, nudges me toward the inner room.

'But—'

'Dear suspicious stubborn one. I'll tell you. I'll tell you everything today. But I must do it in the right place, where mist and air blend into ocean. Where it is easier to confess, and easier perhaps to forgive. Where we'll go as soon as you're ready.'

My American drives a car that is long and low and coloured like rubies, its skin so sparkly-smooth that even the wind cannot hold it back. Inside, it smells like gardenia and jasmine, expensive and seductive and all woman, making me jealously wonder, *Who*. The seat fits around my body soft as a cupped palm (how many other women has it held like this) and when I lean back I see, floating above the glass roof, clouds shaped like pitying smiles.

Tilo have you forgotten that you have no right to this man, his past or his present.

But I cannot hold on to any of it, doubt or anger or sorrow. My dress has settled around me like the petals of a white lotus, and through the window the sun's hand slides warm as permission over my face. The car moves sleek as any jungle beast, that same silence and speed. The clock face on the bank tower says seven-thirty. We are in good time to reach Haroun.

'OK,' he says. 'Where's this place you want to drop by first?'

Most of the street names I remember, and I tell them to him from my head. Ellis and Ventura and one called Malcolm X Lane. The car glides through alleyways where garbage spills onto pavement and mat-haired men and women stare at us from doorways where they've spent the night. Lined up around their feet, like protection, are plastic bags with their lives stuffed into them.

'You sure this is the right place?'

'Yes.' Then suddenly I'm doubtful. 'Wait,' I say. 'I have the directions here in my bag.'

But the piece of paper on which I wrote it all is gone. I take out the packet of *kalo jire*, shake the bag upside down. Only a lone fluff of lint floats out like a taunt.

'I *know* I kept it here.' The words fall from my mouth in cracked chunks.

'Look again. Where can it go.'

A thought jabs at me syringe-sharp so I must bend and press my hands over my eyes.

Spices did you somehow—

'Maybe you left it at the store,' says Raven. 'Want to go back and look?'

I shake my head. Trickster spices, is this why you acted so kindly, to lower my guard and then punish me so, where least I expected it.

'Hey, you're really upset. Is it that important?'

'It's a man's life,' I say, 'that I took in trust.'

'Let me look.' He stops the car, leans over my feet, lifts up the mat. Looks around carefully. A long time seems to pass. Too long. I want to tell him it's no use, but I have no heart to speak.

'Wait, is this it?'

My sheet, scrunched into a wad with jagged edges. But still readable.

Spices what cruel game is this you are playing with me, cat and mouse.

'I wonder how it got under there,' says Raven.

I keep my knowing to myself and read him where to go. I press with my fingertips against the dashboard as if it could make the car go faster.

Raven glances at me, then floors the accelerator in one liquid movement. The car leaps into the alley, takes the corners with a smooth low roar as if it too can feel the hurry pulsing in my hands and feet. We are there sooner than I dared to hope. I jump out, the door left swinging behind me, and climb the dark, stained stairs to the top. I knock on the apartment door, calling his name, knock and knock until my palms are sore, my voice raw and trembling, even my bones.

A sound behind me. I whirl so fast my head spins. A crack in the door of the apartment opposite, two eyes like black candles, a woman's soft accented voice. '*Woh admi* – he left five-six minutes already.'

Tilo, if only you hadn't wasted time talking, putting on this foolish dress.

I sink onto the gouged top step, grip the banister for strength.

The woman comes forward, concerned. 'Are you all right? You want water?'

'Please go, I just need a few minutes sitting alone,' I say, turning from her to the blood that chants its regret-song against my eardrum, my closed lids. *Ah Haroun Haroun Haroun.*

Time drags its slow length over me. I sit there – I do not know how long. Then his hands are on mine, pulling me up.

'Tilo, there's nothing you can do now. Listen, we'll stop here again on our way back, whatever time you want.'

I look into his face. He has a small, earnest crease between his brows. His eyes seem darker, as though they are learning what he'd shied away from all this while: how to feel another's pain, how to desire for one breath-space (ah, but that is enough to change us forever) with every muscle, every bone, every pulse of the beating brain, only to take this pain away.

It is a face, I decide, that can be trusted.

Still, I must ask. 'Before sundown?'

'I promise. Now will you do something for me?'

My *yes* comes out reflexively, I Tilo so trained to granting wishes. Then with new caution I add, 'If I can.'

'Be happy, OK? At least until we come back.'

I say nothing. I look at Haroun's door, I remember the look I saw last on his shut face.

'Please, I need for you to be happy,' says Raven, tightening his hands on mine.

Ah American, you know well how to play the strings of my mind. You know that I will give to you what I feel guilty to give myself. Are all women like this.

'OK,' I tell him and feel it lift, the heaviness I was holding inside.

We walk down the stairs. Behind us on the dim landing, my heart's weight hovers (but I will not think of it now) for evening, for me to return.

He pours a glassful, palest yellow like the sky above, holds it out to me. For a moment I am content only to watch. How is it that some people have about them an elegance in their simplest, most unthinking actions. It is a wonder to me, I who was never elegant, even in my young-bodied days.

When I drink (another Mistress rule I am breaking) the wine travels through me, cold and then hot, points of light that collect in the small space behind my lids, begin to flicker. He takes the glass, turns it and drinks so his lips press where mine were a moment ago. He watches my eyes. My mouth fills with tart sweetness, fear and expectation. I am lightheaded, unmoored. Is it the wine, or him?

Today I am on holiday, I decide, no less than the tourists that flitted around us butterfly-gay wherever we stopped. Fisherman's Wharf, Twin Peaks, the Golden Gate Bridge. On holiday from myself. Today with the ocean like goldfoil rolled out all the way to the horizon, bringing tears.

Would you not agree that even I am entitled to a day like this, once in a life.

And this place where Raven has knelt on the ground careless of his Bill Blass pants and set out for our lunch a loaf of bread long as his arm, chunks of cheese in their thick white skin, a wood bowl heaped high with strawberries shaped like kisses. All exotic to me, though when I tell him that he laughs and says no, it is really quite ordinary. I know he is telling the truth. Yet when I hold up a strawberry I can see it only as a perfect red gem with luminous curves, and when I bite into it I am overcome by its innocent, edenic fragrance. And suddenly it occurs to me that this is how Raven must see the everyday things in my life – cumin, coriander, clove, *chana dal* – and a brief sadness, delicate and inexplicable as fog, drifts over me.

Stop Tilo, for today you are on holiday from your thoughts also.

And so I focus my attention upon this place, with the Pacific waves crashing under us somewhere we cannot see, the gulls' cries wheeling above, this place which I will remember like no other. Where I lean back and am, for a moment, elegant as any empress (yes, *I*) against a cypress bent by a hundred years of wind, and gaze at the salt-stained ruins of a bathhouse that shimmers against the water like a mirage.

'Built,' Raven tells me, 'by a foolish dreamer.'

'Like me,' I smile.

'And me.' He too is smiling.

'Of what do you dream, Raven?'

For a breath-space he hesitates. Shyness sweeps like the shadow of a wing over his face, that look so rare in a man. Then a different look comes over his face, and when I read it something inside me begins to tremble. For it says, I will keep no more secrets from you.

This is what I have waited for, ever since I met him that diamond-dust evening. And yet.

Raven, is it not foolish that I am afraid, I Tilo who have been the keeper of so many secrets for so many men and women. But I fear that when I learn your desire, you will become no different from the others who come to my store. I will give you what you long for, and in the giving pluck you from my heart.

Perhaps that will be best. My heart which once again will belong wholly to the spices.

Even as I think this my mind scurries, frantic, searching for a plan to stop your words. But you are already speaking, the sounds turning to gold-motes on this salt-spray air.

'I dream of the earthly paradise.'

The earthly paradise. The words spin me back to my volcano island with the sea furled green around it, the beckoning coconut fronds. Between my toes the warm grit of sand, the sharp silver glint of it in my eye, bringing tears if only I would allow.

Raven how could you possibly know of—

But he is saying, 'High in the mountains pine and eucalyptus, damp odour of redwood, bark and cone, a stream so cool and fresh to the mouth you feel you've never tasted water before.'

My American, once again I am made to see how we are worlds apart, even in our dreaming.

He continues. 'Nature undiluted, in beauty and harshness both. Where you could live once again the primal life, alongside the bear lifting his mouth to the rowanberry, the antelope standing tall, listening for sounds. The mountain lion springing upon its fleeing prey. In the white sky would be black birds circling. And no man there or woman. Except—'

I look my question.

'I will tell you,' says Raven, brushing back the iridescent curtain of his hair. 'But I must start where it began, my dream and my war.'

You at war Raven, with your certain, gentle hands, your lips so full of giving? I cannot imagine it.

As I think this, a darkness speckles the sun. A flock of crows, their flapping wings the colour of neem leaves, crossing overhead. Their doleful cries fall on us like premonition.

There is a pool of shadows at the corners of Raven's taut mouth. His face is all angles and hollows, the softness gone out of it. It is a face, for a moment, capable of anything.

Tilo how little you know this man. And yet for him you are risking everything. Is this not the crown of foolishness.

There is a high drone, like bomber planes, in my head. It drowns out Raven's words. But already I know the name of the place he is referring to.

The dying room.

'Can you see us in that dim place,' says Raven, 'my mother's hands on my shoulder, guarding me, the old man with his failing body, his fierce heart? And me, a boy in his Sunday suit caught in the animosity sparking like a live wire between them.

'The old man said, Evvie, leave the boy with me, and when my mother's whole body stiffened into a *no*, he said, Please, I only have a little time. There was power in that imploring voice, so much that I couldn't see how she resisted it. And a helplessness that caught at my heart, the broken tones of a man not used to asking for favours.

'But my mother stared into the dark as though she hadn't heard it. No. As though she had heard it too many times before. And for the first time ever, her face looked hard and distrustful, ugly.

'I think the old man saw it too. His voice changed, grew hard as well, and formal. And though it was not loud it boomed against the walls of the room like a waterfall. Granddaughter, he said, I had hoped not to say this but now I will. I ask it as debt-payment for all those years you lived with me, all that I gave which you threw away when you left.

'That was how I learned who he was to her, and to me.

'All I want, he continued, is for the boy to have a choice for his life's path. As you had.

'He's too young to be forced into making a choice, my

mother said in a choked voice. I could feel the fear closing up her throat. *My mother, afraid*, I thought in amazement, because I had never imagined such a thing possible.

'When you chose not to follow the old ways, did I force you? asked the old man, pausing between words as though each were a hill he had to climb. No. I let you go although it was like cutting my rib cage open. You know I would never hurt your boy.

'In the silence I could feel all around me the listening breath of the people. The room filling and emptying with it, like a lung.

'Very well, she said at last, taking her hands off my shoulder. You can talk to him. But I stay in the room.'

'When my mother lifted her hands from me and moved to the back,' says Raven, 'it was like she took all the light with her.

'No. Let me say that again. What went with her was the light of everyday, by which we do our day-tasks and know our day-selves. But it wasn't darkness that was left behind, only a different kind of light, a flickering redness that you could see through if only you had different eyes. And words. The room was full of words, only they needed a different ear than I possessed to hear them.

'The old man didn't move or speak. But I felt the pull of him on my arms and legs, in the middle of my chest. A warm pull, as though he and I were formed of the same substance, earth or water or iron rock, and now that we were close, it called to its own.

'I began to walk to him, feeling all the while that other will tugging me backward. My mother's. She wanted so badly for me to turn away from the part of her life she'd replaced with the shiny furniture and the pretty flower curtains, though even then I guessed that it wasn't those things she'd wanted but just the chance to be ordinary and American.

'Can you understand this?'

Raven in whose eyes I see the desperate memory of your mother's desires, I understand more than you will ever guess. I Tilo who wanted so much as a child to be different, who as an adult now so longs for the ordinary life of kitchen and bedroom, fresh-made bread, a parrot in a cage to call my name, lovers' quarrels and the small joys of kiss-and-make-up.

O the irony of desire, always hearkening after the liquid glimmer beyond the distant-most dune. Sometimes only to find that it is no different from the parched sand on which we stood days, months, years ago, in yearning.

Tilo here is a question for you to consider even as Raven's story pulls you into it, an enchanted well for unwary travellers to sink in: does one ever really know what one wants? Did Raven's mother? Do you? You who begged once to become Mistress, will you ever be happy to be only a woman?

'Step by step,' says Raven, 'I moved without knowing it, and with each step his pull grew stronger and hers less. Until I stood directly in front of him and could hear them finally, the words, stitched together into a song which gathered itself warm as a live animal skin around my body. I couldn't understand the language, but the meaning was clear enough. *Welcome*, it said, *welcome at last. We've been waiting so long.*

'The old man was holding his hands out to me, and when I put mine in them I felt the softness under their calluses. They reminded me of my father's hands. Only, these were old, all bone, with folds of speckled skin wrinkling at the wrists, nothing beautiful about them at all, nothing to explain why I felt so suddenly happy.

'They grasped me with a strength I didn't expect, and then the room went bright with pictures: a host of men and women at the edge of a river, digging up roots in the sweltering sun, cutting branches to weave into baskets. Bent over sick bodies, waving their hands in patterns that left behind little lines of light in the air. Sitting in front of a night fire chanting the wellness songs, sprinkling in cornmeal that sparked as it burned.

'Slowly I understood that he was showing me his life the way it had been, and the lives of those who had come before and passed their power on. I felt the ache in their backs, the elation thudding like horsehooves through their chests when a man given up for dead opened his eyes. I understood that if I wanted that life, it would become mine.'

My breath comes faster as I listen. It is fearful-exhilarating to glimpse the parallels in our lives, the differences. To think that Raven too holds a legacy of power. To wonder why then has he come to me.

And to hope.

Ah my American, perhaps at last I have found someone with whom I can share how it is to live the Mistress life, that beautiful, terrible burden.

'I stood there, scared, not knowing what to do,' says Raven. 'But slowly I noticed how the skin around his eyes was brown and crinkly and kind, like tree bark, how his eyes glowed like there were little fires deep in them. *My great-grandfather*, I thought, and the words were like a cool balm laid on fevered skin.

'Then I saw them behind his head, the other faces stretching all the way into the wall, like when you stand between two mirrors. The faces shifted, their features blending so that they were and were not my great-grandfather's face, were and were not mine. Now he was reaching into his chest and lifting something out. *His heart*, I thought, and for a horrified moment I imagined him handing it to me, purple and bleeding, still beating crazily.

'But it was a bird, big and beautiful, charcoal black, gleaming like oil, which sat still in his ancient hands and watched me with red bead eyes.'

He nods at my unasked question. 'Yes, a raven.

'There was drumming all around me, and the thin, air-filled notes of a pipe. My great-grandfather held the bird out for me to take, and I reached out, too. Then I saw the frames of other pictures rolling past: myself playing base-ball with my friends down at the corner lot, sitting at the table doing homework with my dad, at the grocery with my mother, pushing the cart for her so she turned at the checkstand with a smile like dewdrops in the sun. I knew it was my life I was seeing, the one I'd have to give up before I could take on the other. I smelled again the moist flower-smell of my mother's breath as she kissed me on the forehead. I felt the fear in her fingertips just before she'd let me go, and knew that if I decided to follow the way of my great-grandfather's people, things would never be the same between her and myself. My heart sank under the weight of the terrible sorrow I would bring to her, and suddenly I wasn't sure.

'What would I have decided? I don't know. Over and over and over I've repainted the scene in my mind, trying to see past what happened to what might have.'

He pauses to look at me with a sudden hope in his eyes. But I do not know how to look into the realm of lost possibilities and must with regret shake my head.

His breath falls between us, heavy, solid. 'I keep telling

myself, it's the past, let go of it. But you know how it is. It's a lot easier to be wise up here—' he taps his head '—than in here.' He puts his hand on his chest and rubs it absently, as though to ease an old injury.

Raven, tonight I will lay on my windowsill *amritanjan*, ointment that is like cold fire, hot ice. Which makes you sweat away the pain and what is sometimes worse, the memory of pain that we humans cannot seem to stop clutching to ourselves.

'In the moment of my deciding,' he says, 'this is what happened. From the back of the room my mother said, soft but urgent, in the special voice she kept for when I was about to do something really dangerous, *No*. It is possible that she had not meant to speak, for when I turned to look she had clapped a hand over her mouth. Still the harm was done.

'Hearing her tone I'd drawn back instinctively. It was a small movement, but it was enough. The bird gave a great cry and rose in the air. I could feel the rush of wind as it beat its wings. It rose straight up. I was terrified it would crash into the ceiling and injure itself, but it went through it like it was water and disappeared. Only a feather floated down and landed in my hands. I touched it and it was the softest thing. Then it melted into my palm and was gone.

'When I looked up my great-grandfather had slumped forward. A couple of men ran up, then shook their heads and laid him on his back. A wailing came from the others crowding around his bed, but I was mute with guilt. And loss as I remembered the kindness in his face, and that feather, like silk, like eyelashes in my palm.

'My mother was pulling me toward the door, saying, Come on, let's go, we've got to go. I pulled back. Frightened as I was – for surely it was I who'd killed him

– I felt I had to get to the old man's side, to lay my hands in his one last time. But I had no chance against my mother's adult strength.'

Raven looks at me blindly. 'That was the first time,' he says, 'that I really hated my mother.'

I see the memory of it in his eyes. It is a strange emotion, not the wild and stormy hatred one would expect a child to feel, but as though he had been pushed into a frozen lake and now, having emerged, saw all things with a changed, deliberate, icy vision.

'I didn't struggle anymore – I could see it was no use. Instead I reached out and yanked at her necklace. It broke with a snap so loud I expected people to turn to look, but of course the loudness was only in my head. My mother drew in a sharp, shocked breath and raised her hand to her throat. Pearls flew in every direction, hitting the floor and walls with small, hard sounds.

'You made me hurt my great-grandfather,' I said. 'He's dead because of what we did.' And then I turned and walked to the door. There were pearls under my shoes, smooth, slippery bumps. I trod heavily, wanting to crush them, but they skittered away, and when I looked back, the dark floor seemed to be strewn with tears of ice.

'A shivering had passed over my mother's face at my words, and when it resettled, I saw that it was different, looser, as though the muscles had suddenly grown tired of trying. A part of me, horrified, wanted to stop, but the new, hating part made me go on.

'He was going to give me something really special, I said, and you took me away from it.

'Sometimes I wonder. If I hadn't spoken those words, would my mother have said something different, *I didn't mean to cry out like that, baby, it just happened*. But maybe not. Anger is always easier than apology, isn't it?'

'Yes,' I say. 'Yes – for us all.'

'This is what she said, in a voice so clear and reasonable that only I, who knew her so well, could catch the edge of fury beneath it: He was dying anyway. We had nothing to do with it. I'm just sorry that you ended up being there when it happened. *That* was my mistake. I never should have let that idiot talk me into coming back. And as for something special, don't let all the mumbo-jumbo in that room fool you.

'By now we were out on the porch, where more people had gathered. Thick-necked men wearing dirt-stiff jeans, some drinking out of bottles, a few eating chunks of fried dough dipped in gravy from paper plates. The women sat like pillars, heavy in hip and thigh. If they thought anything of us, a slender, pearl-buttoned woman and a boy in a suit, if they heard the words we hurled at each other, they hid it behind their blank faces. As we passed, one of the women lifted the edge of her dress to wipe a child's nose.

'My mother stopped. This, *this*, is what I'm taking you away from, she said, and I didn't know if she was referring to the entire scene, or to that unshaven woman-leg exposed so carelessly, the ugly folds of flesh and fat.

'Look carefully, said my mother, the disgust clear in her voice. Don't forget it. This is what your life would be if you – or I – had done what he wanted.

'And then we were in the car.'

Now the sun hangs low over the Pacific, a giant burnt-orange *gulabjamun* for the waves to lick at. Raven and I pack the remnants of our picnic. I watch his back as he throws the last pieces of the bread to the gulls, the stiffness he holds in his shoulders and hips, for it has been hard for him, dredging up this story from where he had buried it, giving it, through words, life and power again. I wish to tell him so much: how his story has filled me with sorrow and amazement, how I am honoured that he has given it to me, how in the listening I have taken a part of the pain into my own heart, to hold and understand, and I hope to heal. But I feel he is not ready for me to say these things.

Besides, the story is not over yet.

Now Raven turns to me with a determined smile. 'Enough of the past,' he says, as though he has wrested it back into its lawful place, away from now. As though such a thing were possible. 'Shall we head to the beach? There's just enough time for a stroll along the ocean before we return. If you want.'

'Yes,' I say. 'I want.' And deep in me, under the sorrow and the longing to console – for such is the paradox of the heart – a selfish hope I am half ashamed of stirs: perhaps if I look out. If I call. The snakes.

Hope not built on reason brings disappointment only. That is what the First Mother would say.

But I cannot resist. There is something in the air, a sense of benediction, undeserved gifts floating down on thick dust-gold sunbeams. If ever the snakes were to come back to me, it would be today.

At the very end. I will call to them just before we go back.

We walk on the cold speckled sand, feel the give of it under our weight, the way it wells up to mould itself around our ankles.

Ah ocean it has been so long. Every footstep is a memory, like walking on broken bones. Like that old tale, the girl who wanted to become the best dancer in the world. Yes, said the sorceress, but each time you set your foot on earth will be like knives slashing. If you can stand the pain, you will be granted your desire.

First Mother, who would have thought the taste of salt-spray on my lips as I walk beside the man I must not love would bring this longing for that simpler time when you made all decisions for me.

'There are moments in our lives,' says Raven, 'you of all people surely know them. A few rare moments when we are given a chance to repair what we damaged in unthinking rage. Such a moment came to me once, and I threw it away.'

We are walking back up the beach, retracing our steps. The sea air is like a drug that fires my senses. I am aware of everything with knife-keen precision: the way drops of water hang for a moment in the air when a wave explodes against the cliff, the tiny pink flowers growing from crevices in sea-rocks where one would expect nothing to grow, and most of all the rasp of regret in Raven's voice as he lets himself be taken by the undertow of memory.

'A few minutes into our journey home that day, the car stopped at a red light. My mother took her hands off the wheel to rub tiredly at her eyes. I watched the long, bent line of her neck, and her throat, so naked and fragile, and a thought came to me: *Throw your arms around her, call her by that magic childhood name,* Mommy, *which once made everything right. There will be no need for further words, apology or blame. Let skin speak to skin as you press your face into her neck, that fragrance you have known forever.*

'But something kept me in my seat, immovable, stubborn as a stone. Maybe it was that sense that comes to us all at some point in the growing-up process, that we are separate from our parents and must suffer our own lives, with our own sorrows. Or maybe it was something simpler, a childish spite, *Let her hurt like I'm hurting*. And then the light changed and she started driving again.'

I see them in the car, mother and son, tied together in the bond of blood which is closest and perhaps most painful. I feel in the back of my throat the aching force of the words dammed up in theirs. I know how with every mile it will be harder to say them. Because with every mile they are moving farther from each other, farther from that moment of grace offered to them briefly. Even as their breaths mingle, even as her elbow grazes his when she reaches to change gears. Until the distance that stretches between them grows too vast for human traversing.

'After that day,' says Raven, 'I became a different person. My world was like a bag turned upside down, with all the certainties shaken out of it.

'We'd be doing something ordinary – maybe my mother would be driving me to the dentist's, or we'd be at the store picking out clothes for school. I'd look up to make a remark, and suddenly the memory of that dark room would drop like a film over my eyes, changing everything I looked at. I'd stare stupidly at the Levi's I'd been wanting for months, or the sign on the dentist's wall that said YOU DON'T HAVE TO BRUSH ALL YOUR TEETH – JUST THE ONES YOU WANT TO KEEP, which I'd found so funny the last time I was there. But now they meant nothing.'

Fear breaks over me like a black wave as I listen to Raven. If a single brush with the life of power could leave him so bereft, what would happen to me. I Tilo who have given up all to be Mistress. How would I bear it if the spices ever left me.

And Tilo, by doing what you have done today, are you not pushing them toward such a leaving.

I want to stop Raven. To say, Enough, take me back to my store. But I am in it too deep now, his story. And beyond, Haroun waits.

Tomorrow, I say to the spices, trying to believe my promise. From tomorrow I will be obedient.

Overhead, the gulls' call is like raucous laughter.

'My mother too had become a different person. Something went out of her that day in the car, some core of resolution, some drive, which perhaps she'd used up when she spoke that fateful *no*. She kept on doing all the same things – our home was still meticulously clean and cared for – but not with the same intense belief. Where before she'd liked sound – the radio would always be playing in our house – now I'd come home from school to find her sitting by the window in silence, gazing out at the empty lot across the street filled with high, swaying weeds. Perhaps the journey back to where her life had begun had made her see that in some way she hadn't really escaped it, not in her heart, which is the only place where it counts.

'But all this I thought of much later. At that time I'd look at that brief unfocusedness in her eyes before she hurried to fix me a snack, becoming housewife and mother again, and I'd think, *guilt*. And with the cruelty that perhaps only children can feel toward their parents I would think, *Good. She deserves it*. And I'd think of ways to punish her further.

'One of these was to watch her. Just sit and stare at her as she did her chores – mopping the floor, dusting the furniture – but where before in her movements I'd seen the natural grace I'd so loved her for, I would now see strained effort. The effort to be as different as she could from the women she'd left behind, greasy-haired women with a bunch of kids pulling on their faded dresses, crying. Women who'd lost control of their bodies and their lives the way she was determined never to. I'd pretend to do my homework while I watched her helping my father with the accounts, her fingers moving nimbly over the calculator. I'd sit in a corner of the room with a book and watch her pouring tea into matching cups for her church friends, passing around home-baked shortbread as if she'd done it every day of her life. And all the while I was waiting for the mask to slip, the muscles to slacken, a dullness to overcome her features. But of course it never did.

'I could tell it made her uncomfortable, though. If we were alone, she'd say, What's wrong with you, don't you have anything else to do? And when I shook my head, her eyes would darken – with guilt, I would think again, though now it occurs to me that perhaps it was only helplessness – and often she'd leave the room. If others were present she'd send me a silent, imploring glance, *please go*, and when I looked blankly through it, she'd get flustered so that sometimes she added things up wrong or spilled the tea.

'Her friends would say, What a quiet, polite boy you have, Celestina, how lucky you are, wish mine were like that. And I would lower my head modestly for them and smile a quiet, polite smile, but from under my lashes I would glance up at her. I knew she knew what I was asking her without words: *What would your friends say if they found out where you came from, who you really were? What would Dad think?*'

Raven gives me a rueful smile. 'Coming from your Indian culture, you probably can't even imagine behaving this way toward your parents.'

I smile at the double irony of it. My American, how you have romanticized my land and my people. And most of all me, I who have never been a dutiful daughter, not to my birth parents, not to the Old One. I who have given only trouble wherever I went. Will there ever come a day when I can tell you this.

'The Indian culture isn't quite what you think,' I say wryly.

'But tell me the truth – aren't you thinking how insufferable I must have been, what a deplorable, unnatural son? And you're right, I was.'

I want to say, It is not my place to judge you, nor my desire. As a Mistress of Spices, I should not. As a woman imperfect as you, I cannot. Besides, you have done the judging already, year after year after year.

But I can only put my hand on his arm and say, 'Raven, you are too hard on yourself.'

He shrugs and I see that he has convinced himself otherwise.

'My mother was a controlled woman,' he continues, 'not given to outbursts, but once in a while I'd manage to make her lose her temper. I'd feel a bitter satisfaction when she started in on me, quiet at first, then her voice getting louder as I put on my don't-care face, till at the end she'd be shouting, *I don't know why you're behaving like this, don't know what to do with you!* She always stopped short of saying anything really cruel – even then I felt a grudging admiration for that. But later I'd go in the bathroom and look closely in the mirror. I'd run my fingers through my hair, which seemed coarser each day. Touch the blunted bones of my face. I'd spit out the words which surely had been in the back of her mind all the time: *What else can I expect from you, you no-good Indian.*'

So many years, and still I hear in his voice the dregs of that bitterness, hatred of oneself which must surely be the worst hate of all.

'But why did you feel she'd think this way?' I ask. 'From what you've told me, she doesn't seem the kind—'

'Yeah, I thought that myself sometimes. An old memory would come into my head, a rainy day cuddled under a quilt with her as she read to me, or when I'd been sick and she stayed up all night holding ice packs to my forehead. I'd tell myself I was wrong, that I was overreacting. Then I'd remember the day in front of that clapboard house which smelled of unwashed blankets and dirty diapers. I'd remember the disgust in her voice as she told me to look carefully. Disgust for the men eating frybread with gravy dripping down their chins, the women tipping back their heads with the ease of old habit to drink from bottles. But also for herself, the part which was of them and always would be, no matter how well she hid it.

'And if she hated herself this way, I thought, what chance did I have?

'If we'd been able to talk about that day just once, if we'd fought about it openly, things might have turned out OK. But she couldn't. Her past was too deep in her, like a broken arrowhead. You live carrying it carefully, but you never touch it, because that might set it to travelling again, straight for your heart this time.

'I can see that now, but I was young then, and she was the adult, the one I'd always depended on. So I waited for her to make the first move. Waited and waited, hurting and confused and angry, and then it was too late.'

I watch him in the last of the light as he stops to look out at the ocean, eyes narrowed against the gold glare. It's been a long way from that sliver of bathroom mirror to this ocean which lies open to the whole sky. He holds himself with such assurance that no one looking would think those old words about him. *Hurting and confused and angry.* Yet somewhere inside they are still embedded, and I must find them and pluck them out.

But I cannot until he tells me the entirety of his pain. And so, unwillingly, I must probe.

'What else, Raven, what else made you so angry?'

For a moment he is silent, and I think he will deny it. Then he says, so softly that I must strain to hear, 'The bird.'

'Yes, that beautiful black bird which I'd shied away from when my mother cried *no*, which disappeared into the sky with its sad eyes like rubies, its more-than-human cry. I'd dream about it from time to time, and when I woke, my palm would tingle where the feather had melted into it. And again I'd remember the feel of my great-grandfather's hands holding mine.

'I'd be angriest with my mother then, though in the way of children I included myself in that anger. I'd tell myself she made me lose that bird and all it could have given me. The next moment I'd be kicking myself for not having been quick enough to *do* something. Why didn't I grab hold of it, why didn't I shout a *yes* to counter her *no*? And then I'd think of the power I'd felt for a moment near that bed, an amazing blast of heat like you might feel if you suddenly, unknowingly, pull open a furnace door. I felt somehow – although I didn't have the words to explain it to anyone, not even myself – that that power countered all of what my mother had pointed to with such distaste. It was a more real truth than the dinginess and dirt, the poverty and the alcohol. She knew this, I told myself, and yet she pushed it away so it was lost to me for ever.

'That's when I'd act the craziest.

'I started cutting classes and hanging out with a bad crowd. I got into fights and discovered I enjoyed them – the feel of putting all my strength behind a fist, the *thwack* as it split open flesh; the smell of blood which is like no other, the pain in my hands which made me for a little while forget that other pain inside.

'My mother would be called in to the principal's office. She'd listen in silence and later, in the car out in the school parking lot, she would put her face in her hands and say – she'd stopped shouting when she realized that it was what I wanted her to do – *I can't handle this anymore. I'm going to have to tell your father.* But she never did.'

'Your father,' I say, remembering the quiet man with hands like a forest. 'What did he make of all this?'

We're almost at the end of the beach now, gilt water pooling around outcrops of black rock. The mournful, foghorn calls of seals fill the air. Raven sighs and starts again.

'My father was the real casualty in the silent war between me and my mother. Whenever he was home we were careful to be nice to each other – it was our un-spoken pact, the one thing we had left in common, our love for him. So we talked normally, we smiled, we did our chores together, we even quarrelled about them like we used to. But he wasn't fooled. It was as though he heard the unspoken hate-words I launched at her, every one of them. They made their way into his heart until it was shot through and through, nothing but holes. He went about his everyday work, a sieve of a man, all the will to live seeping out of him.

'The saddest part was how hard he'd try to make us happy. He'd take us special places over the weekend, boat-ing on the lake, the rodeo at Cow Palace. The movies.

We'd be riding in his truck, the three of us pressed up close, my mother dressed pretty and sitting between her two men, as she called us. The people we passed on the road must have thought we were the perfect family. My father would make a joke, a weak one, usually – jokes weren't Dad's thing – and we'd both laugh really hard, harder than the joke merited, harder than we would have *before*. There we would be in the truck, the cab echoing with our fake laugh. Dad would look at us, and there'd be such knowing sorrow in his eyes, I felt I could drown in it. But how could I tell him what was tearing at me without betraying my mother? And no matter how much rage I felt toward her, I couldn't do that.

'Then time ran out on us.

'I remember that afternoon like I'm looking at it. I came home from school and Mother had made brownies. I loved brownies. I'd beg her for them all the time when I was little. But on that day it only made me angry. What did she think, she could make up for messing up my life by baking a bunch of brownies? I didn't touch a single one, though I was starving. I made myself a sandwich instead, poured a glass of milk and went up to my room. I wolfed down the sandwich, drank the milk, and lay on my bed feeling sorry for myself. The whole house smelled of chocolate, making my stomach growl. I paid no attention when the phone rang. I was thinking how I'd like to run away from home, how that would make her worry. Next I knew, she was knocking on my door. I opened it, ready to say something nasty.

'She stood there with the car keys already in her hand.

'We have to go to the hospital, she said, her face like ashes. Something exploded at the refinery.

'Then we were holding each other, both trembling a little. Even through the fear that shot up my veins making my head swim, I remember waiting for it to happen, like it did in the movies. The tragedy to bring us together. But it didn't. Not then, and not later when we sat by the bed where he lay swathed and still in his bandages, doped to the max with painkillers, which was all the doctors could do for him. He must have been hurting, because he'd give a little jerk with each incoming breath. But when he died in a few hours it was quietly, the breath just stopping – the way blessed souls die, I would later read in a Buddhist text. His death was like his life, not even his closest ones really knowing how much he suffered.

'When Mother realized he was dead she started to cry, ugly, gulping sobs that racked her whole body. She cried like her own life had ended, and in a way it had. Because the one person close to her who believed in the self she'd created with such care was gone.

'I pushed back my own shock – somehow I hadn't believed he'd actually die – and told myself I'd have to deal with it later, alone. Right now I had to take care of my mother. I put my arm around her and tried to feel what she must be feeling so that I'd know how best to console her. And you know what?'

I am afraid to look into his stormcloud eyes.

'I couldn't feel a thing. Nothing. Here I was, holding my weeping, widowed mother, knowing all the things I should feel, pity, remorse, protectiveness and love – yes, that most of all – and feeling none of them. I held her because that was what one was supposed to do, but inside I felt disconnected, totally separate, like someone had taken a giant cleaver and chopped off all ties between me and her – no, between me and the whole human race.'

'It was just the shock,' I say. My words sound weak even to my ears.

'If it was, it didn't go away, not in the next few weeks,

or months, or when I went away to college. Sometimes I feel it even now.' And he rubs again at his chest, my American, his eyes empty as holes bored into the night sky. 'Do you know, Tilo, what the saddest thing in the world is? It's when you hold someone whom you'd loved so much that just the thought of her used to be a huge flash of light inside your head, and you feel – no, not hatred; even that's something – you feel this vast coldness ballooning inside of you, and you know you could keep your arm around her or drop it and walk away, and either way it would make no difference.'

'O Raven,' I say, and impulsively I turn to the boy he was to place a kiss of compassion on his cheek. For it seems to me he is right, of all things this must be the worst. Though truly I do not know, I who had so often left the old for the new, caring little for that which remained behind. I who had come to believe that the empty, echoing chambers of the heart are as much a part of the human condition as our yearning to fill them.

Until now.

I think this, and my chest feels as though it is being squeezed between the rollers washerwomen use to wring clothes dry. For the first time I admit I am giving myself to love. Not the worship I offered the Old One, not the awe I felt for the spices. But human love, all tangled up, at once giving and demanding and pouting and ardent. It frightens me, the risk of it.

And I see that the risk lies not in what I always feared, the anger of the spices, their desertion. The true risk is that I will somehow lose this love. And then how will I bear it, I Tilo who am learning that I am not as invulnerable as once I thought?

I want to pull back from Raven to consider this, but somehow it is not his cheek but his lips against mine, and it is not the boy but the man, his arms around me, and it is not a kiss of compassion but one of mutual need. We kiss there by the ocean's last brightness before night falls on us, my first kiss, his coaxing tongue sweet and hard in my mouth a surprise (is *this* what people do), my stomach rising up and then falling away as though going very fast I'd come upon a deep dip in the road. Until I have forgotten to be ashamed of this body and am wishing, yes, like any woman, that this would never stop.

Then I hear a laugh. It peals up clear and true-noted, a derisive bell tolling me back to myself.

And without looking I know who.

Yes, two of them, one leaning lightly on her escort's arm, one climbing out of a sleek low black-shine car with a glint of gold on its hubcaps, on her long legs in suntan-silk stockings. All silver and diamanté, these bougainvillaea girls, tossing their curls, breathing scents whose names waft across the darkening air to me. Obsession. Poison. Giorgio Red. Backless dresses held up as though by magic, a long slit up the side of a thigh. Deep velvet and cream. Their gold-brown bodies warm and humming like the engine of the car, ready for adventure, for distances.

What are they doing here, these girls I last saw at my store, shopping for saffron and pistachios?

'The food's not that great,' says one woman, 'but I love the view.'

I notice it for the first time, the restaurant set into the rock and coloured like it, the discreet carved sign, gleaming glass giving way to more gleaming glass, and beyond, the ocean offered up like a plate of gold.

'Yeah, the view,' says the other woman, and looks for a moment straight at me from under her smoky lashes. Her lips are cranberry and glitter. Curving in a kind of smile.

I realize I am still in Raven's arms and struggle away.

Her escort, a white man, whispers something.

The woman is not so discreet. 'Some people—' she says. 'I guess there's no accounting for taste.' Her glance sweeps Raven now.

A heat begins to pulse behind my eyes, little explosions of red. The other woman laughs again, leaning into her man, his arm around her slim lamé waist. I see with rage the lovely line of her neck, her breasts. 'You know how it is, people get turned on by all kinds of kinky things.'

'And that dress,' says her friend. 'Did you see that dress?'

'It's pathetic, isn't it,' says the other one, 'what some women will do to look young.'

The man's eyes slide over us, bored, as though he's seen worse. As though it isn't worth the waste of his time. 'We'd better hurry,' he says, 'if we want to make it to the theatre on time.'

The restaurant door swishes shut behind them.

I feel a pounding inside me, starting up from my soles. It makes its way in waves up my body. Its colour is boiling mud.

I welcome it. In a moment it will spew from my mouth in the shape of ancient words (where did I learn them), scalding the bougainvillaea girls past recognition.

But.

'Don't pay attention to them,' says Raven. 'They aren't important.' He grips me tight above the elbow as though he knows what I am intending. 'Dear one,' he says, his voice urgent. 'They don't know you, who you really are.

They don't understand about us. You can't let them spoil our evening.' He holds on until the pounding slows.

But the evening *is* spoiled. We make our way to the car in silence, and when Raven tries to put his arm around my shoulder I move away. He doesn't try again. Nor does he go back to his story. In silence we drive back across the bridge, and when I look back I see the fog has dimmed the lights of the City so they flicker like dying fireflies.

Raven stops the car in front of Haroun's, sits for a moment with the engine idling. When I say nothing except a curt 'Thanks' he says, 'I'll come by tomorrow.'

'I'll be busy.' I step out, stiff and clumsy and angrily aware of it, remembering the gold sweep of young legs in nylons.

'The day after, then.'

'I'll be busy that time too.' Ungracious Tilo, says a voice through the whirlwind in my head. What has *he* done.

'I'll come anyway,' he says. 'Give me your hand.'

When I don't, he takes it and presses a kiss into my palm. Folds my fingers over it. 'Dear Tilo.' There is tenderness in his voice but a hint of laughter also. 'And I thought you were the wise one.'

All the way up the stairs I hold the warm shape of his lips in my hand. I am almost smiling.

Then I remember the other thing the bougainvillaea girls took from me and am angry all over again.

The snakes. My only chance at seeing them.

Red Chilli

The door to Haroun's apartment feels brittle as a husk under my hand. Empty as a left-behind shell. Even before I am done knocking I know no one is in.

Where can he be? Have I once again missed him? But this time I am not late. Perhaps he is at *namaaz* and will not answer until.

I wait a while, try again. First polite and controlled, considerate of neighbours. Then I am pounding the door with my palm, feeling the hard *thwack* of the wood against my hand-bones, crying his name.

Behind me she stands at her open door, haloed by backlight, saying softly, 'Today he hasn't returned yet. Why not you come in and have some hot *chai* until he gets back?'

Her eyes are large and luminous as a moonlight lake, her cheekbones carved from softest soapstone. How could I not have noticed earlier.

But my body is beating out a question that will not be ignored. Why is he late why is he late today of all days.

'Come *khala*, only I am at home.'

'I appreciate,' I say through sawdust lips, 'but I must wait out here.'

'Excuse me one minute then,' she says.

She returns carrying a steaming stainless-steel glass wrapped in an embroidered dishcloth. Purple grapes, silk-green leaves. Even through my worry I notice the small neat stitches.

I drink the tea. It is strong and spiced with clove. It gives me heart, makes the waiting a little easy.

The woman – her name is Hameeda – asks if she might sit with me. She has some time. Shamsur has taken Latifa to buy a birthday gift. They asked her to come too but she had homework. Besides, it's better they went without her. She always thinks Shamsur buys the little girl too-expensive things, and then they have an argument right there in the store.

I am glad of her company, the artless way she has of talking, how prettily she moves her hands as she speaks. The water music of her bangles. Day after tomorrow is Latifa's sixth birthday, they will have a small party, two-three children from Latifa's class, a few Indian neighbours. Haroun also, but he is very proper, very shy, he will probably just drop off a gift beforehand. She will have to have Latifa take him a plate of food later.

'He is so shy with women, he hardly speaks to me. If we meet on the stairs he will only say Salaam Alekum and hurry down, not even look in my eyes, not even wait for my response.'

This is a new Haroun I am seeing.

'I think he doesn't realize how good looking he is. Who knows, maybe he doesn't care. His hair is always falling over his forehead! If only he would take a little trouble he could—'

I hear in Hameeda's voice something dangerous that unchecked will lead to a home breaking.

'And your husband,' I ask in hard tones. 'He likes Haroun too?'

'*Khala!*' Hot colour stains her face at what I have presumed, but there is a small laugh in her voice also. 'Shamsur's not my husband, he's my brother.'

'Where's your husband then?'

She looks down. Pain falls like a veil over her face.

I am regretting the words, I Tilo who should know better than to prod like some village gossip.

'Sorry I asked,' I tell her quickly. 'This *chai* is very good. What-all spices did you put in it?'

'No no,' says Hameeda. 'It is all right. With you I feel comfortable to tell, I don't know why. The man who was my husband, one year and half ago back in India he gave me *talaq*. Because I had no boy children. Also he had seen another girl, younger and prettier. And her father owned big shoe-making business in our town. What better combination could there be.' For a moment her voice dips into bitterness.

'But truly I am luckier than many other women to whom this happens because I have such a good brother. Shamsur, when he hears what is happening, he takes one month off from his job saying Family emergency. That time he is head chef at Mumtaj Palace. You know Mumtaj Palace? Very fine restaurant, he has taken Latifa and me there to eat three-four times. Anyway, he comes to India and makes a big noise until he gets me a good divorce settlement, puts the money into savings bonds in my name, then gets me temporary visa to visit here. When I get here he says *Bahen*, why not you stay with me and go to college, get a good job, stand on your own two feet. Also here no one will call names to your Latifa because her father put her out of his house, no one will say bad luck girlchild.

'I am a little afraid of this new country but at last I say Yes. And now I am taking Adult *Angrezi* class for free, learning to read and write the American language. Maybe I will study computer next in the community college, why not.'

'Why not,' I say, and looking at her face like a star my heart lightens a little.

'You know *khala*, what they say is true. Allah helps those who do good to others. Shamsur's boss is opening one more bigger restaurant so he made Shamsur manager of this one. Now we have money to move to a better apartment but I told him *Bhaijaan*, why do we need more fancy things, here with such kind neighbours is good enough.'

I see the blush rise up her throat as she speaks. Her eyes move involuntarily to Haroun's door. And with all my heart I hope for them both what she is hoping.

Now it is late and cold, so much that I have lost count of the hours. My legs are numb from sitting on the naked wood of the stairs. Shamsur and Latifa returned long ago, and Hameeda went in to serve dinner. She returned with food for me, but I couldn't swallow past the lump of dread in my throat.

Haroun where are you?

'Please *khala*, come sit inside on the couch. You'll catch *jukham* out here. I'll leave the door open, that way you'll hear him as soon as he comes.'

'No Hameeda, I have to do it this way.'

I did not tell her that I hoped my pain to be an atonement, a protection for Haroun. But perhaps she understood, for she didn't insist again. She only said, 'Knock if you need anything. I'm a light sleeper.'

The unseen sounds of the night, they are not unfamiliar to me. But tonight they have taken on a strangeness, a peculiar, ominous clarity. Footsteps ring as on a fiery anvil, splintering pavement. Sirens drill through the bones of my skull in corkscrew motion. A cry (human or animal?) arcs through the air at me, a thrown knife. Even the stars beat unevenly, like racing hearts.

So the clumsy climbing sounds on the staircase crash on my ear, like a mad elephant throwing itself at a pile of stones. No. They are the sounds of a man I once saw in my village, that long-ago other life, bumping into a wall, the bottle dropping from his hand. Shatter of brown glass, fizz of foam, the fermented yellow odour of it spreading over the street, turning the ground dark.

Haroun. He's drunk.

I am dizzy with the anger of relief, already forming the scolding words, *You know how worried I've been? Look at the time, shame, for this I wasted my time sitting sitting in the cold? I never would have thought this of you, and you a good Mussalman too.* I am already in my mind making him bitter coffee with the grounds left in, brewed with almonds to clear the head and heart.

Then he rounds the bend of the stairs and I see.

Crusted on his forehead, his face. Deep red like carbuncles.

His blood.

At my knock Hameeda opens the door so quickly she must have been waiting also. She looks in my face, then beyond to where Haroun has fallen crumpled on the stairs like a thrown-away coat, stifles a cry, *Allah, no*, runs to fetch cloth and hot water. Wakes her brother. More efficient than I, she pries the keys from Haroun's fist. Opens his door so we can carry him to his neat bachelor bedroom, whitewashed walls empty except two pictures hanging where his eyes would first fall on waking. A passage from the Koran in a lush curved Urdu script, and a silver Lamborghini.

O my Haroun.

'*Khala*, no time to cry now,' says Hameeda, this slim girl so much stronger than I imagined. 'Hold his head like this. And *bhaijaan*, go phone for help.'

'Hospital?' asks Shamsur, a slightly stooped man with gentle eyes still dazed with sleep and shock.

'No no, who knows who-all they will tell, police-folice,

all kinds of *jhamela*. He might not be wanting that. Call Rahman-*saab* instead.'

Time seems to skip a beat, or is it my mind, for here is Rahman-*saab* already, a dapper, moustachioed man in a maroon velvet nightrobe and matching slippers, opening up a scuffed black medical bag, explaining to me how he used to be a surgeon in Lahore, army hospital, before he came here. 'I am thinking I will be big doctor in *phoren*,' he says as he deftly examines the head wound Hameeda has cleaned. 'But authorities say, take this test, and this one, and this one, and oral examination also. In the exam hall I am not understanding their *taan taan toon toon* American accent, and so now I run my own gas station. Who can say I am better off or worse?'

He gives Haroun a shot, pauses for the anaesthetic to work, for his moans to die away.

'But doctoring I still love, so I help my friends on the side. What-what things I am seeing, what-what things I am having to do! Luckily there is no problem to buy supplies illegal.' He grins as he stitches up the cut, gives a couple more shots, instructs Hameeda on the pills he is leaving behind, discreetly pockets the bills Shamsur has handed him. 'Good for them and good for me, no? Not to worry too much about this fine young man. His kismet was good this time. Next time who knows. Looks like they used an iron rod. Skull could have cracked like snail shells. Call me if fever comes more than one hundred and two.' I hear his voice giving Shamsur stockmarket tips all the way down the stairs.

Just the two of us in the room now. Hameeda didn't want to leave but I told her to get some sleep. 'He will need you more tomorrow when I am gone,' I said.

She nodded and slipped away, this intelligent girl with doe eyes who asks no questions although surely she must wonder who I am, why I am here. Hameeda who I hope will heal Haroun's wounded life with the balm of her holding hands.

But how will she keep him safe.

I lay my palm on Haroun's forehead, willing the pain to rise, to pass out through his skin into mine. His eyes are closed, sleeping or unconscious, I don't know which. His chest moves so slightly that time to time I must hold my hand to his nostrils to check his breath. His face is pale and stern against the bandage. *You failed*, say his drawn silent lips.

Yes Haroun, I have failed you. I Tilo held back by timid prohibitions, distracted by my own desires.

I clasp his hands, place all my attention on them.

Burning, come.

Instead, his eyelids flicker open. For a moment his eyes circle the room in wild panic, not recognizing. My mouth is ashes, my body hot and tight inside its skin. Then 'Ladyjaan,' he says with a smile so pleased that my heart breaks open like pomegranates. Before I can respond he is asleep again.

I walk to the window where in the pre-dawn Dhruva, the star of resolution, stares at me unblinking-bright.

Dhruvastar on you I promise I will not fail again. I *will* bring to Haroun that which will make him safe, whatever the cost.

I take out the bag of *kalo jire* seeds I carried so carefully all day. Pour them into my palm. For a moment I watch them glisten in the moist starlight, then fling them out over the sleeping city.

Kalo jire wasted once again, what apology can I offer you? I can say only what you know already. It is too late for you to work your power. One spice alone is left that can help Haroun now.

What would you have seen if you had been waiting this morning outside the store? In grey first light a bent woman in a grey shawl, carrying the weight of her new promise to add to all else, her guilt and her sorrow. Tired. She is so tired. Her fingers fumble at the knob, fail. Fear stings at her like poison nettle: Has the store set itself against her entering it ever again? She twists the knob once more, leans in with the weight of her body. Pushes. And look, the door swings open, sudden as a taunt or a trick, making her almost fall.

Something is different in the room, she knows it right away. Something added or taken, leaving it out of balance. Uneasiness pricks at the back of her throat.

Who has been here and why.

Then she sees it at her feet – how could she have missed it even a moment – giving off its cold phosphorescent glow. Alum.

She picks up the icecube shape and wonders at how it sits so small and innocent in her palm, alum purifier. But wrongly used she knows it can bring death. Or worse, the death-in-life that imprisons will and desire inside a body turned to stone.

Alum *phatkiri*, what message do you bring to me today.

She runs her fingers idly over its smoothness as she thinks this. Then she feels it, the ridged image rising under her hand. Taking on its inexorable shape. And suddenly. There is no air. To breathe. The room tightens around her like a pulled-in net, red-and-blue-veined wherever she turns, or is it only in her eyes.

She runs her hand over the block again. Once, twice. No error. It is there, clear as thunder, clear as lightning, the outline of the firebird as she has seen it a hundred times on the island, only reversed this time so it is not rising out of the flames. But head-first, plunging in.

'Shampati's fire calling me back,' whispers the woman, remembering the lessons in the motherhouse. Her voice is old, and without hope. There is no bargaining this, she knows. No space for refusal. She has only three nights left.

I shut the door of the shop behind me, my hands firm as though my mind were not a sandstorm whirling and whittling. I keep the CLOSED sign on the door.

Think Tilo think.

Seventy-two hours only, the moments dripping through my cupped palms like silver water faster and faster.

Not that. Think one by one of what you must complete, who you must help before you—

Before I do what I never thought I would again in this life – light Shampati's fire and step into it. But this time without the Old One's protecting eyes. I Tilo who have broken so many rules that I do not know what the spices will—

Stop Tilo. Think one thing only at a time and yourself last of all. Think Haroun.

I close my eyes, will the breath to slow, speak the words of re-creation. And he is there.

Haroun in a neighbourhood he doesn't know well, a

faraway neighbourhood with buildings that crouch in the gloom, the night-fog thick as the voice in the backseat which directs him to take a left and then another. Haroun driving his taxicab yellow as a sunflower, such a frail yellow on this street of warehouses, dim lights pooling brownly over stains and potholes. Haroun thinking *But no one lives here*, thinking, *I should have said no to this fare only he gave a twenty-dollar tip up front.*

'Stop,' says the man in the back and Haroun hearing something else in the voice turns and sees the upraised arm, the rod a bent black thing. Begins to cry out No, don't, don't, you can have the money. But there's a shower of stars, hot silver and stinging inside his eyes his mouth his nose. Through them he hears the hands that grope his pockets and jerk the glove compartment open, the voice shouting, 'C'mon blood, time to split man.' A car starts up somewhere close, no, it is a motorcycle into whose roar he falls and falls and falls.

And I am falling too, into the anger I could not allow myself till this breath-space. Anger that burns the lining of the throat, anger red like the slow glowing of coals like the bursting heart of a volcano like the eye-searing smell of scorched chillies, telling me what to do.

In the inner room I do not need to turn on the light. To open my eyes. My hands guide me where I need to go.

The jar of red chillies is surprising-light. I hold it in my hands, and for a moment I hesitate.

Tilo you know from this point there will be no turning back.

Doubts and more doubts crowd the cage of my chest, clawing and crying for release. But I think of Haroun's face, and behind him Mohan with his blinded eye, and behind him all the others, a line of injustice that stretches beyond the edge of eternity.

The seal is easier to break than ever I had thought. I reach in, feel the papery rub of the pods against my skin, the impatient rattle of the seeds.

O *lanka* who has been waiting so long for a moment like this, I pour you onto a square of white silk, all except one which I leave in the bottom of the jar. For myself, for soon I will need you too. I tie the cloth ends into a blind-man's knot that cannot be untied, that will have to be cut open. I hold the bundle in my hand and sit facing the east, where storms arise. I begin the transforming chant.

The chant comes slow at first along the ground, then gathers speed and strength. It lifts me high so the sun pierces my skin with its trident. It is the clouds, it is the whisper of rain. It drops me to the ocean-bottom where blind fish coloured like mud graze in silence.

The chant like a tunnel I am travelling, and suddenly at the end of it an unexpected face.

The Old One.

The chant coils like smoke, hangs unmoving for a moment, giving me time to ask.

'First Mother, what—'

'Tilo you should not have broken open the red jar—'

'Mother it was time.'

'— should not have released its power into this city that has too much anger in it already.'

'But Mother, the anger of the chilli is pure, impersonal. Its destruction is cleansing, like the dance of Shiva. Did you not tell us this yourself?'

She only says, 'There are better ways to help those who come to you.'

'There *was* no other way,' I say in exasperation. 'Believe me. This land, these people, what they have become, what they have done to— Ah, rocked in the safe cradle of your island, how can you understand?'

Then I see she cannot hear me. I see too the new lines carved into her face, age and worry. The sickness swelling the skin beneath the eyes.

'Tilo time is short let me tell you what I should have earlier. Before I became First Mother who I was. Like you a Mistress. Like you rebellious—'

The chant is restless, climbing again, and I who have tied myself to it must follow.

'— like you recalled. I too was forced to throw myself into Shampati's fire a second time.' She lifts her burned-white hands to show me. 'But I did not die.'

I am pulled faster and faster, the wind a wailing in my ears. 'Stop,' I cry. There is so much I must ask her. But the chant is master now.

Very far and fading I hear her say, 'Maybe you too will be allowed to come through. I will put my last powers to it, intercede on your behalf. Pull you back to the island. Tilo to be Mother for the Mistresses to come.'

I open my eyes not knowing for a moment when or where I am. Around me all is silent, no shape no colour, the chant disappeared, air into air. The only thing I remember is the Old One's voice, the promise in it but the doubt also.

Questions prick me like gadflies. I Tilo to be the new Old One, is it possible, do I want, can I even imagine. Such power, such ultimate power, mine.

Then the weight in my hands brings the present back.

The bundle is different now, heavier. Squat and solid. Glinting a little through the cloth. Whatever the chillies have changed themselves into fits firmly in my hand as though made for it. I feel through the cloth the smooth cylinder shape, the comma-shaped curve of metal where a finger could so easily tighten. My breath comes faster.

For a moment I am tempted. But no. Only Haroun must cut the bundle open.

Besides. I know already in my knocking heart (O elation, O pity and terror) what the spices have given Haroun as final remedy.

I sit dazed, listening to my heart, the urgent uneven stop-and-start sound of it, then realize. It is not my heart alone knocking, but someone at the door. I pull up my stiff limbs to answer and am amazed to find it evening already.

Tilo one day gone.

Outside Geeta is waiting, worry rubbed black into the corners of her eyes like careless mascara.

'I knocked and knocked but there was no answer. Then I saw the sign and thought maybe I got the date wrong. I was about to leave.'

I take her by the hand. Burn of searing iron, prick of poison needle, I feel nothing. That is how far I have come from the first time, Ahuja's wife, so long since I saw her – ah but I cannot think of her yet.

This change, is it good or bad. I can no longer judge.

'I am so glad you didn't leave,' I say. I pull her into the inner room. Before I can tell her my plan I hear someone else at the door, rapping impatiently.

'Be yourself,' I whisper as I shut the door. 'That is all you can do, and I.'

But inside I am praying to the spices. To the unpredictable human heart.

*

'He's really sick,' says Geeta's father. He presses his weight into the counter, hands gripped as though the pain is in him too, a plump man who at another time would be pleasant faced, with wavy humour lines around a kind mouth. A man who only wanted to be happy in his home with his father and his daughter, and is that too much to ask.

'*Baba*, you know. Throwing up, doubled over with the cramps. And stubborn as ever.' He shakes his head. 'Won't let me take him to Emergency. Says Ramu, on your dead mother's soul, I beg, don't make me go to those *firingi* doctors, who knows what drug they are giving me, messing up my mind and body both. Go instead to the old lady at Spice Bazaar, she is good at such things, she will be knowing what to do. I don't know why I even listened to him. He should be at the hospital right now.' He glares at me as though it were all my fault.

He does not know that in a way it is.

'I can help you,' I say, more confident in my mouth than in my mind.

He holds himself tension-tight, not ready to believe yet. 'Never thought I'd be saying this, but life's nothing but one trouble after another. If only you knew the things that have happened this last month.'

Ah Ramu, but I do.

He sighs. 'I tell you, I'm sick of it.'

'I don't blame you. I feel that way myself sometimes,' I say, I who have come to learn through my own meddling what human trouble is.

He moves restlessly. He has had enough of pleasantry. 'Well, what can you give me?'

'It is in the storage room,' I say. 'You will have to help me bring it out.'

'Oh, OK.' Inside he is shaking his head, thinking, What foolishness. I should be at the pharmacy instead.

'Sorry, no electric connection in there. You go first with this flashlight,' I say. 'Look in the corner.'

'What does it look like?'

'You will know when you see. Really, you will.'

The oval of light bobs up and down, elongates and denses, moves over floor and wall. Stops.

I hear the intake of breath sharp as icechips, him and her. I close the door.

At the counter I squeeze shut my eyes. *Tilo focus*. I hope that in his bed at home the old man too is sending his mind power to aid mine.

Kantak thorn with which to remove earlier thorns, what will it be? The trough of hate so easy to remain in? The mask of righteousness so easy for the face to fit to?

With shaking hands I light a stick, incense of rarest *kasturi*, the fragrance the wild deer hunts crazily through the forest, not knowing he holds it in his own navel.

Hard words to say, *I was wrong*. Almost as hard at times as *Love*.

Father and daughter in there so long, what are you doing, are you able to lean across the pain you have carved into a chasm between your two lives, to touch each other's breath.

The flung-open door is a sound like a slap. He comes out. Alone. I hold my breath, try to see behind him.

What has he done to her.

Redrimmed, his eyes are slits. His mouth. His voice thin and sharp, a knifeblade. 'Old woman, did you think such a cheap trick would work? Is it so easy to build up the house walls an ungrateful child has kicked down?'

Incense odour, too sweet, chokes my chest. I try to push

past him to the inner room but he has me in his grip.

A thought flits through my head light as seeds of grass. *Will he hurt me too*. Almost I wish it.

Then he is hugging me, laughing, and behind him in the doorway her laughing face also, wet with tears.

'Forgive me, Grandmother,' he says. 'I couldn't resist paying back the trick you played on me, you and *baba* both. But I am glad.'

And she: no words, but a damp cheek laid against mine saying more than pages.

My hands are still trembling, my laugh also as I say, 'Don't do this to an old woman's heart, one more minute and you are having to take *me* to the hospital.'

'*Baba*, I never knew he was such an actor.'

'The pain is real,' I say, filling a bottle with fennel water. I count in fenugreek and wild dill seed, shake it well. 'Give him this once every hour until the cramps wear themselves away.'

At the door I tell them, 'He did it for you, you know.'

'Yes,' says Geeta's father, his arms around the daughter lost and found. He lowers his eyes.

'Remember this when next he angers you with his talking, I am sure it will be soon enough.'

Father and daughter smile. 'We'll remember,' says Geeta. She hangs back a moment to whisper, 'We didn't talk of Juan, I didn't want to spoil the moment, but next week I'll bring it up. I'll come back and tell you how it goes.'

Through a veil of incense I wave her good-bye from the door. I do not tell her that I will no longer be here.

This morning, my second to last, I am busy. There are bins to move around, shelves to empty, sacks and canisters to drag to the front. Signs to write up. Yet over and again I find myself at the window. Standing and simply looking. The dust-choked lone tree the narrow chink of discoloured sky. The graffiti-clad buildings the smog-belching buses the alleyways smelling of weed. The young men standing on corners or driving around slow, music exploding from their machines. Why suddenly is it all shaded with poignance. Why am I wrenched at the thought that it will all be here, all except me. Why when I may have power more than I dreamed, the entire island, generations of Mistresses to command. And the spices, mine more than ever before.

What is this thought swimming up from the depths of consciousness. As I watch it I realize I have been thinking it without words for a long time.

Tilo what if you refuse.

Refuse. Refuse. The words echo in my mind, ripples of opening-up sound. Circle upon circle of possibility.

Then I remember the Old One's words. 'No choice. A recalled Mistress who does not come of her will is brought back by force. Shampati's fire opens its mouth and all around her are devoured by it.'

I stare out the dusty window at a woman in a red *kameez* getting out of an old Chevy, lifting a child out of a car seat, shouting at her daughters to 'Hurry *up* I have *hazaar* things to do.' Over her shoulder the infant stares at me unblinking, curly head haloed by the morning sun. The girl's oiled braids glisten as she skips through the doorway to offer me a gap-toothed smile.

It is like a fist punching me in the centre of my chest, the love I feel for them, even the mother who mutters loud enough for me not to miss that my *dals* are too expensive, why can't I charge the same as Mangal Groceries?

Strange how many loves there are that we can feel. Strange how they rise in us without reason. Even I a novice at this know so already.

I feel their names moving through me, bubbles of light, all these people I love in opposing ways. Raven and the First Mother, Haroun and Geeta and her grandfather also. Kwesi. Jagjit. Ahuja's wife.

Ah Lalita-to-be, how can I go without seeing you one more time. And Jagjit caught in the gold jaws of America, how—

But for their own good I must leave.

'Listen,' I say to the woman in the red *kameez*. 'You take all the *dal* you want for free.'

She gives me a suspicious stare, certain this is some trick. 'What for?'

'Just like that.'

'No one gives just like that.'

'Then take because the sun is shining so bright, take because of your children's sweet faces, take because I am going out of business and must close up this shop tomorrow.'

Long after she has left with her bags I stare out. The air seems to hold impressions, as when one shuts one's eyes after staring at the sun. Luminous and throbbing, the outlines of people that once walked this way.

Air will you hold my shape after I am gone.

'What's this,' says Raven, walking in.

I have put up signs in the windows. BIGGEST SALE OF THE YEAR, BEST BARGAIN IN TOWN. EVERYTHING MUST GO.

'O just an Indian custom, year end.'

'I didn't realize the Indian year ended at this time.'

'For some of us it does,' I say and swallow the tears crowding my throat. I slip under the counter, before he can see, the sign I have just finished lettering, the one I will put up tomorrow.

SHOP CLOSING, LAST DAY.

Will another Mistress soon be standing here making another sign, UNDER NEW MANAGEMENT. Who will she be. Will Raven come to her too and—

Stop foolish Tilo. Where you are going (but where is that) none of this will matter.

Raven waits patiently for my attention. I notice that he is wearing jeans. A plain cotton shirt white as the sun at noontime. In his simplicity he dazzles me.

'I came to tell you the rest of my story. If you have time.'

'The best time I'll ever have,' I say, and he begins.

'The death of my father cut me free of all ties, all caring. I was like a boat that had come unmoored, bobbing in an ocean filled with treasure troves and storms and sea monsters, and who knew where I would end up.

'Have you ever felt this way, Tilo? Then you know what a lonely feeling it is, and how dangerous. It can turn men into murderers, or saints.

'I had no one to love, for in their different ways both my father and mother were lost to me – and my great-grandfather too, though I was careful not to think of him. And so the laws of the world no longer seemed to apply to me. The opinions of others meant nothing. I felt light and porous, as though I could become anything I wanted – if I found something worth being – or implode into nothingness.

'I spent a lot of time alone in bed, staring at the ceiling, imagining possible lives. My present existence – scraping through classes, getting in fights, partying with the guys, sitting at the dinner table with my mother, swallowing forkfuls of silence – filled me with dissatisfaction. There was no direction to it, no intensity. No *power*.

'For slowly it came to me as I lay in my room while outside the world rushed by that there was only one thing in life worth having. Power. It was what my great-grand-father had offered me in that dying room. It was what my mother had snatched from me. And though I could never go back to *that* moment, *that* power, there were other kinds in the world. I needed to find the one that would be right for me.

'I toyed with wildly different thoughts – becoming part of a gang, going off with the Peace Corps, joining the army. Even going back to that clapboard house to find someone who knew my great-grandfather's ways. But in the end I did none of them. In the end I went to business school.

'You're laughing? I knew you would. But this is what came to me as I lay wondering: money was at the centre of the world – at least the one I lived in. Money was power. With money I could remake myself – not like my poor mother strained to do, but completely, suavely, at once and for ever.

'For the most part I was right.

'The finances were not a problem – my father had had life insurance – but I knew I'd have to work hard and change my habits – pull up my grades, quit hanging around with the guys, things like that. But it was less diffi-cult than I'd thought. I discovered an unexpected hardness in myself, a drivenness, something that shook off all that could hold me back, something that didn't mind cutting through all that was in the way. Maybe it was a quality I'd got from my mother, but in the passing down it had crystallized, grown more adamantine.

'My days took on a silent, submarine quality as I prepared myself for my future. People receded from me, and I let them go gladly. The friends who scoffed or tried to incite me to fight, the teachers who discussed me in amazed whispers in the staff lounge, even my mother who watched me thankfully but without understanding. They were merely distractions, ripples on a distant surface which had little to do with my life. I would feel the same way about my classmates in college.

'This is what I discovered about myself in college: I understood money effortlessly, its strange logic. How it came, how it grew, its ebbs and flows. I delighted in its secret language. I had a knack for investments, and even in those first days – I was still a student – when I started playing the market I knew exactly what to buy and when to sell.'

'And did it bring you the power you dreamed of?'

My American looks down at the lines of his hands, then into my eyes. 'It brought me power, yes. And a – *solidity*. I could see why in the old tales the giants were always counting their gold. It assured them that they were real. There's a headiness to money-power, the feeling that everything in the world is there for you to pick up and examine, choose or discard, like you might do with fruit at a produce stand. And you'll be amazed at how many things you can buy, and people too. I'd be lying if I said I didn't enjoy that.

'From the beginning I decided that I'd have fun with my money. I gathered around me all the things I thought would bring me that fun. You would probably think them infantile, coming as you do from a less materialistic culture.'

I let it pass. Another time, Raven, I think, we will discuss this. (But Tilo, Mistress of only a few hours more, when will that be.)

'I realize now that they were a poor boy's fantasy of the rich life, gleaned from glossies and TV shows. Yachts, penthouse apartments, Porsches, Gucci underwear, vacations on the Riviera or at Vegas. All the stereotypes. People who've always been rich probably spend their money quite differently. But I didn't care, and none of the new friends (if you could call them that) who gathered around me seemed to mind.'

'What about your mother?'

Sharp silence, like a shard of glass between us. Then Raven says, 'When I made my first million I sent my mother a cheque for a hundred thousand dollars. It was the first time I'd corresponded with her since I left home. Oh, she'd write to me, not often but regularly, telling me what she was doing. Nothing exciting – church bazaars, planting petunias in the spring, getting the house painted, things like that. After a while the letters would come and I'd leave them unopened. Sometimes they'd get misplaced before I read them. I never wrote back.

'Why should I, I told myself. There's nothing between us anymore. But I think I wasn't quite honest with myself. Somewhere in the back of my mind I wanted to show her that I'd done what she wanted to better than she ever had. I'd made it in a world she couldn't even dream of being part of. That's why I sent her the cheque, and with it a photo of myself and a bunch of friends – including my latest girl – at a beach house I'd just bought down in Malibu. It was to be the ultimate punishment.'

He gives a harsh laugh. 'Well, the letter came back with a red stamp saying they couldn't find anyone to deliver it to. And when I thought back, I couldn't remember when her last letter had arrived.

'A couple years later, after some other things had happened, I made a trip back to the old neighbourhood – something I'd never thought I'd do again. A Chicano family was living in our house. They told me they'd been there for quite a while. No, they didn't know where the woman who sold them the house had moved to.

'I never did catch up with her, though I tried. I called around, asked the ladies at her church, even hired a detective for a time. I thought of going up to her folks – not that I was sure where that was, but I could have found out. But I couldn't make myself. You know how certain childhood phobias can rule your life. So I persuaded myself they wouldn't have known any more than I did.'

Ah Raven. I am wondering if you still search for her in all women, the lost mother. Forever beautiful forever young.

'I needed to tell her so many things,' says Raven. 'That I was sorry for my earlier coldness, that I understood, at least a little, why she'd left her home and denied who she was.' He sighs. 'I wanted to say, Let's try to forgive each other and start over. And most of all I wanted to tell her about my dream. Because she might have known what it meant. After all, her grandfather had taught her, and you don't forget those things even if you try.'

'What dream?' I say. My mouth is dry. Tilo, says my pounding heart, this is it.

But Raven continues as though he had not heard. 'Things changed somehow when the letter was returned to me. Without my mother to show it to, my golden life seemed to lose some of its glitter. Some mornings, lying in bed next to my sleeping girlfriend, I'd feel boredom, just a twinge of it, like the first signs of age in one's muscles. It frightened me.

'To counter that boredom, I began to take risks. First on the market – but I couldn't seem to lose. Everything I touched went higher and higher, and there was no excitement there. Then I turned to physical things – whitewater rafting, skydiving. I even went on a trip down the Amazon. But that wasn't satisfying either. There'd be a few moments of adrenaline rush, and next an irritated tiredness with a question pushing through it: *What the hell am I doing here*.

'Then one of my friends brought the mushrooms.

'I'd never been into drugs before. I'm not pretending virtue – I had nothing against providing them at parties. But I looked down on the people who took them. I thought of them as weak. It was distasteful to watch them come down from their high, to see them dragging through the rest of their lives until the next one. The way they behaved when the craving was on them. And no matter what they claimed I never knew a single one who wasn't in the grip of their drug of choice. Now that I was free (or so at least I believed) from all that I had once leaned on, I wasn't about to take on a new dependency for the sake of a few moments of questionable delight.

'But the mushrooms, claimed my friend, were different. They were potent and sacred, not a commercial drug at all. You couldn't buy them from a dealer, not for love or money. He'd managed to get hold of these only because he was lucky enough to possess a friend, an Indian from Guatemala, where they used these during special ceremonies to induce trances.

'You won't believe the visions, said my friend. It'll be like you died and went to heaven, only better. Ecstasy, acid, none of them can hold a candle to this one. And safe. Safe as mother's milk.

'I was intrigued. Not that I had much trust in this particular friend's capacities, mental or ethical. Still, all that talk of visions and Indians went straight to the vulnerable part of me that I tried to believe no longer existed.

I'd maintained a surreptitious interest in Indians all through college. Whenever there was a campus event involving them, I'd go sit in the back and watch. Earnest young men and women dressed neatly and formally spoke to us about the importance of the Native American Rights Fund or described the work being done by the United American Tribal Youth. I appreciated their struggles and admired their energy, but try as I might, I didn't feel I was one of them, not in the gut-wrenching way I'd felt it on my great-grandfather's porch. And for all their knowledge of tradition and history, their lives seemed as bland, as lacking in mystery as mine.

'And so something leaped in me when my friend handed me the mushrooms.

'I didn't show it, of course. By now I was a master at hiding what I felt. I'd discovered that that was an important part of being powerful. I tossed the packet of mushrooms in a drawer, spoke a perfunctory word of thanks, handed him some money over which he protested profusely, and waited for him to leave. But as soon as the door closed behind him I took them out. They were black and shrunken in my palm, and of an old rubbery texture. A strange excitement came over me as I looked at them, a feeling that perhaps at last I was back at the door which connected two worlds, the way I had been when my great-grandfather died.'

His breath grows quick and shallow, remembering. And mine, in fear of what is to come. I know of such substances. The Old One spoke to us about them many times. *Daughters, they will show you the forbidden, and in that showing break apart your mind.*

'My friend had told me that evening was a better time for the experience, but I couldn't hold back. I put the first one in my mouth and chewed. It was the worst thing I'd ever tasted. He'd warned me about that – no pain, no gain, he'd said – but I hadn't expected this – bitter is not the word for it – this vileness. I had to use all my willpower not to spit it out.

'Then I waited.

'Fifteen minutes max, my friend had said, and you'll be zooming, but nothing happened.

'After half an hour I chewed another mushroom – it seemed less disgusting this time. I guess that's the nature of repeated assault. After another half hour I took two more.

Nothing.

I was furious at being cheated. I went to the bathroom to wash out my mouth. Next I was going to call my friend – make that *ex*-friend – and have a few words with him. If he showed a reluctance to return my money I was prepared to phone certain gentlemen who had offered their services to me for just such tiresome situations. You're shocked? I told you I'd hide nothing. This was the black side of the life of power I lived. Will you think too badly of me when I say that I found it as attractive as the other?'

I shake my head, I Tilo who know more than enough about the pull of darkness.

'I splashed water onto my face and looked in the mirror. And saw – no, nothing horrifying like you might expect, a monster head, or someone with snakes crawling from his mouth. And yet it *was* horrifying.'

'What was it?'

'Just myself, but when I looked in my eyes, they were dead. Dead eyes looking back at me. It struck me then that my life had been a total waste.'

'Why a waste, Raven?'

'Because in all my adult remembering I had not made anyone truly happy, nor been happy myself.'

American, the truth of what you speak strikes close. In the lightning flash of it I must re-examine my own life. I who pride myself on having fulfilled so many people's desires, how happy have I made them? How happy have I made myself?

Raven continues, 'My eyes showed me my heart, and it too was dead. What use was it, then, to keep this body, this sack of excrement, alive? I looked for something with which to end it. Nothing in the bathroom, so I started toward the kitchen for a knife.

'On the way the cramps hit me. I doubled over with the pain, vomiting. I vomited until there was nothing left, until it felt like I would throw up my guts. Between bouts of retching I remember thinking, At least I won't have to kill myself, this'll do it. I briefly wondered if my "friend" had known this would happen, and had done it purposely. And then I passed out.

'I woke in the hospital. My housekeeper had found me the next morning and called the ambulance. They'd pumped my stomach, but it was too late to do much good. Some of the poison I'd vomited out, but some had spread through my system. I was lucky to be alive, they said. I had to smile at the irony of that. They kept me under close observation.

'I was feverish and sweaty in turns, and in between I shivered violently. My palms were clammy and my throat dry as sand. That was the worst part. I couldn't drink anything because the doctors were afraid it would start the

retching again. They'd put an IV in me but it didn't help
with the thirst. I couldn't stop thinking of water, water in
tall, cool glasses, water in pitchers and buckets, vats full
of water that I could cup in my hands and drink and
drink.

'Somewhere in that thirsty night the dream came.

'I stood on a hill of ashes amid a lake of fire while a
searing wind blew over me. Grit of ash was in my mouth
and nose, choking my throat. There was a smell like
singed flesh all around. The thirst was worse than ever. I
burned from it, literally, for when I looked down my body
was blistered and crisped, like my father's must have been
under the bandages. The pain was so great I couldn't
stand it. Help me, I cried through cracked lips. Someone
help me. But no one approached me who had cut myself
off from the human race in my heart and gloried in it. I
knew then that there was one solution alone left to me.
Death. And so I threw myself off the hilltop into the burning lake, and even as I fell I wondered. What if I don't die,
what if I continue to burn?

'That was when the raven came.

'I don't know where it came from, but it swooped to
catch me in its wings. It was more beautiful than ever
before, and its feathers glistened a rich blueblack with
each wingbeat. As it soared, the rush of air on my face
wiped off the stench of burning flesh. Ah, it was the best
thing I'd ever felt. There was a song in my ear, harsh but
not bitter, filled with strength, the bird's voice. I realized it
was giving me its name. I closed my eyes, drank it down,
and my thirst receded.

'When I opened them the raven was gone, and I was in
the place I told you of. Eucalyptus and pine, California
quail, deer. Crags and ravines filled with sweet water
which I drank without craving. A place of wildness and

wet, to labour in and grow strong and pure again. A place with no people to spoil it. Then I woke up.

'I'm not sure what the dream means. Perhaps my mother could have told me. Can you?'

But I do not know.

'It's a real place,' says Raven. 'I'm sure of that. It's the place where my happiness lies. I think that's what the bird came to tell me. To stop wasting my life on trivialities and find it. To go back to the old ways, the ways of the earth before it was spoiled. To the earthly paradise.

'Only, I didn't know how to get there. I went into the wilderness a number of times, with guides, then later alone. Found a lot of beautiful solitary places, but none that touched me like the place of my dream.

'Slowly I lost heart and convinced myself that it had been just a fever-hallucination. I resigned myself to living – if you could call it that – in a world from which the magic has been drained away.'

Now he reaches across the counter to put his hand over mine. In his changed breathing I feel it coming, dense and frightening-bright, the core of the story, the reason why.

'But lately I've been dreaming it again. Clearer each time. The raven too. It circles the sky there. When I wake I have a warm feeling, as though that clean sunshine is inside my chest, growing. As though I have a chance at last to find it, live it, discover who I really am.

'You know when the dreams started?'

'No.' The word is a whisper in my throat. But I know what I want the answer to be.

'Yes,' he says, Raven who reads my heart. 'When someone told me, There's a woman down in Oakland, go see her. She isn't what she seems. She can do things. After the mushrooms, I couldn't allow myself to believe. But on a whim I came to the store on a Friday evening. And met you.

'In the last few dreams you've been there with me, you and I, in that perfect place. Only, you look different, the way I know you are, under this skin.'

He runs a fingernail, like fire, up my arm.

I allow his words to wrap me in their shimmer. Why not, I say stubbornly to myself. Why should it be impossible.

'I want to try it once more, this time with a companion who sees clearer than I ever can.' His eyes are deep and pleading, but also in them a dare. 'Will you come with me, Tilo? Will you help me find the earthly paradise?'

I am still thinking my answer, what I want to say what I should, when the bell at the door tinkles. I look up and they are there, three bougainvillaea girls, the prettiest and youngest yet, all fizzy laughter and flutter lashes. In miniskirts their legs are long and tan, cocoabutter smooth. Their lips are dark and pouting. They toss back their crinkle-cut hair and glance around and laugh again as though they can't believe they are actually here, that they are doing this.

They look like they've never cooked a meal – certainly not an Indian meal – in their lives.

One of them detaches herself from her friends and comes forward. She wears a thin silk blouse through which I catch the hint of a lacy bra. Beige eyeshadow that sparkles. Scent of roses. Tiny gold and diamond heart earrings, a matching pendant that rises and falls in the hollow of her throat.

The effect is charming, even I must admit this. From the

look in his eyes, Raven seems to agree.

'Excuse me, you understand English? Our office, they're having a potluck, we're each supposed to bring something ethnic, you know, from our culture, make it ourselves. We didn't have a *clue*.' She smiles an ingenuous smile. 'Maybe you can help us?'

That word *help*. I cannot steel myself against it. I put aside my annoyance to think. It's a challenge, to find a party dish simple enough so they couldn't ruin it in fixing.

'Maybe you can do vegetable *pulao*,' I say at last. I tell her how it's cooked, the water measured and boiled, the Basmati soaked just the right amount of time, the *kesar* sprinkled in, the peas, the roasted cashews and fried onions for garnish. I list the spices: clove, cardamom, cinnamon, a pinch of sugar. Ghee. Maybe a dusting of black pepper.

She looks a little doubtful but she is game. She takes copious notes in a little gold-edged pad with a matching pencil. Her friends smother giggles as they look over her shoulder.

I tell them where to find the ingredients. Watch them wander toward the back of the store, all sway and undulation. Raven too is watching. Appreciatively, I think. There is a pricking like pins in the centre of my chest.

'Quite amazing,' he says, 'how women can balance themselves on heels no thicker than pencil points.'

'Not all women,' I say wryly.

He smiles, squeezes my hand. 'Hey. You can do things these girls couldn't in a hundred years.'

The pinpricks begin to fade.

'You're authentic in a way they'll never be,' he adds.

Authentic. A curious word to use. 'What do you mean, authentic?' I ask.

'You know, real. Real Indian.'

I know he means it as a compliment. Still, it bothers
me. Raven, despite their fizzy laughter, their lipstick and
lace, the bougainvillaea girls are in their way as Indian as
I. And who is to say which of us is more real.

I am about to tell him this when one of them calls,
'Help, we can't find the cardamom.'

'That's because we don't know what it looks like,' says
another. They laugh at the delicious humour of it, that
such arcane knowledge should be expected of them.

I am about to go back there but 'Let me get it,' says
Raven. He disappears behind the shelves – for a long time,
it seems. More laughter flits through the store, flocks of
swallows. I gouge the countertop with a thumbnail, force
myself not to follow.

Finally they are back, Raven carrying packets and
sacks. Cans. They have bought enough to feed the entire
office ten times over.

'You were *so* helpful,' one says. She looks up at Raven
from under her lashes. 'The crispy *papads* and mango
nectar will go great with the *pulao*.'

'Yeah, and it was a great idea to buy enough so we
could practise at home before the party,' says another,
training a brilliant smile on him.

The third bougainvillaea girl, the one in the silk blouse,
puts a hand on his arm. Bright as a blackbird's, her eyes
take in his high cheekbones, his trim waist, the firm
muscles of arm and thigh. 'I know what,' she says,
'you can come and be our taster. Tell us if we did it
right.'

'No, no.' But he is grinning, quite at ease with all this
attention. In his manner I see how many beautiful women
have invited him thus, and perhaps how many he has
accepted.

Unaware of the blister of heat building inside my skull,

he nods at me. 'She's the expert, she's the one you should be calling.'

She of the lacy bra dismisses his suggestion with a flicker of lashes. 'Here's my card,' she smiles, scribbling something on the back and putting it into his hand. I see her fingers brush his, lazy, deliberate. 'Call me if you change your mind.'

The heat blister bursts. When the swirl of steam has settled I see clearly what I will do.

He helps them out with their sack of purchases. Closes the car door solicitously, gives a last friendly wave.

Raven you are no different from other men, pulled by the high arch of a foot, the curve of a hip, the way a diamond shines moistly against a woman's silkskin throat.

He is leaning over the counter now as though there had been no interruption, reaching for my hands again. 'Tilo, dear one, what do you say?'

I draw my hands back out of his reach. Busy them with busywork, folding tidying dusting clean.

'Tilo, answer me.'

'Come back tomorrow night,' I say. 'After the shop closes. I will give you your answer then.'

I watch him all the way to the door. Smooth spring of step, soft glint of hair, under his clothing the glide of his goldriver body. There is a wrenching in my heart.

O my American, if youth and beauty is what you want, the joy of what you can see what you can touch, I will give you your fill. I will draw on the powers of the spices to fulfil your deepest fantasies about my land.

And then I will leave you.

When I look down at my gnarled hands I find I have torn to bits the card the girl gave to Raven. Which he chose (but why) to leave behind.

Makaradwaj

On its own shelf in the inner room sits *makaradwaj*, king among spices. Has sat all this time, certain in the knowledge that I will one day come. Sooner, later. Days months years. It does not matter to *makaradwaj*, who is the conqueror of time.

I take the long thin vial in my hand, hold it till it grows warm.

Makaradwaj I am here as once you predicted, I Tilo for whom time is running out. I Tilo ready to break the final, most sacred rule of all.

What, asks *makaradwaj*.

Makaradwaj who knows my answer, why must you make me say it.

But the spice waits in silence until.

Make me beautiful, *makaradwaj*, such beauty as on this earth never was. Beauty a hundred times more than he can imagine. For one night so that his skin will dazzle, his fingertips be branded with it for always. So that never again will he be with another woman without remembrance and regret.

The laughter of the spice is low and deep, but not unkind.

Ah Tilo.

I know I am wrong to ask this for myself. I will not pretend repentance, I will not act shame. I will say to you with my head high that this is my desire, give or withhold it as you may.

Do you desire it more than you desired us on the island, that day when you would have thrown yourself off the granite cliffs had the First Mother said no.

Spices why must you always compare. Each desire in the world is different, as is each love. You who were born in the world's dawning know this far better than I.

Answer.

Weigh it yourself: to him I will give one night, to you the rest of my life, whatever you choose it to be, one hundred years on the island or a single moment, conflagration and consuming, in Shampati's fire.

As I speak the last of my doubts fall away, the last of my hopes. I see my future distinct in the vial's glow. What I cannot have. And I accept.

Tilo it was never for you, the ordinary human love, the ordinary human life.

My answer has satisfied. The spice speaks no more. The vial is hot now in my hands, its contents melting. I raise it to my lips.

And hear the Old One's long-ago voice: '*Makaradwaj* most potent of the changing spices must be handled with most respect. To do otherwise can bring madness, or death. Whatever a person weighs, measure out one thousandth of it, mix in milk and *amla* fruit. It must be sipped slow, one spoon an hour, over three nights and days.'

I drink it all at once, I who in three nights and days will be gone who knows where.

The jolt of it hits me first in the throat, like a bullet, a burning such as I have never felt before. My neck is exploding, my gullet, all the way to my stomach. And my head, expanding, a giant balloon, then shrinking to a nugget of iron. I am lying on the floor. The nausea pulses out of me like blood from a torn artery. My fingers are stiff and splayed, my body bends and buckles beyond my will's controlling.

Tilo too confident, who thought you could absorb the poison like Shiva of the blue throat, who have risked all for nothing, die now.

For nothing. That thought is the hardest to take.

But wait, the pain is less now, enough that I can breathe in gasps. Through it I feel a different sensation, deep in the body, a shifting, a tightening. A reknitting of bones. *Makaradwaj* doing its work.

And a voice: *By tomorrow night Tilo, you will be at beauty's summit. Enjoy well. For by next morning it will be gone.*

Ah spices, why should I worry about the next morning. By then will I too not be gone.

And will you be happy going, or will you come to us with your heart stained with the colours of regret.

For myself I have no regrets, I say. And almost believe my words.

But, I add. There are two left in my care whom I have not helped. I cannot go in peace unless I know the end of their story.

Ah, the boy, the woman. But their story has only begun. It is yours that is ending.

I understand. But though I have no right to request this, I want to see them one last time.

More wishes, Tilo? Have you not already asked your final desire?

Please.

We shall see, say the spices, their voice indulgent, knowing they have won.

My last day dawns heartbreaking-bright, the sky coloured palest indigo, the air smelling of roses, though how in this city I do not know. I lie on my thin mattress a while, afraid to look, but then I hold up my hands. The knotted knuckles are gone, the fingers are long and tapered. Not yet fully young but growing toward it.

I release my breath in a great sigh. Spices I apologize that until now I had not dared to hope.

O you who are young, you will never know the delight with which I rise from bed, how the simple act of stretching these newly middle-aged arms upward makes me giddy with forbidden pleasure.

I shower, running my hands over my body, feeling it grow firmer even as I touch. I let my wet hair fall over my face, half darkness, half light.

Already this. By night how much more.

Impatient Tilo, put aside night thoughts. First there is a full day's work to be done.

I pull back my hair in a no-nonsense coil, pull on my American dress from Sears. I open the front door to tape up the LAST DAY sign.

On my doorstep, a bunch of them, spilling red velvet. Roses the colour of virgin blood. *Until tonight*, says the note.

I gather them tight to me. Even the thorns are a pleasure. I will place them in a jar on the counter. All day we will look at each other and smile our secret.

News of the sale has travelled. The store is busy as never before, the cash register rings without pause, my fingers (younger, younger) are tired from punching buttons. The register drawer grows full. When it can hold no more I stuff the money into a grocery sack and smile at the irony of it, I Tilo to whom these banknotes are of no more use than dead leaves.

I would have given it all for free, for affection's sake. But it is not allowed.

'What's happening?' the customers ask over and over, eager for a story.

I tell them only that the old woman is closing the shop for health reasons. Yes, something sudden. No, not so serious, not to worry. I am her niece, helping out this last day.

'Say good-bye to her for us. Say thanks for all her help. Say we will always remember her.'

I am moved by the warmth in their voices. Even though I know that what they say, what they believe, is an illusion. Because in time all things are forgotten. Still, I imagine them walking this street next month, next year, pointing. 'There once was a woman here. Her eyes like a magnet-rock drew out your deepest secret,' they say to their children. 'Ah, what-all she could do with spices. Listen carefully.'

And they tell my story.

Late in the afternoon he comes slowgaited, Geeta's grandfather pausing to catch his breath.

'Is still hurting a bit, *didi*, but I had to come to thank you, to tell what hap—'

He stops in midword, scowls at me. Keeps scowling even after my explanation.

'How can she leave us like this? It is not right.'

'She doesn't always have control. Sometimes she must do as she's told.'

'But she has so many powers, she could—'

'No,' I say. 'That's not why the powers are given. You in the wisdom of your age should know that.'

'Wisdom.' He gives a wry smile, then grows serious. 'But I am needing to let her know things.'

'I'll make sure she knows them.'

He frowns distrustfully, adjusting his glasses, Geeta's grandfather, all the enjoyment taken from his tale.

'Did Geeta return to your house last night?'

His head jerks up. 'How are you knowing this?'

'My aunt told me. She said to watch for you, you might come.'

He stares a long moment. Finally he says, 'Yes. She came back with Ramu. Her mother is so happy that late at night she is cooking all over again, mustard fish, *cholar dal* with coconut, all Geeta's favourites. We all sit around the table and talk, even I, because I have taken the medicine and feel better, though unfortunately I cannot still eat.' He clicks his tongue at the thought, all that good food gone to waste. 'Anyway, everyone is being very happy and very careful, talking of jobs and movies and cousins back in India, not to get any more anger going, I most of all. Your aunt will be proud how I am holding my tongue, not asking this or that, only making comment about American political news.

'Then just before we get up to wash our hands Ramu says Well maybe you should ask your young man to come over for a visit. And Geeta very quiet says If you wish Daddy. Ramu says Mind you don't take this as permission, and Geeta says I know. And that's all. Each goes into their bedroom but smiling.'

He looks up, that smile still caught in the folds of his face.

'I am so happy for them,' I say. 'For you too.'

'That father-daughter, so alike, so proud. I'm sure they are having many more fights.'

'As long as they don't forget the love,' I say.

'I will remind.' He taps his chest proudly.

'Without too many words, my aunt told me to tell you. And here, she said you were to have all the *brahmi* oil in the store. Keep your head cool, she said. No, no, it's a farewell gift from her.'

He watches me wrap the bottles in newspaper, place them in a sack. 'So she's really not going to come back.'

'I don't think so. But who knows what the future holds.' I strive to keep my voice light, though sorrow swells in my throat.

'You have her eyes,' he says as he turns to go. 'I did not realize all this time they are so beautiful.'

He does not ask more, this spectacled old man who sees deeper than many with perfect vision. Nor do I offer. It is our unspoken pact.

'Tell her,' he says, 'I am wishing her all happiness. I am saying a prayer for her.'

'Thank you,' I say. 'She is much in need of prayers.'

But look who comes into my store now, a young woman I've never seen, her skin the clean dark of a plum, her crinkly hair caught in a hundred tiny braids, a smile like fresh-baked bread.

'Wow, this is neat. I've never been in here.'

She is offering me something, an envelope. I hesitate and then, by her sky-colour uniform and carry-bag, the curve-beaked bird on her armband, I know. She is the mailwoman.

'My very first letter,' I say, taking it in wonder. I glance at the handwriting, but it is not known to me.

'You just get here?'

'No. In fact I'm about to leave.' I want to confide more in this friendly-faced woman, but what can I say that she – that anyone – would understand.

'It's my last day,' I tell her finally. 'I'm glad I got a letter on my last day.'

'I'm glad for you too. It took a while because this person didn't have a zip. No return address neither, or else they'd have sent it back. See.'

I look where she's pointing, but my eyes stray to the name on the letter.

Mataji.

Only one person has ever called me that.

My lungs have forgotten how to breathe. My heart hammers so hard surely it will break my body into pieces. The edges of the day curl into burned brown.

'This letter means a lot to me,' I say. 'Thank you for bringing it.'

Blindly I grope through the brown air to find something to give her. Return with a bag of golden raisins, *kismis* for energy that endures.

'From my country. A gift.'

'Thanks, that's real sweet of you.'

She is looking through her bag. For what? Why does she take so long? When will she leave so I can open the letter?

Then it strikes me that she too wishes to give something.

She finds it, hands it to me.

Thin silver rectangles all tied together with green paper, soft to the touch. The sweet fresh scent of mint rising.

'Chewing gum,' she says at my questioning look. 'Thought you might like it. Something from America, you know, for your journey.'

I hope she sees it in my eyes before she goes, my appreciation for this unasked gift, I Tilo who for once cannot think of what to say.

At the door sunshine catches on her face, as it did so long ago for Ahuja's wife.

I lock the door behind her. I need to give this letter my full attention, all the words and in between.

I unwrap a stick of gum, fold it into my mouth. The

generous sweetness on my tongue gives me the courage to read.

Mataji.
Namaste.

I don't have your full address so I don't know if this letter will ever get to you, but I have heard the U.S. postal system is a good one, so I will hope. Because I want so much for you to know.

I am not at home anymore. I am in another city, though I am not allowed to say where for safety reasons.

All this happened one week ago although I have thought and thought of it for months.

You know that magazine you gave me? In the back were notices. One said, If you are a battered woman, call this number for help. I looked at it for a long time. One minute I would think Why not. Next minute I would think Chee chee, what sharam to tell strangers your husband is beating you. Finally I threw the magazine in the pile of old papers he takes to the dump for money end of every month.

I decided to try one more time. Put the past behind. How much choice did I have. I told him, Why not I go see the doctor and see what is wrong, why I am not becoming a mother.

He had no objection. Even the money he was willing to spend. Maybe he too thought a baby will make things better, tie us in a shared love. OK, he said, as long as it is a lady doctor. Indian is better.

I didn't find an Indian doctor but the American lady said everything was fine with me. It could well be your husband, she said. Maybe his sperm count is low. Have him come in for a checkup. Tell him not to worry. Plenty of things can be done nowadays, easy.

But when I told him this, his face turned dark as the monsoon sky. The veins in his forehead were like blue knots. What are you saying, he said, I'm not a man? You want to look for someone better? He started shaking me so hard I could hear the bones in my neck make snapping sounds.

Please, I said, I'm sorry, my fault, let us forget it, you do not have to go anywhere.

He slapped me hard, two, three times. This is all part of your plan, no? Get the American doctor on your side?

He pulled me to the bedroom, threw me on the bed. Take off your clothes, he said. I'll show you whether I'm a man or not.

Mataji I was so terrified my hands went to the buttons of my sari-blouse, like usual. Then I remembered what you said, No man, husband or not, has the right to force me to his bed.

I sat up. One part of my mind said, He will kill you for this. One part said, How can that be any worse. I forced my voice to tell him, I will not go to bed with a man who beats me.

For a moment he stood surprised like a stone. Then he said, Oh yeah? We'll see. He lunged forward, grabbed the front of my blouse and tore it. I can still hear the ripping sound, like it was my life.

I cannot write what else he did to me. It is too shameful. But in a way it was also good. It broke my last hesitation, my fear of hurting my parents. I lay there afterward, listening to him crying, begging my forgiveness, putting ice compresses on my face, saying, Why do you make me do these things. When he *fell asleep I went in the shower and stood under hot water scrubbing, even the bruises, till my skin felt as if it would come off. I watched the dirty water being sucked down the drain and knew I had to leave. If my parents do not love me enough to understand, I thought, then so be it.*

Next morning he told me not to go out anywhere, he'd take a half-day, be back at lunch with a surprise for me. I knew his surprises, jewellery, saris, things we can't afford. Him believing they would make me forget. It made me ill to think I'd have to wear them for him. As soon as his car turned the street I went to the old paper pile. At first I couldn't find the magazine. I was so scared. I thought somehow he'd seen it and thrown it away, that I would have to live with him forever.

I went through the pile again. My head was feeling dizzy, I was so nervous he'd come back early. When I found it I started crying. I could hardly talk when I phoned.

The woman on the line was very kind. She was Indian like me, she understood a lot without my telling. She said I was right to call, they would help me if I was sure of what I wanted to do.

I packed a bag, took my passport, some wedding jewellery that was in the house, whatever money I could find. I didn't want to touch anything of his, but I knew I'd have to survive.

Two women picked me up at the bus stop. They drove me to this house in another town.

I don't know what I'll do now, Mataji. They've given me lots of books to read. My rights. Stories of other women like me who now lead better lives. Stories of women who went back and were beaten to death. They tell me if I want to file a police case they'll help me. Also they can help me set up a small tailoring business if I like. They warn me things won't be easy.

There are other women here. Some cry all the time. Some don't talk at all. They're afraid to press charges, afraid to leave this place. One woman had her skull fractured with a wrench. Sometimes I hear her praying, He Ram, forgive me for leaving my husband. *I can't even pray. Who shall I ask to bless me? Ram, who banished poor pregnant Sita to the forest because of what people might say? Even our gods are cruel to their wives.*

Somedays I'm afraid too. And so depressed. I look at the room I share with two women, all of us living out of suitcases. I have no place to be alone. One bathroom in the house for six of us, underwear hanging everywhere. The smell of monthly blood. I think of my neat home. And then my mind plays tricks, reminds me of the happy moments, how sometimes he could be so kind, how he would bring video movies and pizza on Friday nights, how we would sit on the sofa watching Dev Anand, laughing.

There are voices in my head every day. They whisper, He's learned his lesson, things will be different now, would it be so bad to go back?

I try to push them away. I remember what you said to me just before I left. I tell myself, I deserve dignity, I deserve happiness.

Mataji, pray for me that I will remain strong enough to find it.

Yours,
Lalita

The letter blurs as I clench it in my hands. Are these tears of sorrow or of joy. Yes my Lalita, coming at last into your own, I am praying for you. O spices, O all the forces of the world, do not let her give up. Daughter, the birth passage is always narrow, suffocating. But that first free gulp of air filling the lungs, ah. I pray it for you.

Meanwhile, I will pound almond and *chyavanprash* for mental strength and physical and set it outside the door for the wind to carry to the woman-house where you wait. I will do it now, in the thinning sliver of time left to me.

I open the door to set out the *chyavanprash* and there he is on the step, his face startling-close to mine, Jagjit in a jacket of real leather, looking through the milky glass at the poster of Kwesi's One World Dojo. Jagjit whose homeboys call him Jag.

Thank you spices I had let go of hope.

He snarls backward, Jag short for Jaguar, his hand going for his pocket, then steadies.

'Hey lady, shouldn't creep up on a dude like that. You might get hurt.'

I smile, think of telling him, *It's my doorstep after all.* But is that any longer true.

'You scared me too,' I say instead.

'Scared, who said anything about being scared?' Silver glint of an earring as he tosses his head. Then he takes a closer look through the dusk-light. 'Wait a minute. You're not the old woman who owns the store.' His eyes hold new interest, Jagjit not yet fourteen growing up so fast in America.

I tell him the niece story. Then I say, 'But I know who *you* are.'

'How come?'

'My aunt told me to look for you. Said, That Jagjit is one fine young fellow, lot of potential. Could become anything in the world he wants.'

'She said that?' For a moment his face is boyishly pleased, then the shadows take it back again. His thoughts are full of violent sounds.

Jagjit world conqueror, what have you been doing, who have you—

Haroun's face pale in bandages flashes in front of me but no it cannot be I will not think it.

Tilo sooner or later it will happen, the path he is going.

'You want to buy something?' I ask. I want him inside the store. I point to the sale signs. 'Today's a good day for it. Maybe your mother needs?' But already I know he no longer shops for his mother.

'Nah. I was just passing by, don't even know why I stopped. Maybe it was the poster.' He jerks his chin at it.

'You like karate?' Spices, make it happen make it happen.

He shrugs. 'Never tried it. Costs too much to keep up. Besides, I got other things to do. Gotta go now.'

His feet are already turned toward the night alleys.

I think fast, I who am not good at this. And then it strikes me.

'Oh, I almost forgot. My aunt left something for you.'

'She did?'

'Yes. She said it was very important. I'll find it for you if you come in.'

He hesitates. 'I ain't got the time.' But then curiosity pulls at him, Jagjit who is still just a boy. 'Only for a minute.'

'Only for a minute,' I say. In my mind I am already in the inner room. Stapling the ends of the money-sack, writing the note to go with it.

'Do you think I did the right thing?' I will ask Raven later as we lie in bed. 'It seemed the perfect solution then, all that money which would otherwise be wasted. But now I'm not so sure.'

Crease of doubt between his brows as well. But he wants me to be happy. So he will say, 'I think you did the best thing possible.'

Still, misgiving will gnaw at me.

'There was more than a thousand dollars in that sack. What if he uses it for something bad, you know, drugs, weapons, instead of taking it to Kwesi's and enrolling.'

'Trust,' he will say. 'Trust in him, trust in the universe. It's a fifty-fifty chance. More than you and I had of ever meeting.' He will lift my hand from the coverlet, kiss each fingertip.

I will rub his jaw, the slight prickle of beard, the clean lime smell. He's right.

'Think of his face. What kind of look was on it when he opened the package? When he walked out the door?'

I will remember Jagjit's not-believing eyes. 'For *me*?' How he re-reads the note over and over.

'You know what it says?' he asks.

'No. Will you read it to me?' I say, lying shamelessly.

'It says, *For Jagjit my world conqueror, to start a new life over*. And underneath, *Use power, don't be used by it*.'

'Sounds good to me. This aunt of mine, she is wise,' I smile. Then I take down the poster from the door, give it to him. 'Go for it,' I say.

His eyes hold a new shine, visions of impossibly high kicks, edge of the hand breaking a brick in two. Kiais fierce enough to shatter the walls of an opponent's heart, katas delicate and precise as a dance. Fame and fortune, perhaps the movies, like Bruce Lee. An escape from now into for ever.

But also a worry. Jagjit who already knows that the way back is twice as long. Blockaded with steel blades where there were none before.

'I don't know if my homies will let me.'

I give him a bag of *laddus, besan* and rock sugar, for protection. For resolve that does not crumble. I tell him, '*How will you know unless you try*, that is what Aunt would say.'

He gives me his smile, a little scared but open and full also. 'Tell her thanks. Tell her I'm going to give it my best shot.'

'I trust,' I will whisper from Raven's bed on my last night, seeing again Jagjit vanishing into night-milk fog, my prayer my hope, the only thing left that I can do. 'Jagjit, I trust you will.'

Lotus Root

At last the day is over, the customers gone, everything in the shop sold or given away except what I will need for Shampati's fire.

Shampati's fire, blue flame green ember, the sound of blazing not unlike the sound of rain, what will you do to this body given me by the spices. Where will you take this heart I have promised back to them.

And pain. Will there be—

Stop. Time enough for that later. Now the moment is ripe for the seed you not-knowing plucked that day in the Sears store, to plant here and water every night from the unending river of desire.

I put on the white dress Raven gave me, all foam and flower-scent falling over slimness of waist and hip, all whisper and glide around my bare legs. I fill a small silk sachet with dust of lotus root, herb of long loving. Tie it on a silk cord around my neck so the sachet lies between my breasts that smell of ripe mangoes.

Now I am ready. I go to the back where it hangs on the wall, remove the covering from it, I Tilo who have broken too many rules to count.

How many lifetimes since I looked into one.

Mirror what will you reveal of myself.

I am dazzled by the face looking back at me, young and ageless at once, the fantasy of fantasies come to life, spice power at its fullest. Forehead flawless like a new opened *shapla* leaf, nose tipped like the *til* flower. Mouth curved as the bow of Madan, god of love, lips colour of – there are no other words for this – crushed red chillies. For kisses that will burn and consume.

It is a face that gives away nothing, a goddess-face free of mortal blemish, distant as an Ajanta painting. Only the eyes are human, frail. In them I see Nayan Tara, I see Bhagyavati, I see the Tilo who was. Wide elated eyes, but also telling me something I did not expect.

Can beauty frighten? I see in my eyes that mine terrifies me.

And now at the door, knocking.

I move as through deep water, I who have waited all my life – though I see it only now – for this brief moment blossoming like fireworks in a midnight sky. My whole body trembles, desire and fear, because it is not for Raven alone I am doing this but for myself also. And yet.

With my hand on the doorknob I freeze.

O Tilo what if the real night falls short (as surely it must) of the imagined one. What if this love of man and woman, lip to lip body to body heart to heart is less than—

'Tilo,' he calls from the other side. 'Open.'

But when I do, it is he that stands frozen. Until I cup my hands around his face and say with gentleness, 'Raven it is only I.'

At last he says, 'I had not dared to dream such beauty. I do not dare to touch it.'

I take his arms and place them around me, half laughing half dismayed. 'Does the body make such a difference? Can you not see I am still the same Tilo?'

He looks some more. Then his arms tighten. 'Yes,' he says against my waterfall hair. 'I see it in your eyes.'

'Then take me with you Raven. Love me.' And inside my heart I add, O don't waste time.

*

But there is one last thing for me to do.

Raven brings his car to a smooth halt. Eyes the dark stairwell darkly.

'You sure you don't want me to come?'

I nod, clench closer to my breasts the package I am carrying. I push from my mind what he would say if he knew its contents.

All the way up the spiral of stairs smelling like old socks, a voice like a rusty nail scratching inside my skull. Is it the First Mother's is it mine. Is there anymore a difference.

Tilo do you know what you are doing.

I set my teeth against that voice because I do not really. Because from time to time imagining this moment I have been struck dizzy with the fear that it is all wrong. But this is what I say aloud: 'Violence for violence. Sometimes that is the only way.'

When I push at Haroun's door it opens. I am glad for it but also angry that he is not more careful. Haroun haven't you learned yet.

His room is full of still, dark shapes. His bed, his body, a pitcher of water, an unlit table lamp, a book someone has been reading to him. Only his bandages shine like a warning. The oval of his head is turned away. I think he sleeps.

I am reluctant to wake him into pain, but I must.

'Haroun.'

At the whisper he moves a little, as in a dream.

'Ladyjaan.' His tongue staggers on the word, but there is pleasure in it.

'How do you know it is me,' I ask in amazement.

'It is how you call my name,' he says, his voice tired but smiling through the darkness. 'Even though your voice is different today, sweeter stronger.'

'Are you OK? Has the doctor been by again?'

'Yes. He is being very kind, and also Shamsur-*saab* and his sister.' His voice lifts a little on the last word. 'They are not taking one penny from me. She is cooking all meals, changing bandages, sitting by my bed telling stories to keep me company.'

Ah Hameeda. It is as I hoped.

'Haroun, are you not angry at what happened?'

'*Ai* Ladyjaan.' His mouth grows razor-thin as he speaks. 'Of course I am. If I catch those bastard pigs, those *shaitaans*—' He is silent for a moment, replaying the past, imagining the future. Then he takes a deep breath. 'But also I have been lucky. Left eye is a little blurry still, but Doctor-*saab* says by Allah's grace and his skill it will be good as new. And I have found such friends – like family they are. Even Hameeda Begum's little girl with her voice like a mynah bird. Already we are planning to go to the circus as soon as I get better.'

'Haroun I came to say good-bye.'

He tries to struggle up. 'Where are you going?' His fingers grope for the bedside lamp.

'No Haroun no.'

But he has switched it on already. He draws in his breath sharply, presses his hand against the sudden pain in his ribs.

'Lady what *jaadu* is this, and why?'

I am blushing under his gaze. I have no words that he will not think frivolous. But Haroun with his heart new-opened understands more than I hoped.

'Ah.' The word is his compassion but his concern also. 'And after? Where will you go? What of the store?'

'I don't know,' I say, and the fear is a salt wave I am once more drowning in. 'I think I am returning home, Haroun, but is there ever a way back.'

He holds my hand in his, Haroun comforter, our roles reversed.

'Not for me, Ladyjaan. But for you – who knows? I will do a *dua* to Allah for your happiness.'

'I have here something for you. And then I must leave.'

'Wait simply two minutes, Ladyjaan. Hameeda is coming back as soon as she gets cooking done. Special tonight, goat curry with *parathas*. She is so good in cooking, all spices nicely mixed, you will certainly like.' I hear the glad pride in his voice. 'She will be so pleased to see you again. We will be honoured if you stay and eat with us.'

Then he asks, my curious Haroun, 'What have you brought me?'

And suddenly I know what I must do. And am glad of it, like a person on a night precipice who just before taking the last step sees, lightning-etched, the fatal edge.

'Actually it is for Hameeda, for you both together.'

I push the bundle which had once been red chillies behind me. Then I reach around my neck and lift out the sachet of lotus root. Put it in his hands.

If regret wisps over my heart (O Raven) like a snatch of fog, I pay it no mind.

'She must wear it on the night of your *nikah*,' I say, 'for a lifetime of passionate loving.'

Now he is the one who blushes.

'Give her my *mubaarak*,' I say from the door. 'And Haroun. Be careful.'

'Yes, Ladyjaan. I have learned my foolishness. Hameeda too is scolding me about same thing. No more late-night work, no going in dangerous neighbourhoods, no taking customers that I get a bad feeling for. Also I will keep in front seat a baseball bat. Shamsur is getting it for me already.'

He waves me *Khuda hafiz*, Haroun who has so much

to live for, for whom the immigrant dream has come true in a way he never thought.

'You were gone for ever,' says Raven. In the muted street-lamp his eyes accuse me just a little. 'How come you look so glowing?'

'*Raven!*' I am laughing, remembering the bougainvillaea girls. 'Are you jealous?'

'Can you blame me? Look at you.' He touches my cheek. Pulls me to him for a long breath-stopping kiss, nuzzles my throat, Raven learning the contours of my body. Then he grows serious. 'It's more like – I know this sounds foolish – but I feel like you might disappear any minute. Like we have only a little time.' He draws back to fix his gaze on mine. 'Tell me it's foolish.'

'Foolish,' I say, looking down at my fingers, their shell-pink glow.

'Hey. You still have that package. I thought that's why you came here, to give it to your friend.'

'I changed my mind. Raven. Will you take me to one more place.'

He sighs. 'Woman, don't do this to me.'

'It'll take just a few minutes.'

'Oh very well. Try to be quick, OK?'

When he turns off the engine I kiss his eyes, let my lips linger over the brows, the soft hollows beneath. 'To keep you till I return,' I say.

He groans. 'I think I just ran out of patience.'

I laugh with the power of it, I who can for the first time in all my lives make a man speak this way.

The dim-lit pier seems very long, the water very black, the package very heavy. Or is the weight in my heart. My breath is a jerking in my chest. I fear I will never reach the end.

Unbidden, that old longing comes to me again. *Snakes, are you—*

The words are a tumble of snowflakes in a car's head-lamps, gone already. I know this is not the time.

Spices I am sorry, I say, standing at the water's inky edge. But finally I think I have done right. It is best for Haroun to live a life of love, not hate and hurting which brings only more of its kind.

You should have thought that before, Tilo. Their voice comes from nowhere and everywhere, as in a trickster play. *Now you have roused us, we must work our power. Something must be destroyed. You tell us what.*

Spices I am singing the chant of propitiation. Can you not this once travel the path of forgiveness.

The world does not work that way, foolish Mistress who thinks she can roll up the falling waterfall, can make the forest fire suck in its blaze-red tongue. Or as that man waiting in his car would say, hold again in your hands the bird already flown.

Leave him out of this, spices, this is between you and me.

The package in my hand glows with heat. Or is it rage. *Tilo who should not have played with forces beyond your understanding, the destruction you have set in motion will touch every life around you. The entire city will shake with it.*

There is no more then to say, I tell them, my lips dry with a sudden fear I would shake off but cannot. I lower the package into the water, let it go. It sinks slowly, incandescent. When finally it has disappeared I let out my breath. And this is what I say before I turn to walk the long way back.

Spices start with my life if you must. Take me first. Spend your hate on me.

Tilo how little you have understood. From the deep the voice is a hiss, like water on hot iron. Or is it a sigh. *Like the waterfall the avalanche the forest fire, we do not hate. We only do what we must.*

Raven lives on the topmost floor of a building that seems to me the tallest in the world. It is walled with glass. As the elevator rises we see falling away beneath us the entire glittering city. Almost it is like flying.

He throws the door open with a flourish. 'Welcome to my home.' There is a slight tremble to his voice. I am amazed to realize he is nervous, my American. Deep in me, a surging. Love and a new desire, to reassure this man.

'It's beautiful,' I say, and it is. Light wells around us, though from where it comes I cannot tell. Soft white carpet into which my feet sink ankle deep. Wide low sofas of smooth white leather. A coffee table that is a simple oval of glass. One large painting on a wall, swirling with sunrise colours, or is it the beginning of the world. In the corner, under a large ficus, the statue of an *apsara*. I kneel to touch the sharp-honed features. It is not unlike touching my own face.

In the bedroom, the same understated luxury, the same surprising spareness. A bed covered with an embroidered silk bedspread, white on white. A lamp. One large bookshelf filled to the top with books that have been read late into the sleeping hours. The outer wall is all glass. Through it I can see lights, tiny yellow holes punched into the night-time, then the dark swatch of the Bay. The only decoration in the room is a batik of Buddha, lotus hand raised in compassion.

Playboy Raven, my American of the party scene, I never would have guessed this.

As though in answer he says, 'I've been redoing things, throwing out a lot of my old junk, picturing you here. Do you like it?'

'Yes.' My voice is low. I am humbled that someone should build his home around his imagination of me. And guilt-filled because.

'Although it doesn't really matter, does it,' he adds, 'since pretty soon we'll be gone.'

'Yes, soon,' I say through stiff lips.

Raven turns off the lamp. In the cool silver moonlight I feel his breath behind me, smelling of almonds and peaches. He twines his arms around my waist. His lips against my ear, his whisper warm as skin.

'Tilo.'

I close my eyes. He is kissing my shoulders, my neck, little kisses on each separate nub of the backbone. He is turning me to him, unbuttoning my dress and letting it fall in a silken swirl to my feet. His hands move like doves over my body.

'Tilo, look at me, touch me too.'

I am too shy to open my eyes but I slip my hand under his shirt. His skin is firm and smooth everywhere except at the collarbone, where there is a small puckered scar, vestige of some long-ago fight. It rouses in me a tenderness I am amazed by, I who have always craved the power of perfection and find now that human frailty has its own power too. I kiss it and hear the breath sharp in his throat. Then his lips are everywhere, his tongue, teasing, drawing me out of myself. I Tilo who never thought I would learn the ways of pleasure so surprising-fast, pleasure that flows over the body like warm honey, fingertips, toes, each pore of the skin.

We are in bed now, the walls fallen away, the stars shining in our hair. He lifts me on top, lets my hair cover his face like a song of water. 'This way, dear one.'

But I know already. *Makaradwaj* kingspice tells me what to do so that Raven laughs low in his throat, '*Tilo!*' then gasps and shudders.

The voice of the spice is in my ears, *Use everything. Mouth and hand, yes, nails and teeth, flutter of eyelash against his skin, that special look in your eye. Give and take back, teasing. As did the great courtesans in the courts of Indra the godking.*

Let him be discoverer of the land that you are, mountain and lake and cityscape. Let him carve out roads where none went before. Let him enter finally where you are deepest and most unknown, thick vines, jaguar cry, the dizzying odour of rajanigandha, *the wild tuberose, flower of the bridal night. For isn't love the illusion that you will open yourselves totally to each other, suffering no distance to be kept.*

O *makaradwaj*, why do you say *illusion*. I am willing to give this man all my secrets, my past and my present both.

And your future? Will you tell him when your loving is done that this first time is also the last? Will you tell him of Shampati's fire?

'Tilo,' cries Raven urgently, pulling my hips into him, again, again, bone to bone, till I feel the hot release take us both. Till we are one body and many bodies and no body all at once.

It is then I feel the sadness, a heat forsaking my skin like the last colour forsakes the evening sky, making me shiver. A part of me dying, a receding song I feel in every hollowed bone, every brittled hair, every limb slumping toward its old shape. Does Raven feel it too.

Is it the spices, leaving me?

Tilo don't think of it now.

For now let us lie holding each other under this bed-spread white as faithfulness, our breath slowing. For a moment his arms circling me are a battlement time cannot storm. Mouth against mouth we whisper sleepily, little endearments that make no sense unless you are hearing with the heart. Smell of love-sweat on his skin. The rhythm of his blood that I already know as intimately as my own.

This tenderness after desire is spent, what can be sweeter.

Just before I fall into dreaming I hear him say, 'Tilo, dear one, I can't believe we'll be together for a lifetime of such nights.' But I am too deep in the dreaming waters to answer.

You who have more knowledge than me of loving, I ask you this: Do you, sleeping in your lover's arms, dream his dreams? For that is what I see behind my closed lids. Red-barked sequoia and innocent blue eucalyptus, squirrels with their silk-brown eyes. A land to grow into, to be transformed by. Its winter of chill caves and smoky fires, its waterfalls frozen into soundlessness. Its summers of gritty earth under our bare feet, under our bare backs as we make love in fields of wild poppies.

Raven I know now you are right, the place you call earthly paradise *is* somewhere waiting. And so I ache more wanting it, knowing that I will never go there with you, I Tilo whose time is running out.

He stirs with a groan as though he is hearing my thought. He murmurs a word that sounds like *fire*.

I stiffen. My American, are you dreaming *my* dream?

He emerges from sleep for a moment to offer me an unfocused smile, to nuzzle my shoulder, my throat. 'My tropical blossom,' he says. 'My mysterious Indian beauty.' Then he is gone again, unaware that I have drawn back.

American, it is good you remind me, I Tilo who was at the point of losing myself in you. You have loved me for the colour of my skin, the accent of my speaking, the quaintness of my customs which promised you the magic you no longer found in the women of your own land. In your yearning you have made me into that which I am not.

I do not blame you too much. Perhaps I have done the same with you. But how can the soil of misconception nurture the seedling of love? Even without the spices standing guard between us, we would have failed. And who can tell if we would have come to hate each other.

It is better this way.

The thought gives me strength to tear my reluctant body from his warmth. To do what I must before he wakes.

In a kitchen drawer I find paper and pencil. Begin.

The note takes a long time. My fingers are numb. My disobedient eyes wish to weep. My mind brings forth love-words only. But at last I am done. I open the bathroom cabinet, wrap the note around the tube of paste where Raven will find it tomorrow morning.

Then I wake him.

We have a disagreement, our first lovers' quarrel. (*And our last*, says the voice in my head.)

I must return to the store, I tell Raven. He is upset. Why can't we stay together till morning, make love once more in early light? He will bring me breakfast in bed.

O Raven if you knew how much I would love—

But by dawn, when Shampati's fire will blaze whether I wish it or not, I must be far from him.

I make my voice cold, tell him I need to be alone, think things through.

'Are you tired of me already?'

Raven, Raven, I cry inside.

I tell him there's something urgent that needs to be done which I cannot explain.

His mouth sets in a line of hard hurting. 'I thought we were to have no more secrets. That we were to share our life, all of it, from now. Isn't that what you just promised me with your body?'

'Please, Raven.'

'And what of our special place? Aren't we going to look for it together?'

'What's the hurry?' I am amazed at the calm deceit of my voice even as my stomach tightens and churns.

'We shouldn't waste any more time,' Raven's voice is urgent, 'now that we've found each other. You of all people should know how uncertain life is, how fragile.'

In my ears the blood beats an echo, *fragile, fragile*. Outside his window the stars are hurtling dizzily toward morning.

'OK,' I say to Raven finally, I who am too cowardly to watch the truth shatter in his eyes. 'Come back in the morning and I'll go with you.' Under my breath I add, 'If I'm still there.'

I know I will not be.

*

We drive in silence. Raven, still displeased, fiddles with the dial of his radio. The animals in the Oakland zoo have been acting strange, crying and calling all evening, states a late-night newscaster. A singer with a voice like reeds in wind informs us that if we travel faster than the speed of sound, we must expect to get burned.

Shampati's fire, how fast will I travel, how brightly will I burn.

I am seeing the note as Raven will see it in the morning, stumbling into the bathroom, his sleep-filled eyes still imprinted with the shape of my lips. Eyes that in surprise he will open, shaking the wool of dreams from them.

Raven forgive me, the note will say. *I do not expect you to understand. Only to believe that I had no choice. I thank you for all you have given me. I hope I have given you a little too. Our love would never have lasted, for it was based upon fantasy, yours and mine, of what it is to be Indian. To be American. But where I am going – life or death, I do not know which – I will carry its brief aching sweetness. For ever.*

Sesame

I do not unlock the door of the spice shop until after Raven has roared away. I am afraid of what retribution I will find for this last act, love snatched in a way a Mistress never should.

But everything is as I left it. I laugh. Almost I feel let down. All this time I have been a worryheart for no reason at all. It will be as the First Mother said – I will step into Shampati's fire, wake on the island to take up her load. O, there will be punishment, I do not doubt that. Perhaps a scorching branded on my skin to make me always remember, perhaps (for I feel it changing already, the bones gnarling back) a body older and uglier, with all such a body's pains.

I walk the emptied aisles, saying good-bye, remembering the moments. Here Haroun first offered me his palm to read, here Ahuja's wife leaned admiring over a sari coloured like the silken heart of a papaya. Here Jagjit stood behind his mother, innocent in his turban green as parrots. But already their names are slipping from me, their faces, even this sadness of forgetting muted, as though I were long gone already.

Raven will I forget you too.

Only after I am halfway across the store do I sense it, subtle, like the shift of light and shade in a night sky when a star has gone out. The old Tilo would have known it at once.

The shop is a shell only. Whatever was in it giving heat and breath has long left.

Spices what does this mean.

But I have no leisure to ponder it now. The third day is ending. I hear the planets spinning faster, the hours hurled like rocks through the sky. There is barely time to prepare Shampati's fire.

I bring all that is left in the store – spices, *dals*, sacks of *atta* and rice and *bajra* – and make a pyre in the centre of the room. Over it all I sprinkle my name-spice, sesame, grainy *til* to coat and protect me through my long journey. I let fall the white dress, shivering a little. I must take nothing from this life, go from America naked as I came into it.

Now I am ready. I dip my hands in turmeric, spice of rebirth with which I began this story, and pick up the stone jar that had held the chillies. I sit in lotus asana on the pyre of spices (but already my limbs are groaning a protest) and for the last time I open the jar. I draw my mind back from all that I have loved, and as it empties (is this what death is like) I feel a surprising peace.

I hold up the single chilli I had left in the jar for this moment, and speak the invoking words.

Come Shampati, take me now.

First Mother, are you at this very moment singing the song of welcome, the song to help my soul through the layers, bone and steel and forbidding word, that separate the two worlds. Or have you in illness or perhaps disappointment let me fall from your mind.

Fear beats against my ears like a storm-scared bird. Any moment now the flames—

But nothing happens.

I wait, then say the words again. And again. Louder each time.

Nothing.

I am sobbing the words, trying other chants, even the smallest magic, please, please.

Nothing still.

Spices what are you doing what teasing trick is this.

No answer.

Spices, in my mind I am gone already, plummeting through space and time, my skin grazed by meteors, my hair on fire. Don't prolong my agony, I beg you, I Tilo humbled at last and terrified, as you wanted.

Silence more profound than ever I have heard it, even the planets ground to a halt.

And in that silence I see the spices' punishment.

They have left me here, alone and reft of magic. For me there will be no Shampati's fire.

Shampati's fire, which I have feared for so long. Now suddenly I fear more my life without it.

Ah beautiful body in whose veins already the blood grows thick and sluggish, I see it now. I am doomed to live in this pitiless world as an old woman, without power, without livelihood, without a single being to whom I can turn.

O spices who know so well my deepest weakness, pride, it is the perfect sentence. For how can I go to those I helped, who feared and admired me all this while, who loved me for all I gave, as this naked eroded self. How can I stand the pity in their eyes, and under it the revulsion as I hold out my begging hand.

Raven, especially you I can never face this way.

So. My life lies twisting in front of me like the alleys I will inhabit, toothless and smelling of the body's wastes, hiding my face from all who might know me, pushing the weight of my life in a stolen cart, sleeping in doorways and praying that one night someone—

Every fibre of my aching body cries, *Better to climb the redgold girders of the bridge, to feel the dark water closing overhead, seaweed winding around the limbs, sinuous as snakes. Better to be done with it at once.*

No.

Spices, I Tilo accept your decree. In spite of terror and heartbreak, the loneliness of love lost and power turned to ash, I take it upon myself to live this way as long as I must.

For ever, if you so decide.

This is my atonement. Willingly I undergo it. Not because I have sinned, for I acted out of love, in which is no sinning. Were I to do it over, I would do the same again. Step across the forbidden threshold of the store to take Geeta in her glittering tower mango pickles and re-assurance. Hold Lalita's hand steadfast in mine and tell her she is deserving of joy. I would give again to Haroun lotus root for a love that is worth more than his immigrant dream. And again, yes, I would make myself as ravishing as Tilottama, dancer of the gods, for Raven's pleasure.

But I know that rules broken must be paid for. Balance upset must be restored. For one to be happy, another must take upon herself the suffering.

A tale comes to me from my forgotten childhood: in the start of the world, searching for the nectar of immortality, the gods and demons churned up *halahal*, bitterest poison from the primal ocean. Its fumes covered the earth, and all creatures, dying, cried out their terror. Then the great Shiva took in his cupped hands the *halahal* and drank it. The dreadful poison burned in his throat, turning it a bruised blue that remains to this day. Ah, even for a god it must have been painful. But the world was saved.

I Tilo am no goddess but an ordinary woman only. Yes, I admit it, this truth I have tried to escape all my life. And though once I thought I could save the world, I see now that I have only brought brief happiness into a few lives.

And yet, is that not enough.

Spices, for their sake I will take on whatever burden you wish to lay on me. Only give me an hour of sleep. One hour of oblivion so I do not have to watch this body twist back into misshapenness. One hour of rest, sheltered from the thorn-fingered world that waits for me, for I am tired and yes, afraid.

The spices do not say no.

Thus I lie down, for the last time, in the centre of the store of which I am no longer Mistress.

I wake to a faraway voice, carrying distress as the wind carries dust, carrying my name. It seems only moments since I slept. But I am no longer sure of anything.

The voice calls again. *Tilo Tilo Tilo.*

Is it not one I know, and love?

I start to my feet so fast it dizzies me. The floor tilts up, the flat of a huge hand that wishes to fling me off. A sound all around me like tearing, is it my heart.

No. See, it is this shop built of spice-spell, cracking apart like eggshells around me. The walls shake like paper, the ceiling snaps in two, the floor rises like a wave bringing me to my knees.

Ah spices, you need not have wrested my last refuge so rudely from me, I who was gathering the courage to leave.

Then a word comes to me. *Earthquake.*

Before I can think it fully, the ground jerks and shudders again. Something flies through the air – is it the stone jar is it a slab of mirror – to shatter against my temple. Red stars explode in my skull. Or are they seeds of chillies.

But even as I plunge into pain I know with hopelessness that it will not kill me.

Maya

I am wrong again.

I am dead.

Or have I waked too early, on my way to afterlife.

O Tilo (but this is no more my name), trust you to fail this too.

For what else can this place be, warm as a womb and as dark, throbbing with power as it surges through the void.

I try movement to see if it is possible. My limbs are wrapped in something silk soft – is it my death-garment, or my birthing sheet. But I can turn my head, a little.

The panther of pain has been lying in wait. It pounces, making me cry out.

It seems unjust that there should be so much pain even in afterlife.

Tilo who is no longer Tilo, since when have you known enough to judge the universe, whether it is just or not.

'Since never, I admit it,' I say. My voice is rusty with disuse.

'Are you awake?' asks a voice. 'Does it hurt a lot?'

Raven.

Is he dead too? Did the earthquake kill us all, Haroun and Hameeda, Geeta and her grandfather, Kwesi, Jagjit, Lalita just opening into newness in another town?

O don't let it be so.

'Can you move?' asks Raven's voice, coming from somewhere to the side of the swollen stiffness that is my head.

I put out my hand toward the sound and touch a wall of fur. The lining of a sarcophagus, I think, a communal sarcophagus where lovers are buried, their dust left to mingle till world's end. Only, this one is flying through galaxies, swerving to dodge meteor showers that streak us with sudden light.

Then I hear a long, angry beep.

'Wish people would watch where they're driving,' Raven says. 'It's been this way ever since the quake, everyone acting crazy.'

'I'm in your car,' I say. The words fall from my mouth like flat pebbles. They do not express the wonder I feel. I touch my wrappings. 'This is your bedspread,' I say. Even in darkness I can feel the raised threads, the intricate design, silk on silk.

'That's right. Do you think you can sit up? There are some clothes near your head. You can put them on. Only if you want to, of course.'

I hold on to the smile in his voice. It spreads in me like underwater light, gives me strength as haltingly I unwind myself from the bedspread. My head is a chunk of concrete balanced precariously on my aching shoulders. The heavy silk fabric keeps slipping from my awkward hands which have forgotten a hand's duties.

Or is it that I wish to delay for as long as possible the baring of this decrepit body.

Gingerly I touch. Having known beauty, how much harder will it be this time to accustom myself to ugliness. And that thought which I cannot bear to face yet: Carrying me to his car, as he must have, what did Raven see. What did he feel.

But what is this. Against my fingers the flesh is not prune-dry, nor the hair thinned to balding. The breasts sag a little, the waist is not slim, but this is not a body quenched of all its fragrance.

How can it be.

I touch again to make sure. Arc of calf, triangle of cheekbone, column of throat. No mistake. This is not a body in youth's first roseglow, but not one in age's last unflowering either.

Spices this game is beyond my comprehension. Why have you not punished me. Or is this your doing First Mother. But why this kindness to an erring daughter who does not deserve.

My questions spiral up and up into the night. And it seems to me that after a moment an answer floats down, whisper soft, or is it only what I wish to hear.

Mistress who was, when you accepted our punishment in your heart without battling it, that was enough. Having readied your mind to suffer, you did not need to undergo that suffering in body also.

Raven's voice pulls me from the whirlpool of my thoughts.

'If you feel up to it you can climb between the seats and come sit up here by me.'

I slide awkwardly into the front seat, glancing quick at Raven, who looks the same as ever. I am self-conscious in my new clothes – a pair of jeans that I must hold up with a belt cinched tight around my waist. A too-large flannel shirt which smells of Raven's hair. Different, indeed, from that dress of moonlight and gossamer at our last meeting. Fortunately it is dark in the car – darker than I remember.

I wonder why. Then I notice that most of the street-lights we are passing have burned out.

'Tell me what happened.' This voice, hesitant and husky – I cannot think of it yet as mine.

What else is different, Tilo who once was.

'After I dropped you off I couldn't sleep,' says Raven. 'I was too upset. I started to pack for the trip. I'll go alone, I said to myself, if she won't. But I knew I didn't mean it. Even at the height of my anger I couldn't imagine a future without you.'

His words flow like honey wine through my body, warming me. But even as I listen, my eyes are on his rearview mirror. When he stops at a crossroad I turn it toward me.

'I need to look,' I say. My voice trembles a little, apologetic.

Raven nods, his eyes full of compassion.

She is different, the woman in the mirror. High cheekbones, straight brows with crease lines between. Some grey hair. Not particularly pretty or ugly, not particularly young or old. Just ordinary.

And I who have through my many existences recoiled from ordinariness or rushed toward it longing, see that it is neither as hateful as I thought, nor as full of quaint charm. It is itself, and I accept it, I who was lovely Tilottama for one night only.

The only regret in my heart is for what Raven seeing me must feel.

'You know,' says Raven who has been watching my face, 'this is more like how I always imagined you.' He touches my cheek with a gentle finger.

'You're being kind,' I say stiffly. I do not want his pity.

'No, really.' His voice says *please believe me*.

'You don't mind? All that beauty gone?'

'No, at first I thought I might, but I don't. Frankly, it was a bit intimidating. I felt like I had to stand tall all the time, suck in my stomach. Things like that.'

We both laugh the brittle, lightheaded laughter of people who have not slept enough, who have nearly died, who have seen things in the last dayspan that it will take a lifetime to figure.

I look in the mirror again.

And see that the eyes are the same. Tilo eyes. Still curious-bright. Still rebellious. Still ready to question, to fight.

They remind me of my note. Remind me that what I

wrote in it hasn't changed.

I snatch back my hand which he is raising to his lips.

'What now, dear one?' He is half concerned, half amused.

'My note. Did you read it.'

'Yes. That's how I got to you so quickly. I found it when I was packing my bathroom stuff. It scared me, how you wrote you were leaving, but didn't know where you were headed. It was like being at my great-grandfather's death-bed again, faced with a strangeness beyond my under-standing. I've always known you have this other side to your life with no place for me in it.'

'Not anymore.'

Raven hears the sorrow in my voice, reaches to touch my hand.

'In our paradise you won't need it. You won't need any-thing except me.' He gives my hand a squeeze.

I do not say yes or no, and after a while he starts again.

'Reading your note brought me back, too, to that moment in the car with my mother, the one I'd botched so miserably. It was like I was being given another chance. This time I was determined to do the right thing. So I left. I was only half packed but I didn't care. I had to get to you before you were snatched from me forever. And it's a good thing I did, because soon after I crossed it they announced' – he taps the radio with his finger – 'that the Bay Bridge was damaged. I could have so easily been stranded on the other side.

'As I got closer to the store I felt this ominous weight pushing down on me, getting heavier with each moment. I floored the accelerator – it's as though I was in a race with something unseen, I can't explain it. Luckily there was hardly anyone on the freeway. Then – I was about a cou-ple of miles from the store, near the water – the quake hit.

It was like a giant fist slamming up from underground, right under my car. Like someone had targeted me. Except that's a crazy thought, isn't it? I was thrown against the door. I lost the wheel. I could feel the car tipping. I was sure this was it. I screamed your name over and over, only I didn't realize it until later. But somehow the car righted at the last moment. Then I saw a wave come over the embankment, shining like phosphorous. A solid, power-packed wall that could smash a semi to bits. Missed me by inches. *Inches*. By now my hands were shaking so much I could hardly hold the wheel. I had to pull off the road. I sat there for a good ten minutes and listened to the noise. It was a roar from deep under, like some kind of earth-animal waking up. I didn't know how long it actually went on, but I kept hearing it inside my head for quite a while.

'I'll admit it. I've never been this scared in my life.

'But then I thought of you and made myself get back on the road. It was tough. My legs were still trembling like they do after you've run a long race. I couldn't control the pressure on the accelerator. The car kept jerking and shuddering, and I was afraid I'd go off the road again. There were big cracks slashed across the freeway, fissures with gases rising from them. A stench like sulphur covered everything. Buildings were burning, and every once in a while you could see glass explode. Even with my windows rolled up I could hear people screaming. Sirens. Ambulances. For a while I was afraid I wouldn't be able to get through.

'And all the time, you know what I was thinking? *Please God, let her be OK. If someone has to get hurt, let it be me.* I don't remember thinking something so intensely ever in my life.'

I move closer, lean my head on Raven's shoulder. 'I appreciate,' I whisper. 'No one has ever been willing to suffer in my stead before.'

'It's new for me too, thinking of someone before myself, not really seeing them as separate from me.' His lashes sweep his cheek as he looks down, my American shy to speak of these things. Finally he adds, very soft, 'I guess that's what love is.'

Love. The word reminds me of my note. But before I can speak, Raven continues.

'I took some side roads, finally managed to get to the store. The building was totally gone, not even a wall left standing. As if – yes, it's a foolish thought, I know – as if someone went at it with particular vengeance. But at least it wasn't on fire.

'I'm not quite sure what I did next. I know I kept shouting your name like a madman. I called for help, but there was no one. I pushed through, clawing at debris – what I wouldn't have given for a shovel – cursing because I couldn't move any faster, not knowing if I was getting any closer to you. I was terrified you'd suffocate by the time I got to you. I've read of that happening. Or maybe I'd step on something you were trapped under and crush you. Finally, when I'd almost given up, I saw a hand. Clutching a red chilli, of all things. I dug through the rubble like crazy, and finally found the rest of you – only you weren't wearing any clothes.'

He stops to give me a glance.

'Someday you must tell me what you were doing.'

'Someday,' I say. 'Maybe.'

'You didn't even look like you, not like when I dropped you off, and not like before either. But I *knew*. So I got you into the car. Wrapped you up. Hit the road going north. We've been moving for about an hour. We had to take some detours – parts of the freeway are pretty bad. But we're almost at the Richmond Bridge. It's the only one left undamaged – almost as though it's fate, don't you think, so we can cross it and keep going north, to paradise.'

He pauses for a response. I say nothing, but I feel strangely weightless, my whole body a smile, like an obstacle runner who never thought she would make it and now has just sailed over the last hurdle. Raven you have made my decision for me. Perhaps the rest *is* fate, and it is time for me to relax into it, I who have fought my destiny so hard all my life.

But there is still one unresolved thing.

I move back to my corner of the car. 'Raven, did you read my note?'

'Yes, of course I did. Didn't I say—'

'Did you read all of it? The part which explains why we can never—'

'Listen, can't we discuss it later? Please? In our special place these things will take care of themselves. I'm sure of it.'

'No.' My voice sounds ungracious, adamant. I wish I could acquiesce graciously, as women – Indian and not Indian – are asked so often to do. Kiss away conflict. But I know I am right not to.

Raven sees the look on my face, pulls over to the side of the road.

'Very well,' he says. 'Let's talk.'

'Don't you see what I mean? Don't you see why it would never work? Each of us loving not the other but the exotic image of the other that we have fashioned out of our own lack, our own—'

'That's not true.' His voice is raw with hurt. 'I love you. How can you say I don't?'

'Raven, you know nothing of me.'

'I know your heart, dear one. I know how you love. Doesn't that count for something?'

Yes, I want to cry. But I hold myself hard against my

desiring. 'All the things that attracted you to me – my power, my mystery – they're all gone anyway.'

'And see, I'm still here.' He holds out his hands for mine. 'Doesn't that prove you wrong?'

My hands move of their own will, their longing to lie in his. But I pull them back. Fist them in my lap.

Raven watches me a moment, then sighs.

'OK, maybe my ideas about you and your people were wrong. And maybe, like you said, you don't know that much about who I – we – are. But if you go off on your own, things are never going to get better, are they?'

When I say nothing, he continues. 'Let's teach each other what we need to know. I promise to listen. And you – I know you're good at listening already.'

I bite my lip, debating. Could he be right.

'Please,' says Raven. 'Give me – us – a chance.' Again he holds out his hands. And I see what earlier I had not: the torn palms, the broken nails.

For me.

You who were foolish Tilo once, who are perhaps foolish still, is that not worth all the knowing in the world.

'Raven,' I whisper. And I lift his wounded hands to my lips.

When we have finished saying what lovers say after they have almost lost each other, when we have held each other long enough so that his breath is mine and mine his, Raven starts the car.

'There's a box of maps near your feet,' he says. 'Different routes into the mountains up north. Why don't you look through them and choose the one you like best.'

'Me? But I know nothing of these roads, which is good, which is otherwise.'

'I trust your intuition. And hey, if we go wrong, we'll just try again. We'll keep searching until we find our paradise, and enjoy each step of the way together.'

His laughter is a golden fountain from which I drink thirstily. Then I run my fingers over the maps and by feel pick one out. It pulses its promise into my fingertips.

Yes, Raven, together.

One last stop, the tollbooth, then it will be only us and the night.

The bridge comes up smoothly, its lights calm and unconcerned as once the eyes of the spices were. They give me permission. *Yes, yes.* I whisper the words to myself, put my hand on Raven's knee. He smiles as he slows to pay. Afloat on that smile, I dimly hear him say something to the man in the booth.

'Yeah, real bad,' says the man. 'Worst one in years. The fire's done more damage than the quake. Where you folks coming from? Oakland? They say that's where the centre was, near downtown. Strange, huh? No one ever thought there was a fault line over there.'

I snatch back my hand as though its touch might scorch, look down at my palm. Ah Raven, here's where the fault lines are.

The car is moving again, smooth, fast, confident. I stare north over the choppy water, its broken reflections of stars. Beyond it land, beyond it mountains, beyond it somewhere the earthly paradise with a black bird hanging motionless in a silver sky.

It exists for Raven. But can it exist for me.

*

When we reach the other end of the bridge I put my hand on his arm.

'Stop, Raven.'

'Why?'

He's upset, I can tell. He doesn't like this, doesn't quite trust what I might do. His whole body strains to keep going.

But he pulls over to the viewing area.

I swing open the door, step out.

'*Now* what are you doing?'

But he knows already. He follows me to the edge and looks on with me.

Down south across the water, a dirty red glow, a city burning. Almost I can hear it, the fat hiss of flames, the houses bursting open, fire engines, police cars, bullhorns. The people crying their pain.

'Raven,' I whisper. 'I made it happen.'

'Don't be crazy. This is an earthquake area. These things happen every few years.' He wedges his hand under my elbow and tries to guide me back into the car. In his mind already we're walking under the redwoods smelling the cleanness. Gathering acorns for food and wood for kindling. If only I would quit this foolishness.

I know what burning smells like. I have not forgotten the death of my village, though it was lifetimes ago, for that too I caused. Smoke and scorch. Smoulder. Each thing that fire takes has a different odour. Bedclothes, bullock cart, cradle. That is how a village goes up in flame. A city would be different, buses and cars, sofa sets covered with vinyl, an exploding TV.

But the smell of charred flesh is the same everywhere.

Raven looks at me. There are new lines, tight and tired, around his mouth. A new wariness in his eye: the fear that his dream will fail, here at the last, after the final bridge has been crossed.

Regret rises in my throat like lava. Raven, I who love you more than I have ever loved anyone in all the worlds I've travelled, to think that I should be the cause for that look.

It would be so easy for me to turn my back on that burning city. To take your hand. I can see it, the car flying true as an arrow through the dawn, sunlight shimmering off its flanks, not stopping until we reach happiness.

Every pore of my body cries out for it.

'Raven.' The words are crooked bones I must pull, bleeding, from my throat. 'I cannot go with you.'

A part of me hates myself for the pain that leaps in his eyes.

He puts out a hand as though to grip me. Shake me into sense. But after a moment he lets it fall. 'What do you mean?'

'I have to go back there.'

'*What?*'

'Yes, to Oakland.'

'But *why?*' His voice is jagged with frustration.

'To try and help.'

'I told you, it's crazy to think you were responsible. Besides, they've got lots of other people who are trained for these things. You'd just be in the way.'

'Even if you are right,' I say, 'even if I did not cause it, I cannot just leave such suffering behind.'

'You've been helping people all your life. Isn't it time you did something different, something for yourself?'

His face so raw in its pleading. If only I could give in to it.

Because I cannot, I say, 'Isn't everything we do for ourselves, ultimately? When I was Mistress, too . . .'

But he is in no mood to listen. 'Shit,' he says. '*Shit.*' He slams his fist into the railing. His lips are thin and white.

'What about the earthly paradise?' he says at last. In his

mouth the phrase is a broken sound.

'You go on. Please. You don't have to take me back. I'll get a ride.'

'So you're going to go back on your promise, huh? Just like that?' Unshed anger fills his eyes.

My heart is so full of sorrow I have to hold on to the railing just to keep standing. Is it ever possible for two people, no matter how deep the love, to explain our lives to each other? To tell our motives? Is it even worth to try?

I am about to sigh. To say, Leave it, you'll never understand.

Then I think, No. Raven, because I have placed you in my heart I must say to you what I believe to be truth. Whether you understand. Whether you believe or no.

I turn to him, and for one last time I cup his chin in my hands. How soft the night-growth on it, like new pine needles.

He looks as though he will push me away. Then he lets it be.

'It wouldn't work, Raven. Even if we found your special place.' I take a deep breath, then say it. 'Because there *is* no earthly paradise. Except what we can make back there, in the soot in the rubble in the crisped-away flesh. In the guns and needles, the white drug-dust, the young men and women lying down to dreams of wealth and power and waking in cells. Yes, in the hate in the fear.'

He closes his eyes. He does not wish to hear any more.

Good-bye Raven. Every cell in my body cries out to stay but I must leave, for in the end some things are more important than one's own joy.

I turn to start back over the bridge, I, once Tilo, who is just now learning that the love flower grows only on the nettle tree.

'Wait.' His eyes are open, and in them a resigned,

faraway gaze. 'Then I guess I'll have to come too.'

My heart lurches so hard, I must grip the rail to stand. O ears, what cruel trick are you playing. Is it not burden enough, the thought that I must spend my remaining life alone.

Raven nods in response to the disbelief in my eye. 'That's right. You heard me.'

'Are you sure? It'll be difficult. I don't want you to regret it later.'

He laughs a gritty laugh. 'I'm not sure at all. I'll probably regret it a hundred times over even before we reach Oakland.'

'But?'

'But,' he says. And then I am holding him tight, laughing against his mouth.

We kiss, a long, long kiss.

'Is this what you meant?' he asks when we pause for breath. 'Is this what you were saying about the earthly paradise?'

I start to speak. Then I see he needs no answer.

Later I say, 'Now you must help me find a new name. My Tilo life is over, and with it that way of calling myself.'

'What kind of name do you want?'

'One that spans my land and yours, India and America, for I belong to both now. Is there such a name?'

He considers. 'Anita,' he says. 'Sheila. Rita.'

I shake my head.

He tries a few more. Then says, 'How about Maya?'

Maya. I try the sound, like its shape. The way it flows, cool and wide, over my tongue.

'And doesn't it have an Indian meaning, something special?'

'Yes,' I say, remembering. 'In the old language it can mean many things. Illusion, spell, enchantment, the power that keeps this imperfect world going day after day. I need a name like that, I who now have only myself to hold me up.'

'You have me too, don't forget.'

'Yes,' I say. 'Yes.' And lean into his chest which smells of open fields.

'Maya, dear one,' he says against my ear.

How different this naming is from my last. No pearled island light, no sister-Mistresses to circle me, no First Mother to give her blessing. And yet, is it not as true? As sacred?

I am looking over his shoulder as I think this. Smoke hangs grey-green in the sky, like fungus moss in a dying forest. But the bay water is pink pearl, the colour of dawn.

And in it a movement. Not waves. Something else.

'Raven, do you hear a sound?'

'Only the wind in the girders, love. Only your heart beating. Let's go now.'

But I am hearing it clear, loud, louder now, the sea serpents' song. That shining in the waves is their jewel eyes holding my gaze.

Ah.

You who have followed me through my up-and-down life, I leave you with one last question: The grace of the world, taken or given back, is there any accounting for it.

'I Maya,' I whisper. 'I Maya thank you.'

The jewel eyes blink their acceptance. Then sun struggles through a rent in the smoke and they are gone.

But not gone too, inside my heart.

'Come on,' I say to Raven, and hand in hand we walk toward the car.

Arranged Marriage
Chitra Banerjee Divakaruni

'THESE EXQUISITE STORIES ENTICE US WITH THE
AUTHOR'S GIFT OF STORYTELLING AND HER
CHARACTERS' ORIGINALITY, INDEPENDENCE AND
INSIGHT'
San Francisco Chronicle

The possibility of change, of starting anew, in this stunning,
beautiful and poignant collection of short stories, is at once
terrifying and filled with promise. For those Indian-born women
living new lives in America, independence is a mixed blessing. It
means walking the tightrope between old treasured beliefs and
surprising newfound desires, and understanding the emotions
which that conflict brings. Together these stories create a tapestry
of existence as colourful, as delicate and as enduring as the finest
silk sari.

'AS IRRESISTIBLE AS THE IMPULSE WHICH LEADS HER
CHARACTERS TO SURFACE TO MATURITY, RAISING THEIR
HEADS ABOVE THE FLOODS OF SILVER IGNORANCE'
New York Times Book Review

'RAVISHINGLY BEAUTIFUL STORIES . . . DIVAKARUNI NOT
ONLY CONVEYS EMOTIONS WITH STUNNING ACCURACY,
SHE ALSO TRANSFORMS THE OUTER WORLD INTO
REFLECTIONS OF THE SOUL'
Booklist

'YOUNG AND OLD, MALE AND FEMALE, EAST AND WEST,
MODERN AND TRADITIONAL, ALL ELEMENTS BLEND IN
THIS EXQUISITE COLLECTION . . . SENSITIVE, ELEGANT
AND BEAUTIFULLY DESCRIPTIVE'
Library Journal

0 552 14477 0

BLACK SWAN

Sister of my Heart
Chitra Banerjee Divakaruni

'CHITRA BANERJEE DIVAKARUNI IS A TRUE STORYTELLER.
LIKE DICKENS, SHE HAS CONSTRUCTED LAYER UPON LAYER
OF TRAGEDY, SECRETS AND BETRAYALS, OF THWARTED
LOVE . . . [A] GLORIOUS, COLOURFUL TRAGEDY'
Daily Telegraph

Born in the big old Calcutta house on the same tragic night that
both their fathers were mysteriously lost, Sudha and Anju are
cousins. Closer even than sisters, they share clothes, worries, dreams
in the matriarchal Chatterjee household. But when Sudha discovers
a terrible secret about the past, their mutual loyalty is sorely tested.

A family crisis forces their mothers to start the serious business of
arranging the girls' marriages, and the pair is torn apart. Sudha
moves to her new family's home in rural Bengal, while Anju joins
her immigrant husband in California. Although they have both been
trained to be perfect wives, nothing has prepared them for the pain,
as well as the joy, that each will have to face in her new life.

Steeped in the mysticism of ancient tales, this jewel-like novel shines
its light on the bonds of family, on love and loss, against the realities
of traditional marriage in modern times.

'DIVAKARUNI STRIKES A DELICATE BALANCE BETWEEN
REALISM AND FANTASY . . . A TOUCHING CELEBRATION
OF ENDURING LOVE'
Sunday Times

'A PLEASURE TO READ . . . A NOVEL FRAGRANT IN
RHYTHM AND LANGUAGE'
San Francisco Chronicle

'DIVAKARUNI'S BOOKS POSSESS A POWER THAT IS BOTH
TRANSPORTING AND HEALING . . . SERIOUS AND ENTRANCING'
Booklist

'MAGICALLY AFFECTING . . . HER INTRICATE TAPESTRY OF
OLD AND NEW WORLDS SHINES WITH A RARE LUMINOSITY'
San Diego Union Tribune

0 552 99767 6

BLACK SWAN

Like Water For Chocolate

A Novel in Monthly Instalments with Recipes,
Romances and Home Remedies

Laura Esquivel

'THIS MAGICAL, MYTHICAL, MOVING STORY OF LOVE,
SACRIFICE AND SIMMERING SENSUALITY IS SOMETHING I
SHALL SAVOUR FOR A LONG TIME'
Maureen Lipman

The number one bestseller in Mexico for almost two years, and
subsequently a bestseller around the world, *Like Water for
Chocolate* is a romantic, poignant tale, touched with moments of
magic, graphic earthiness and bittersweet wit. A sumptuous feast
of a novel, it relates the bizarre history of the all-female De La
Garza family. Tita, the youngest daughter of the house, has been
forbidden to marry, condemned by Mexican tradition to look after
her mother until she dies. But Tita falls in love with Pedro, and in
desperation he marries her sister Rosaura so that he can stay close
to her. For the next 22 years Tita and Pedro are forced to circle
each other in unconsummated passion. Only a freakish chain of
tragedies, bad luck and fate finally reunite them against all the
odds.

'WONDERFUL . . . HARD TO PUT DOWN . . . IT IS RARE TO
COME ACROSS A BOOK AS UNUSUAL'
Steve Vines, *South China Morning Post*

'A TALL-TALE, FAIRY-TALE, SOAP-OPERA ROMANCE,
MEXICAN COOKBOOK AND HOME-REMEDY HANDBOOK
ALL ROLLED INTO ONE . . . IF ORIGINALITY, A
COMPELLING TALE AND AN ADVENTURE IN THE
KITCHEN ARE WHAT YOU CRAVE, *LIKE WATER FOR
CHOCOLATE* SERVES UP THE FULL HELPING'
Carla Matthews, *San Francisco Chronicle*

The worldwide bestseller – now a major film.

0 552 99587 8

BLACK SWAN

A SELECTED LIST OF FINE WRITING
AVAILABLE FROM BLACK SWAN

THE PRICES SHOWN BELOW WERE CORRECT AT THE TIME OF GOING TO PRESS. HOWEVER TRANSWORLD PUBLISHERS RESERVE THE RIGHT TO SHOW NEW RETAIL PRICES ON COVERS WHICH MAY DIFFER FROM THOSE PREVIOUSLY ADVERTISED IN THE TEXT OR ELSEWHERE.

☐	99588 6	THE HOUSE OF THE SPIRITS	*Isabel Allende*	£7.99
☐	99820 6	FLANDERS	*Patricia Anthony*	£6.99
☐	99630 0	MUDDY WATERS	*Judy Astley*	£6.99
☐	99618 1	BEHIND THE SCENES AT THE MUSEUM	*Kate Atkinson*	£6.99
☐	99853 2	LOVE IS A FOUR LETTER WORD	*Claire Calman*	£6.99
☐	99687 4	THE PURVEYOR OF ENCHANTMENT	*Marika Cobbold*	£6.99
☐	99686 6	BEACH MUSIC	*Pat Conroy*	£7.99
☐	99715 3	BEACHCOMBING FOR A SHIPWRECKED GOD	*Joe Coomer*	£6.99
☐	99669 6	ARRANGED MARRIAGE	*Chitra Banerjee Divakaruni*	£6.99
☐	99767 6	SISTER OF MY HEART	*Chitra Banerjee Divakaruni*	£6.99
☐	99587 8	LIKE WATER FOR CHOCOLATE	*Laura Esquivel*	£6.99
☐	99622 X	THE GOLDEN YEAR	*Elizabeth Falconer*	£6.99
☐	99770 6	TELLING LIDDY	*Anne Fine*	£6.99
☐	99656 4	THE TEN O'CLOCK HORSES	*Laurie Graham*	£5.99
☐	99681 5	A MAP OF THE WORLD	*Jane Hamilton*	£6.99
☐	99796 X	A WIDOW FOR ONE YEAR	*John Irving*	£7.99
☐	99758 7	FRIEDA AND MIN	*Pamela Jooste*	£6.99
☐	99810 9	THE JUKEBOX QUEEN OF MALTA	*Nicholas Rinaldi*	£6.99
☐	99608 4	LAURIE AND CLAIRE	*Kathleen Rowntree*	£6.99
☐	99650 5	A FRIEND OF THE FAMILY	*Titia Sutherland*	£6.99
☐	99700 5	NEXT OF KIN	*Joanna Trollope*	£6.99
☐	99780 3	KNOWLEDGE OF ANGELS	*Jill Paton Walsh*	£6.99
☐	99673 4	DINA'S BOOK	*Herbjørg Wassmo*	£7.99
☐	99592 4	AN IMAGINATIVE EXPERIENCE	*Mary Wesley*	£6.99
☐	99769 2	THE WEDDING GIRL	*Madeline Wickham*	£6.99
☐	99651 3	AFTER THE UNICORN	*Joyce Windsor*	£6.99

All Transworld titles are available by post from:

Bookpost, P.O. Box 29, Douglas, Isle of Man IM99 1BQ

Credit cards accepted. Please telephone 01624 836000,
fax 01624 837033, Internet http://www.bookpost.co.uk or
e-mail: bookshop@enterprise.net for details.

Free postage and packing in the UK. Overseas customers allow
£1 per book (paperbacks) and £3 per book (hardbacks).